D1551626

strange unearthly things

strange unearthly things

Kelly Creagh

VIKING

VIKING

An imprint of Penguin Random House LLC, New York

First published in the United States of America by Viking,
an imprint of Penguin Random House LLC, 2023

Visit us online at PenguinRandomHouse.com.

Library of Congress Cataloging-in-Publication Data is available.

ISBN 9780593116081

10 9 8 7 6 5 4 3 2 1

Printed in the United States of America

BVG

Design by Kate Renner

Text set in LTC Kennerley Pro

For my friend Jeannine.
Jane has Helen, and I have you.

"All my heart is yours, sir: it belongs to you; and with you it would remain, were fate to exile the rest of me from your presence forever."

—*Jane Eyre* by Charlotte Brontë

Mr. Elias Thornfield
Fairfax Hall
Bakewell
Derbyshire
DE45 5LA
United Kingdom

20 June

Miss Jane Reye
Lowood School for Girls
1847 Gateshead Way
Corydon, IN 47112
United States

Dear Miss Reye:

Though I am pleased to receive word of your acceptance, I consider it my duty to reiterate one final time that this is not an endeavor you should enter into lightly. The spiritual forces troubling Fairfax Hall are uncommon and no trifling matter. I share this warning from a position of firsthand authority.

Clearly, you feel equal to the task of expunging the aforementioned oppressive forces from my property or I would not have received your signed waiver of liability. However, as previously specified, there are reasons why the compensation for the successful completion of this unusual assignment is so high.

Simply put, the hazards intrinsic to this issue are not to be overlooked and cannot be overstated.

You may take comfort, however, that you will not be alone in your efforts. You will be joined by a small number of other gifted individuals with the aspiration that someone among the assembly, or perhaps the collective, will succeed.

If, after this last forewarning, you are still eager to engage in this undertaking, then please find enclosed your ticket information, room assignment with map, and schedule.

Upon arriving at Fairfax Hall, you will be greeted by my valet and housekeeper, Mr. Poole. He will show you to your quarters and attend to any concerns you may have.

Your stay at Fairfax Hall is extended to the point of my absolution from my aggressor (which I hope will be expedient) or, at the latest, 16 July.

All provisions and amenities will be supplied.

Cordially,

Elias Thornfield

1

reat. It's back.

The entity.

More likely, it never left.

Awesome. A second shadow—just what I always wanted.

Per usual, this ghost—or whatever it is—is currently just an impression on my mind. A picture and a feeling combined into one, except the details are blurred, obscured by the noise and action of the waking world.

Concentration is the flashlight that illuminates the shades I encounter. But I never get the whole picture until I put charcoal to paper and draw what I "see."

I don't want to look too closely at *this* shadow figure or render it into more solid shapes of black and white. I've successfully avoided doing so for four weeks now, assuring myself all the while that this creeper will eventually scram.

I've learned the hard way how bestowing attention of any kind can invite certain spirits closer. More than that, I'm afraid that if I *do* sketch my sketchy tagalong, I'll discover that it's something other than a ghost.

But then, isn't that what my intuition has been whispering all along?

To find out if my instincts are right . . . well, I'll *have* to draw it.

Cringing, I focus on the passenger seat in front of mine, tuning my ears to the hum of the Boeing jet that, like my life, carries me forward at a velocity unfelt.

Night occupies the skies we fly through, and thousands of miles below, the Atlantic churns, as do the lightning-illuminated clouds outside the little window.

Rain slashes the layered glass, and my mind is as turbulent as the weather.

Because there's so much that I don't know.

Even outside of what this thing is that's following me, or what it *wants* already.

I don't know, for instance, what to expect at Fairfax Hall—who I'm going to have to contend with there or what. What *else*.

More troubling than that—I don't know what comes after this job. And that mystery, the yawning void of the whole rest of my life? Well, that's scarier than *any* incorporeal lurker.

Gritting my teeth, I fight the urge to think too far ahead.

Ugh. This *thing* is stressing. Me. Out.

I hadn't expected it to follow me to freaking England.

I guess my hope had been to escape from it like everything else. Leave it behind like an ugly sweater that I conveniently "forgot." Now, though, my fear that Fairfax Hall and this spirit are linked begins to seem less improbable.

Either way, the last thing I want is to arrive on the scene of this gig the way I have for most situations in life: with built-in issues.

There is, after all, a lot of money on the table. Enough to keep me flush until I can figure out how to survive on my own. Enough that I can buy the name-brand cream cheese . . .

A definite plus since I don't currently possess enough cash for a return flight. Not that I'm *ever* going back. To Lowood at least.

Of course, there's also the little problem that, oh yeah, I'm supposed to help *clear* Fairfax Hall of its skulker, not import a new one from America.

The salt-and-pepper-haired man seated next to me, closest to the window, draws a sudden breath, making me jump. He has his chair reclined and his eyes shut.

Envy for the rest he's getting prods my already sour mood.

I had hoped to sleep on the plane before landing in another time zone, another country. Another world.

Steeling myself, I finally give in and glance behind me down the aisle, toward the seat that my senses—the extra ones—tell me holds my stalker.

The seat appears empty, though the one across from it is occupied by a blond woman wearing headphones. She flicks me a dirty look, then goes back to perusing her magazine.

If only she knew what sat across the aisle from her. She might drop her magazine in search of a parachute.

I sit forward again when the plane hits another pocket of turbulence.

Usually, lurkers—the ones I choose to ignore—eventually get bored with me.

For whatever reason, this one wants my attention. Enough that it's willing to wait for me to acknowledge it.

Is that what it's waiting for?

From what I can tell, I've got two equally terrible options.

One, I can keep ignoring it, and assure by doing so that it'll still be on my heels when I walk into this job—which I need—or two, I can unmask it and start to deal with its janky ass.

Helen. What would *she* do?

I sigh and lean forward, jerking my carry-on knapsack out from beneath the seat in front of me. After yanking my sketchpad free, I scrounge for one of my charcoal pencils.

Setting the sketchpad on my lap, I go to work, tracing a faint black outline. My pencil flits here and there, following the orders of my intuition. My irritation—and, yeah, my fear—lends the lines a frayed look.

A tatty, not-cool shape comes together.

Narrow frame. Lean limbs. Sharp and gaunt features half-lost beneath the hood of a heavy black cloak. Ashen skin like cracked and peeling plaster.

Next come the eyes, which are . . . *informative.*

Not that I need more evidence to confirm my instincts regarding this thing.

Like a pair of high beams, two orbs of penetrating firelight-orange blaze through the shadowed hood, each slit through the middle vertically by a blade-thin pupil of pure black. My charcoal can't convey the color I "see," but it does illuminate a gaze full of intent.

Think feral predator in the dark, except with lava eyes.

But there's more.

Against pale skin he wears a thin black necklace adorned with a single matching bead pendant.

Because accessories are everything.

Thin dry lips are parted, almost as if he doesn't want me to miss this detail: the razor teeth that lie beyond. They make me want to ditch the sketchpad and start looking for *my* parachute.

But . . . I don't stop. It's too late, like I'd known it would be the moment I started.

Like the moment after I signed that waiver. Got on this plane.

Told everyone at Lowood what I really thought of them . . .

My heart speeds up as my hand keeps going, almost like it's possessed, the tip of my pencil trading off between outlining and filling in details.

Locks of long, silken, snow-white hair escape the hood that, on either side of the entity's head, hides something . . . bulky. The heavy fabric of the hood conforms to curled shapes that conjure the image of a ram's horns.

I keep going.

His hands tell a story, too. White fingers, cracked as well, degrade into long, sharp black claws.

After finishing his obsidian manicure, my pencil flits back to those *eyes*. Because there's something about them. Flashlights of soul-searing doom.

Those onyx gashes that serve as pupils . . . It's like I *know* them.

Saw them once in a nightmare I never remembered until now.

And somehow the blackness of the shadows that cling to him isn't black enough.

Shit, though. My *pencil's* not black enough.

I see you, too, those eyes seem to say.

Along with so much else I don't know how to translate—or capture—with the tools at my disposal.

I go after answers anyway and, against my better judgment, continue to excavate from my inner perception the terrifying image of a . . . a . . .

"The F are you?" I whisper under my breath.

And what do you want from me?

I don't dare ask this second question aloud. Instead, it echoes through my mind as I pause to examine my work. But then all thought derails the moment those eyes, the ones on my paper, blink.

Terror detonates in my gut. My hands tremble to the point that there will be no more drawing. My heart hammers even harder, beating a warning I know from experience to heed.

If only I knew what, exactly, that warning was.

When the overhead lights flicker, I make myself pause and reevaluate. I make myself think *logically.*

This thing. I don't know what it is and I'm too afraid to guess. But am I letting my fear give it more power than it truly has?

It's entirely likely, for instance, that what I'd perceived as movement had just been an optical illusion caused by the rattling of the plane and the sputtering lights. Because drawings don't move.

Not even mine . . .

The plane jolts. My hand slips and my pencil jumps. An unintended slash of black now splits the entity in two. The slash also seems to break the spell that, so far, hasn't allowed me to look away from the sketch.

I glance to the window, to the storm outside, only to find that my neighbor has awakened. Perhaps he was never really asleep. Whatever the case, his crow-footed eyes are on my paper. But then they lift to me, one wiry brow rising in question.

I make no excuses for either myself or the drawing, but, pressing my lips into a line, I close the sketchpad and shift my gaze forward.

The man continues to watch me, his stare burning with grim curiosity. I'm sure he's about to ask me some question that'll trash our symbiotic no-interaction relationship, then I'll have to tell him to mind his own business and he'll get offended and the rest of the ride will be awkward for all involved.

Hoping to avoid human interaction altogether since it's massively overrated, I snap off my light, recline my chair, and, shutting my eyes, play his own trick back on him.

Lights out, mister. No one home.

For several long minutes, I try to force myself to relax. But that's a big fat nope because my drawing stays emblazoned against the backdrop of my eyelids like a possessed photo negative from *hell*.

Ignoring it, I do the anger-management slow-breathe crap they always tried to push on us at Lowood until my heart stops jackrabbiting in my chest and my hands settle.

Only when I have my peace back—mostly back—do I allow my awareness to stretch out a second time. Cautiously, I take a mental peek.

The wraith is gone now.

This fact? Not as comforting as I want it to be.

I scan a second time, stretching my awareness all the way to the back of the plane and then up to the cockpit.

Once again, though, I'm just surrounded by people.

Surrounded Yet Alone—title to the album of my life, featuring tracks like "Not Again," "WTF," and "Why Me?"

Thunder booms and the plane again jars—harder this time. I grip the armrests, bearing down while I refuse to open my eyes and let go of the hard-won calmness I'd *almost* dovetailed into. That's when a cool, dry, claylike hand falls upon mine. My eyes pop wide.

I scowl at the fingers now clamping my own, but they are not the man's.

Papery digits mapped by hairline fissures curl and tighten around my hand, threatening to crush bone.

I snap my head up, my gaze meeting with slit pupils. From the depths of sooty sockets, those molten eyes blaze into me.

"You dare return?" he asks in a deep and melodious voice that doesn't fit with his monstrousness, dark lips writhing around black gums embedded with serrated teeth.

"Last time should have proved this is no game," hisses the spirit—the creature—his accent rounded, faintly trilled, and unplaceable. "But if you are determined to play savior, *Jane Reye*, then I must again play executioner. You know that."

With those final three words, the cracks netting his skin flare to life with the same orange firelight of his eyes—like he has magma for blood.

The heat wafting off him engulfs me.

With an earsplitting screech, I tear my hand from his unyielding one, strip off my seat belt, and launch myself into the aisle.

I trip, my sketchpad flipping out of my lap. Sketches go flying as I drop to the carpet.

The concerned murmurs of too many voices fill the night-darkened plane as I find my nose two inches from the drawing of the creature I just met face-to-terrifying-face.

"Young lady?"

I twist toward the seat next to mine only to find it occupied again by the man from before.

Concern pinches his brow. He has his hands on his seat belt, trying to unbuckle it so as to get to me. First person, place, or thing to touch me, though, is getting cracked.

"Is there an emergency?" asks the anxious female flight attendant who approaches.

"I think she was having a nightmare or an episode," answers the man. "I tried to wake her, but . . ."

As he trails off, I lift my right hand for inspection. The echo of pain from its being squeezed in that murdering grip remains, the sensation arguing against the man's claim that I'd been asleep.

"Miss, are you all right?" asks the flight attendant, her shadow drifting to fall over both me and my sketches, which lie scattered all around.

Somewhere in the back, a baby wails.

I mutter an unintelligible reply before lifting my eyes to the hundred others projecting judgment. While half the passengers survey me with worry, the other half regard me with irritation.

Headphones Lady lays it on thick with a sneer, her gaze bouncing between me and my drawings, several of which depict screaming faces, twisted figures, and, yeah, some naked people.

After tucking my hair, black, long, and straight, behind my ears with quaking hands, I begin to gather the pages, not caring when I bend or crinkle them. Then the flight attendant crouches next to me.

Her lilac perfume makes me gasp.

Because *Helen*.

"Can I help you with this?" She hands me one of the sketches among the mix that doesn't depict a spirt.

"I'm good" is all I say as I collect from her the surrealist drawing of a girl peeling her skin off like a T-shirt to reveal a skeletal rib cage stuffed to bursting with flowers.

This one, I take more care with, sliding the drawing back into the sketchbook along with the others.

I force myself to inhale deeply, take in the comforting floral aroma that my best friend—my only friend—Helen, loves more than any other.

Strengthened by it, I rise, pretending not to see the attendant's outstretched hand.

"Are your parents on board?" she asks. "Or someone I can seat you next to for the remainder of the flight?"

"I'm . . . by myself," I say. She doesn't need to know that I don't have parents. She doesn't need to know there's no one other than Helen or that, at eighteen years old, I'm finally and officially—thank God—on my own.

"Can I bring you something to drink?" She ushers me toward my seat and my neighbor, who now raises both brows at me.

"Ginger ale?" I tell her, but only because "back off" will probably just lead to more trouble when all I want is for her to stop fussing over me so that I can go back to being invisible.

The attendant touches my seatmate on the shoulder. "Keep an eye on her?" she says, then heads down the aisle, giving him no time to refuse.

"You don't have to do that," I assure the man as I hurry to secure my sketchpad back in my bag, where I should have left it. "It was just a dream, like you said. I'm not going to flip out again."

Also, I don't need him to look out for me. I don't need anyone.

He remains silent for a moment. Then he gestures to my bag.

"It's all those monsters you draw," he says through a nervous laugh. "Might try drawing something a little more . . . peaceful. Like rainbows or bunnies."

I offer him a polite smile.

So many things are about to come spilling out of my mouth.

I eat them and they go down like pinecones.

Because when it comes to other people, I've learned it's better to let them think and say what they want. One, they're used to it. Two, no one gets me anyway.

No one but Helen ever does. Ever will.

But that doesn't mean I can't slap up a few more metaphorical keep-out fences for the duration of one flight.

One life . . .

"I would draw those things," I say, peering past him through the rain-speckled window to the sky that finally begins to lighten. "If they were what I saw."

To this, he makes no reply.

Instead, he turns to stare forward.

Only now it's *his* hands that grip the armrests.

2

Fairfax Hall is not a hall. It is not a manor.

It. Is. A. Freaking. *Castle.*

I power down the window as my taxi winds up the snaking drive, conveying me toward the gray behemoth that looms like a slumbering dragon, its spine jutting with chimneys, spires, and finials.

"Holy flying fish sticks," I mutter, because that's what Helen would have said.

Well, she probably wouldn't have said "flying."

Sticking my head out the window, I take in the gothic facade that glowers at me from behind an emerald mask of crawling ivy.

As we round the last bend, the rich scent of honeysuckle invades my nostrils, its bright, mellow perfume a blasphemous aroma next to this grim, stoic chimera of stone. There's something to the heady scent, too. A nuanced pungency that conjures a flickering, far-off sense of nostalgia.

I'm too distracted to dig for the attached memory.

Two stories high with turrets that support witch-hat rooftops, the edifice dominates the hill we now climb, its two wings spread wide.

Empty and dark, its eyelike windows seem to watch us as we swing into the circular drive at the top of the hill. We also pass a carriage house that's been converted and upgraded into a sprawling garage with several big bay doors—all closed. The windows are tinted, too, and reflective, so I can't see in, but the structure is big enough for a fleet.

Sooo. "Cheese" is to "Dairy" as "Thornfield Dude" is to "Loaded."

Finally, the taxi eases to a halt beside an imposing mouth-like stone portico.

While I climb out, the driver retrieves my bag from the trunk before I can insist on doing it myself. I pay her, including as generous a tip as I'm able.

She's maybe ten years older than me and covered in piercings, her dyed black hair long on one side and buzzed on the other.

It's the edgy, I-will-cut-you kind of look I wish I could pull off—and afford to maintain. Still, it clashes with her wobbly, anime-eyed, let's-be-besties vibe.

While I'd been consumed in my worry over the incident on the plane, preoccupied by my increasing fear that the entity I'd encountered ties into this job, she'd chattered at me the whole way here, asking tons of questions. Where was I from, what was I doing in the UK, how long did I plan to be in Britain, did I have friends here—why was I headed to Fairfax? Coke or Pepsi. Dogs or cats.

My answers, short, sharp, and vague, eventually delivered the message I wasn't the share-y, elbow-rubbing, secret-handshake-y type.

Now that it's time for her to ditch me, though, she finds room for one more inquiry.

"You're meeting someone here, right?" she probes. "Like, people you know. This place doesn't have a winning reputation. Supposed to be cursed or haunted or both. My supervisor had to call me because no one else wanted the job. I rather like ghosts myself, though. I just feel they're . . . misunderstood."

Oh, you sweet summer child.

For a second, I'm tempted to ask the powers that be to swap our brains—and jobs.

"I know the owner," I semi-lie, and hold my hand out for my suitcase.

Clutching the tip I gave her in one hand, she keeps my bag hostage in the other. Like she's trying to decide if she'll be able to sleep tonight if she abandons me.

"Really?" she presses. "Word is that no one's seen him in years. Bit of a recluse. Travels a lot. Jane, can I ask again what you're doing here?"

"It's the tip," I say, deflecting. "Is that it? Not enough, I get it. Look, I've got another twenty you can have."

If you go away.

"No," she says, hurt entering her voice, though I can't fathom why. "It's not the . . ." Trailing off, she glances to the manor, then back to me. "I can at least watch you go in."

"Look, I'm fine on my own," I assure her.

She hesitates, mauve lips pinched like she's got more questions. But then her phone chimes from inside the car, and she gives up on me—as eventually everyone does. After relinquishing my bag, she climbs back into the taxi.

"Cheers, then," she says. "My name's Aubrey if you need me to come back."

Then, cranking her indie rock, she gives a tattooed wave before speeding off.

For a long time, I linger in the manor's engulfing shadow while the car slithers down the hill, shrinking as it winds the serpentine path that will take Aubrey, the care-a-lot cabbie, back to the known world, which I seem to have officially left behind.

Maybe I should have told her about the job . . .

Quizzed her on what she knew about this place.

Nervousness chewing at me anew, I pivot to take in this stone ogre—the second monster I've so far managed to encounter on this excursion.

My eyes climb its walls and rove the dormers of the second floor and the windows below. Maybe I'm looking for someone—anyone—because I've finally realized just how alone I am here. I might have been on my own in Indiana, too, but I still knew people there. There were all the comforting NPCs of life—familiar faces attached to familiar places. Helen waits for me back at home as well, and now I'm far, far away from her, too.

Though really no farther than usual . . .

Giving myself a mental shake, I pick up my bag and start toward the enormous front door. I use the knocker and wait, but no one answers or comes, so I try the knob and it turns. Because, this far into the countryside, why not?

I venture into a cave-like coolness where the aroma of stale candle wax permeates the atmosphere, along with the musty but not unpleasant odor of neglected books. Polished to a high gloss, the dark wood-paneled walls still exude the essence of another age, soaked like everything else in centuries of comings and goings.

Despite the horror movie ending to my plane ride, the tiniest of smiles fights its way onto my face as I inch inward, eyes treated still more by the lavish furniture that populates an equally luxurious foyer.

This corridor. These walls. All of it bleeds familiarity.

Like I've been here before. Except this weird wistfulness has to be misplaced because, until now, the farthest I'd ever traveled was to the Cincinnati Art Museum on a field trip I got written up on for sneaking into the *Victorian Pictures* exhibition.

Speaking of . . .

A smattering of oil paintings depicting regal, decorated men and lushly attired women adorns the walls. One portrait in particular portrays a girl my age with tawny hair and an intense expression—her dark brown eyes penetrating.

We stare at each other for a long time, me and this chick. Almost like *she's* the one I came here to meet.

Whoever she is, she's seated in one of the same wooden chairs from the foyer. A fancy hat with an enormous brim is perched on her head and her arms are looped through a pale pink shawl. Wine-red tea roses spill from her lap.

The portrait itself is pretty epic, though it's hard to say why at first glance. Something about the girl's gaze. Like she's really there, staring straight into me. Like if I said something to her, she might reply. Or like she has something to tell me. Warn me about . . .

The artist. How had they captured that *look*?

Also, where had I seen this girl before? Maybe in that exhibition. Maybe this is a copy. Or maybe *this* is the original.

Leading up from the portrait, an imposing staircase marches toward a second floor that promises to be as posh as this one. The stairway beckons to me, too, enticing me to make myself . . . at home.

I blink several times with a new thought and frown. Because this place. There's something trippy about it. Something *else*. The energy. Like there's some element missing. Amputated.

Which is especially weird since this manor is supposed to house something extra—something that *needs* amputating.

Going still all over, I shut my eyes, "listening" in my way for the spiritual heartbeat of this place.

It would be a lie to say my first inclination isn't to search for the thing from the plane.

Especially since he knew my name. Not that it's unfathomable a spirit would know something like that. Not hard to find out someone's name, after all.

Far more disconcerting had been the whole "Last time should have proved this is no game" line.

Like we knew each other. Had met before.

We hadn't. Dude didn't exactly have a forgettable face.

Yet, at the same time, the fact that he'd known my name also suggested he didn't have, as I'd wanted to believe, the wrong psychic artist, either.

Luckily, he's not here.

But then, nothing is.

I open my eyes and turn in a circle, jolting to find someone standing in the decorative archway leading into the parlor.

A boy.

A. *Hot*. Boy.

He's my age, or maybe a year older, with a warm bronze complexion and a head full of coal-black curls I find it hard not to envy.

Tall and broad chested, with a heavy brow and a smoldering gaze, the stranger—dripping sexy—gestures at me with an apple.

Unbidden, I get a flash of the *David* statue and flush.

"Hey there, fellow pulse haver," he says. "Man, am I glad to see *you*. Been walking around this funeral parlor all by my lonesome for the past hour. Was starting to think that maybe *I* was the ghost here because, let's face it . . . we've all seen that movie."

Code red.

Say something.

Don't be a weirdo.

"You . . . don't look like the housekeeper."

Gah. I said don't be weird.

He laughs, revealing dimples and mint-gum-commercial teeth.

"Why . . . thank you—I think." He polishes the apple against one shoulder before taking a bite.

"The letter said there'd . . . be a housekeeper," I explain.

"Ih ahso saih dere'd bhe foo." Even talking with his mouth full, he's hot. And who needs manners with a jawline like that? He takes a moment to chew and swallow. "But so far, it's just stuffy rooms, empty halls, and spotty cell service. So, I had to dig out my reserve Red Delicious. I have another. You want it?"

I shake my head, too distracted by the fact he doesn't have a detectable accent.

Which must mean . . .

"Are you American?"

"As a hamburger." He spreads his arms in a way that should not entice me.

And it doesn't. Because I won't let it.

"You're here because of the job," I say, though by now, the answer is obvious.

"I'm here because of the *money*," he corrects, the final syllable turning his mouth into a foxy grin.

He wags his brows at me, looking every bit the part of a rock star pirate, with his perfectly disobedient hair, torn dark-wash jeans, roll-top boots, and careless white T-shirt.

I shuffle back an inch while my insides squirm. In response, he takes a few steps toward me. And this boy, who is really closer to being a man, commandeers my total awareness with all his angles and corners, muscles and sharpness.

He terrifies me. More than any spirit I've encountered in recent years—even the thing from the plane. But . . . I can't let *him* know that.

"You are, too, I'm guessing," he says.

I am too what? What had I said to him?

"Yeah," I say. "Here for the job."

"Nah," he says. "Which state you from?"

Oh. Both American. God, Jane, stop ogling and keep up.

"Indiana," I blurt, just to get back on track.

"Iiiindiana," he repeats, as if it's the first time in his life he's ever needed to enunciate the word. "That's the one that looks like a leaky square. What's that the state of?"

"Nothing."

"You live in a state of nothing?" He smiles again, and I want to die because of what that smile does to me—how it twists up all the parts of me that he has already shredded just by existing.

"What about you?" I ask him, somehow, against all odds, still managing to function.

"Maryland," he replies with a slow and soulful blink.

"You live in a land that is merry?"

I don't know where this question comes from, but it makes his smile grow and that, in turn, makes my face an inferno.

"I live there on and off these days," he says. "I wouldn't call Baltimore merry, though. *Lively* is a better word."

"Corydon isn't," I tell him. "So . . . maybe I *do* live in a state of nothing."

Shut up, Jane. Stop talking. He doesn't care. He doesn't think you're funny. He is big and from a big city and you are small and from nowhere.

"Giovanni," he says, pointing at himself.

Because why *wouldn't* he have a name as gorgeous as he is?

"That's Italian," I inform him.

"As a cannoli." This time he laughs, and after skewering his apple on the spear of a nearby statue of Athena, he extends a palm to me.

And now I have no more room to hide. I set down my bag and do the adult thing and accept his hand, which, warm to the point of almost being hot, all but engulfs mine. Instead of shaking my hand, though, he draws it toward him, and places his other hand overtop of it, capturing me. As he does this, his hazel eyes bore into mine, as if seeking to excavate the soul he must be trying to reassure himself I do, in fact, possess.

I blink and resist the urge to pull away. Could I if I wanted to?

His brow furrows, and his smile becomes more musing.

"Your name's . . . Dorothy? No . . . wait. Scratch that. It's Helen."

I jerk my hand from him as if he's burned me. And my skin *does* still bear the searing heat of his.

"You're a telepath," I accuse.

Of course he would have abilities. Isn't that why we got hired?

"Telepath-*ish*," he corrects, one hand waffling between us, one eye squinting.

Shit. He knows what I think of him.

Oh hell. Did he get the *David* flash?

"I read energies," he explains. "From people and objects that I come into contact with. Physically, I mean. Some people call it psychometry. I call it scargazing because, for some reason, it's usually the brutal stuff that bubbles up first."

My knees grow weaker with every word he says, while the smell of him, a mixture of teakwood and amber, makes my head swim.

"My name's not Helen," I snip. "And you shouldn't just go around using your stuff on people like that without telling them. It's rude."

And invasive. And petrifying.

Hands on his hips, he regards me as though I've officially become a puzzle.

"I didn't think—"

"You didn't," I say, cutting him off. "And if you treat everybody like this . . . Well, it's a wonder you haven't gotten burned."

I grab my bag and start for the stairs, heading to find my room, the first place I should have gone instead of playing art history major in the foyer.

"Something sure burned you, though, didn't it, Bird?" he calls after me. "That's why you've got all that armor on."

Halfway up the stairs, I wheel on him and glower. "Bird?"

"You won't tell me your name and now you're flying away. So, what else do I call you?"

I don't like his game. I don't like him. At all.

"Don't try touching me again," I warn.

"I won't," he says, seriously enough. But then a coy smirk teases at one corner of his perfect mouth, making my heart flutter like the creature he's branded me. "Not unless, of course, you invite me to."

"That will never happen," I assure him.

"I know it will," he says, and though his tone suggests he's agreeing with me, his words imply just the opposite.

To this, I don't respond. Instead, I turn and clear the stairs.

"Don't be mad, Bird," he calls after me just before I round the corner. "You never would have been offended if I hadn't told you what I was."

"And yet," I pause to say, "you would still have offended."

With that, I pass out of sight, my nerves—along with my lingering optimism about this job—officially in ruins.

3

With the help of the map included in Thornfield's letter, I'm thankfully able to locate my room on my own since the supposed housekeeper is still MIA. And said room? It's huge.

Like . . . I don't know what to do with myself.

The *bed* is the size of my last room. Well, my *half* of my last room.

It's a four-poster and has a heavy scarlet canopy and curtains, like the kind in a medieval queen's chambers.

Yea, verily. Yon bed needeth its own zip-eth code.

Most arresting of all? There's no one in here but me.

No roommate. So, no sharing the connecting bathroom. No time limits on showers. No lights-out schedule. No one watching every move I make. Telling me what to do . . .

I should be celebrating.

I glance behind me toward the shut door. Closed doors don't keep out ghosts, though. Or whatever that thing on the plane was.

Also, I sort of signed up for a few tango sessions with whatever is here—Flashlight Eyes or something else.

Because money.

Stepping farther into the room—the "Red Room"—that is laid out in such a way that it's kind of two, I dig my phone out of my knapsack because I need to tell Helen I'm still alive.

After opening Messenger, I start typing.

Made it to England in one piece. Barely. Bad storm end of the flight. Disturbing moment during. Visitor. U know what I mean. Before you ask, no. Not something to worry about. Not yet. Yes, I promise to give a full report on Snake Eyes on a Plane later. Should tell you about the guy instead tho. Yes, that kind of guy. Except I hate him. Long story. Just wanted to check in. ttyl.

I hit send, but as I read over the block of text, my gaze shifts to the little bubble that holds Helen's profile picture. Snow is falling and the ground is blanketed by several inches. She has her back to the camera and her arms spread wide, like she's inviting the winter day that bought us freedom from school that afternoon in for a hug. Her red hair, which tumbles down her back in a mass of curls, blazes bright as an inferno against the backdrop of white.

This is one of the last photos I took of her before . . .

Click. I drop the device back into my bag, catching sight of my sketchbook as I do.

It's true the job doesn't officially kick off until tomorrow, but maybe getting a head start is better than sitting in the Red Room and waiting for the walls to bleed.

Or for my spackle-faced tagalong to return.

Looping the strap to my knapsack over my head, I venture back out into the manor.

After making my way down to the first floor again, I hunt through corridors and past countless chambers until I discover the colossal stone-walled kitchen.

I'm not sure if Giovanni ever found food. I, however, hit the jackpot.

There's no one around. Just a huge pile of sandwiches and some bottled teas and water laid out on the island counter in the middle of the room. Like the ghosts of Fairfax Hall had been the ones to prepare the spread.

At first, I only load a single sandwich onto my plate before dropping a green tea into my bag. But then, because there isn't anyone around to mark down what I'm eating, calculate its cost, and build that integer into a submittable report, I snag two more.

All three go with me, balanced on my plate, as I navigate through labyrinthine halls.

After entering a snug study that has low lighting—provided by standing candelabra—I wait to see if whoever lit the candles will appear. When no one does, I meander between a giant black desk and a devouring fireplace to peek behind a decorative folding screen covered in peacocks.

Someone has shuttered the window next to the chair, blocking out the daylight, though there's a standing lamp that I flick on.

I climb into the chair and tuck my legs under me. My plate goes to the huge armrest, and I retrieve my sketchbook. Situated, I again tune in to the house, sending my feelers through its corridors, up its floors, and out over the grounds.

Whispers of things tickle my brain in feathery brushstrokes—flickers from the past. Ghosts of ghosts, but . . . no actual spirits.

Zoning in on the paper, I set my pencil to the whiteness and start building an image.

I don't know why I'm drawing *her*. Maybe it's because of the lilac perfume on the plane. Or maybe it's because Giovanni picked up on her and I want there to be a reason for that. Or maybe it's because I hadn't drawn her since before things got bad. And maybe I want (need?) to see if I still remember her face. The way it used to look.

I *don't* draw Helen's face, though. I just . . . draw around it. Because, in addition to usually needing a visual reference, I guess I'm too scared to get it wrong. Too scared to get *her* wrong. Spoil the picture inside my head by realizing it's not as accurate as I've spent the last two years pretending it is.

As a result of my avoidance of her features, Helen surfaces as a faceless head, her hair everywhere because there's no getting *that* part wrong.

Next, I place my pencil point on the guidelines for where her nose should go, tempted to just start peppering the page with freckles since she's got so many.

Her face. Hasn't it always been my sky? Her expressions the weather, her freckles the constellations that, for a time, seemed to hold the map to our destiny . . .

Voices in the hall cleave the sanctity of my concentration.

"—serious *asshole*." Giovanni.

"Well, he certainly hasn't been doing his job, has he? The letter said he was supposed to greet us and here he's been loafing about in the garage the whole time."

The second voice is feminine and British. Like . . . top-shelf-cat-food-commercial British.

"Thornfield needs to show up already because I can tell you right now that this Poole jerk gets one more dry wisecrack before he's munching on a fist sandwich."

The girl snort-laughs. "Perhaps Mr. Thornfield is waiting for everyone to arrive. Though I haven't run into anyone else yet besides you."

I lean forward in my chair as their voices float nearer, the leather soft enough not to creak, and I peek through one of the hinged slits in the folding screen.

"You're in for a treat," says Giovanni. "In addition to Poole, we've got a flighty, bite-y brunette from Indiana."

He appears in the doorway, half-eaten sandwich in hand, scowl on his face until he spots the desk. "Hey, Ingrid, in here."

He wanders in, followed by a girl his age. Our age.

"A brunette?" asks the girl—Ingrid—who is supple curves and dyed baby-pink curls, the very essence of lushness with her rosebud lips and swaying hips. She pulls off a stud nose piercing in a way that irks the shit out of me, too. Probably because her makeup is flawless and she does the whole girly-girl thing well. Something I struggle with because makeup isn't cheap and it's hard to fight somebody in a dress.

"Yeah," says Giovanni. "She wouldn't tell me her name because she decided she hated my face, too. But . . . I dunno, maybe it's me."

"It's *not* you," says Ingrid as, shuffling a large deck of cards, she rounds the desk and plunks herself in the seat. "But just to be sure, let's ask, shall we?"

Giovanni pulls a chair over and suddenly I can't see either of them anymore.

"Who is the mystery girl and why does everyone hate poor Giovanni?" Ingrid asks over her shuffling.

Cards flip and snap, presumably landing on the desktop. For one moment, I urge myself to walk out of hiding before this can go any further.

But then Ingrid starts talking again.

"Hm. Five of Cups. Whoever she is, she's a bit of an Eeyore. More than a little pitiful—glass-half-empty type. Yearning for something better but prevented from achieving it by circumstances and/or poor decisions. The Tower card next to it signifies how a tumultuous past or catastrophic event has shaped both her personality and current reality. No taste for life and few prospects for betterment. Consumed by her issues and obsessed with negative thoughts. In short? Bitter with baggage."

She's reading tarot cards. I think.

"Maybe that's Poole you're seein'," corrects Giovanni. "Dude on that card even *looks* like him."

"The figure's back is turned on this card," argues Ingrid.

"Probably for the best, because that asshat was ugly AF."

"Well, what about this mystery girl of yours?" prompts Ingrid through a charmed laugh, her voice lowering as if, ironically, she's afraid of being overhead. "What does *she* look like? Is she prettier than me?"

My hand curls into a fist around my charcoal pencil. I grit my teeth.

"Well, she's certainly prettier than *me*," says Giovanni.

A statement that has me blinking—and unclenching my fist.

"Darling," says Ingrid, snapping down yet another card, "I doubt there's *anyone* prettier than you."

"Oh, I dunno," says Giovanni, "I feel like a few of these cards are. Like that one. What's that one?"

"That's the Knight of Cups and, actually . . . that *is* you."

"Then who is *that* sad sack nervous wreck?" asks Giovanni.

"Also you," quips Ingrid. "Nine of Swords in the past position indicates you've been trying to escape some stressful situation. Additionally, it can indicate nightmares and intense mental anguish. Basically, it says you've been waking up from nightmares to realize you're in a nightmare. Anything you'd like to share?"

"What's that next card?"

"The Moon," answers Ingrid. "In the future position, it signifies secrets and confusion. Your current path is unclear."

"This is really helpful," says Giovanni, and it's the flat dryness in his tone that has me stifling a snort.

"Did you hear something?" asks Ingrid.

I draw a breath and unfold myself from the chair. So much for escaping people, places, and awkwardness.

"Plot twist!" shouts Giovanni as I step out from behind the folding screen, my sketchbook tucked under one arm.

"Were you listening to us?" Ingrid demands.

"I was working," I say.

"In the corner?" She asks this like the idea is unfathomable.

"Mystery Girl, in the corner, with the sketchpad," drones Giovanni. "Never would have guessed."

"*You're* Mystery Girl?" asks Ingrid.

"My name is Jane."

"*Jane?*" exclaims Giovanni. "Man, was *I* off. I usually get the first syllable right. Or, at the very least, the *number* of syllables. Jeez. I am just rackin' up those ego burns."

"Well, *Jane*," says Ingrid, "I think you ought to have announced yourself before now instead of eavesdropping in your nook like some creepy little spider."

My eyes flash. Once again, my pencil becomes a dagger. *Words*, most of them profane, leap to my lips.

But Giovanni holds his hands out to me and Ingrid in a halting gesture.

"I would just like to point out," he says, peering back at Ingrid, "that you and I are both psychic, and we *still* didn't know she was there."

"She's not psychic," I snap. "She's a con artist. Everyone knows those cards are a scam."

"I will have you know," says Ingrid, "that these cards were handed down to me by my great-grandmother, because my *whole family* is psychic."

"More like your whole family is a bunch of crooks."

"You take that back right now, you little prat."

"Can I say that I think we've all gotten off on the wrong foot here?" says Giovanni, who launches out of his chair to stand between us. "Let's start over, shall we? I'll do the roll call, if I may." He points at me. "That's Jane, a.k.a. Bird." He gestures to Ingrid, who glances behind, toward the door. "That's Ingrid, the Sadistic Mystic, and I'm Giovanni, a.k.a. the Knight of Cups."

Ingrid gasps, her deck of cards slipping to splatter the carpet.

"Where do you think you're going?" I demand of her as she rushes to peer out into the hall.

For several beats, she's quiet.

Then . . .

"Did either of you see that just now?" she asks, whipping her head back toward us, eyes wide, pink curls bouncing. "Someone pass by the door?"

I didn't see. Neither, it seemed, did Giovanni.

Though I want this to be Ingrid just trying to avoid a scrap, my gut tells me it's not.

"Who was it?" asks Giovanni.

"More like . . . *what* was it," murmurs Ingrid, voice shaking as she slinks back into the room, moving toward us.

I shoulder between her and Giovanni, heading to the door. I peer either way down the hall, finding both directions empty.

"What did it look like?" I ask Ingrid, wheeling on her.

"A hooded figure," she says, lips trembling, "with glowing eyes and a terrible mouth full of sharp teeth. His skin, it was like an ashen log left in the fireplace."

All this is sounding horribly familiar.

"I know you don't believe me," says Ingrid, though it's unclear which of us she's speaking to, unless she's saying this to both of us. "But he *was* there. Walking by. He peered in at the last moment before . . . Those eyes. They . . ."

Giovanni stoops to gather Ingrid's cards. Giving herself a shake, Ingrid crouches to help him.

With a frown, I flip my sketchbook open to the drawing I did on the plane.

"This look familiar?" I ask.

Both Ingrid and Giovanni halt in their gathering, gazes lifting to me.

"Oh, sick," says Giovanni, setting his portion of cards on the desk before heading my way. He wants to reach for the drawing, take it for closer inspection, but, probably remembering my warning, he stops himself. "Did you seriously draw that?"

I don't answer, but my cheeks flame.

I don't like attention on me, let alone my work. I don't like showing off my drawings, either. And I'm not doing that now.

I'm just . . .

"You saw it, too?" Ingrid asks, her nervousness pinching all previous anger out of her voice.

"Uh," says Giovanni, tilting his head at the image. "Actually . . . *I* might have had a brush with that thing as well."

I blink and almost start.

"What?" Ingrid and I ask in unison.

But then the door slams, the candles snuff, and flames roar into being within the fireplace.

4

"Soooo," says Giovanni, breaking the momentary, heart-stopping silence, "that letter was *not* playing."

Bathed only in the light of the erupted fire, the room dances with shadows. They leap along the walls, taking shapes I don't like. We're trapped, too—another thing I hate.

I lift my hand toward the doorknob.

"Wait," says Giovanni, who hurries to my side. My instinct is to ignore him until he presses a palm flat to the wood. Only then do I lower my own hand. Because, obviously, he's doing his thing.

"Oh," he says after a beat, "that is *grody*."

"What is it?" asks Ingrid in a whisper. "What *was* that thing?"

"I don't know," Giovanni admits, though he turns those gemstone eyes on me as he speaks. "Whatever this energy is, it's all fuzzy, like static. But also numb, like a dead car battery. Like it's . . . missing something. And by something, I mean everything."

The room grows warm, too warm.

I grab the doorknob and twist. Though I expect to find it locked, it gives, and I'm able to push out into the hall.

"Hold up, Bird," calls Giovanni as he starts after me, but I ignore him, too focused on hunting down our hunter.

"Where are you two going?" cries Ingrid. "You can't just leave me here by myself!"

"Is that all you can do?" I call as I march past paintings and doorways—rooms filled with more empty furniture. Rooms that whisper to me like they know me. Like this place does. "Slam doors and start fires? Oh, you're *so* bad."

"Bird," says Giovanni, still tailing me, "can we not poke the snake-eyed bear? Feels like we need a huddle or something before we start diving into provoking."

"You're *so* scary," I say, raising my volume, "talking shit on a plane and then playing poltergeist with some trash, B-horror-flick scare tactics."

"Good talk," mumbles Giovanni. Then, after a pause, "Look, can you just . . . wait up?"

I turn another corner, then another. And then . . . I freeze.

Because I'm not in Fairfax Hall anymore.

Or . . . am I?

Blackened and charred walls now flank me—at least where they still stand. Seared debris and sooty rubble litter the burnt and ashen carpet. Above, much of the ceiling has ceased to be, providing a clear view of a roiling auburn sky.

Flaring embers float up from several of the artifacts around me as well as the earth's craggy, glowing surface, which fumes thin screens of smoke.

Wasted black trees, brittle as spent matchsticks, bow to one another in sparse pockets across the lifeless landscape.

I glance behind, toward the direction I came, and then reroute that way.

Giovanni's gone now, though. And there's no returning from this realm.

Instead, I'm funneled through a path of still-smoldering destruction wrought by extinguished flames.

Fairfax Hall is gutted, its interior a crumbling shell of itself.

"You surprise me."

I whirl toward the voice—the same from the plane.

He stands at the far end of what's left of the hall, head tilted down, the acrid and moaning wind tugging at the shadowing hood from which spills his spider's-silk hair. Again, from within that hood, those luminous, serpentine eyes train themselves on me.

"Truly, I did not think you would come so far," he says, speaking with that too-human voice, a voice at odds with the image he cuts. A contrast that makes him all the more frightening.

"I crossed an ocean for money," I snip. "People do it every day."

"You crossed a line for *nothing*. And now you've come to do it all again. It makes no sense."

"I don't know what you're talking about," I growl. "Why are you following me? What are you? And what is this?"

Gesturing to our surroundings, I try to keep my voice steady, to not betray the terror I'd managed to hold at bay until he showed up. Showed up *again*. Fear has me by the throat enough, though, that my voice tremors, giving me away. Because this isn't how my "gift" works. I don't see things. I *draw* them.

But then, maybe that's where I went wrong.

Right along with taking this job.

"You don't remember me," he says. "I remember you, though. And *that* is why I've been following you."

"You don't know me."

"*You* don't know you," he snarls through a sneer. Then, catching his temper and reining it in, he smiles, which is worse. "*I* do, though."

With that, he passes out of sight, vanishing behind an intact corner.

I spur myself forward, *making* myself go after him. Maybe not the best idea. At the same time, staying put isn't going to get me out of here—wherever here is.

When I round the bend, though, he's gone. As is the burned-up Fairfax.

I'm back in the here and now. In the restored manor. Watching someone *else* walk away.

"Giovanni," I blurt.

He freezes and peers over his shoulder at me, brows arched.

"Okay." He turns to face me. "Where the heck did you go? I was just in that hall. Were you on the ceiling or something? I was calling for you."

I glance back down the pristine hallway, eyes climbing the unscorched walls and roving the spotless plaster and perfectly hung pictures. Surely, I hadn't just blipped into some kind of alternate dimension.

But then, what other explanation was there?

"The figure in my drawing," I say, my hand tightening on my sketchpad. "You said you saw it, too."

"Dreamed of it," he replies, one of his shoulders lifting in an almost-shrug. "Week before coming here. In the dream, it was just . . . those eyes. You really captured those eyes, you know?"

"Are you serious?"

"Yeah. You're really good. I'm guessing that's *your* thing? You draw spirits?"

"No," I say, a new rush of heat climbing up my neck. "I mean, you're serious you had a dream with that . . . thing in it?"

"At the time, I just chalked it up to a stress nightmare," he says.

"Stress nightmare?"

"Nightmare induced by stress," he offers.

I level him with a glare. "You mean you were stressed about coming here?"

"Yeah," he says, like that should be obvious enough. But also like he's lying.

I start to ask another question, but then I shut my mouth. Because boundaries are something I understand and here, apparently, is one of Giovanni's.

Fine. Not important anyway.

"Where's Ingrid?" I ask instead.

"Went back to her room, I think," he says. "She was pretty shook."

I frown. Because I want to talk to her, too. Mostly to see if she'd experienced anything like I had. But I don't have the fortitude to go chasing anyone down right now. Especially not her.

Thornfield. Where *is* he?

"I heard you say you met Mr. Poole," I say.

Giovanni's expression darkens. "Out in the garage. He left, though. Punk almost ran me over on his way out."

Not good. *None* of this is good.

Well, what did you expect things would be like here? You didn't exactly sign up for a disco picnic.

Done with questioning, I brush past him, heading back in the direction of the room with the candles because I left my knapsack in there. And my phone.

I have to tell Helen about this.

"Bird," Giovanni calls, and again he's on my heels. "What's going on? Just now, did you see something? What was it?"

I don't answer, and when I reenter the candelabra room, I find it Ingrid-free. Her cards are gone, too. All except for one, which sits on the middle of the desk—a place where it shouldn't have been missed.

Approaching the desk, I peer down at the image the card depicts. One almost as unwelcome as the sight of the entity itself.

A red bird-legged creature with yellow eyes dominates the card, its bat wings spread wide against a black backdrop. A woman and a man are chained to the pedestal it's perched on. Everyone on the card has horns.

THE DEVIL reads the title in all caps below.

I flop my sketchpad on top of the card, blotting it from view. But that puts my drawing of the wraith into focus.

This thing, whatever it is, didn't start messing with any of us directly until after I'd drawn it. Maybe that *wasn't* the trigger, but just in case it was . . .

I tear the drawing free of the sketchpad's spiral spine. Then I chuck it into the now-dying fire in the hearth. New flames flare to devour the paper.

The image curls in on itself and blackens as it burns, the wraith being consumed.

"Oh," says Giovanni, "you saw *that* guy. Again."

I don't reply. Because really, I'm not sure what to say.

But . . . this latest turn of events *does* bring one small yet cold comfort.

I no longer think *I'm* the one who brought this thing here.

Instead, it's starting to feel like *it*—or *something*—has brought me.

5

If Mr. Thornfield or Mr. Poole have made their appearance, I'm none the wiser.

After the incident in the hall with the wraith, I'd gone back to my room, dodging Giovanni, who could *not* take a hint.

Dude is like a Muppet sidekick.

A hot Muppet sidekick with eyes like rough-cut gems and a butt like smooth sculpted marble. At least . . . that's what I've imagined (more than a few times now) Giovanni's butt must be like. Except imagining Giovanni's ass is a problem, and isn't my dance card already full of those?

Probably, I am going to have to spell it out for him that I'm not here to swap life stories, or tolerate his BS.

But here I am, tolerating someone's.

Because where is our host? And this housekeeper?

I'm not going to go looking for them—or anyone—again tonight. Not until I get more information about what *exactly* we are all doing here. What *exactly* we are all dealing with.

Though, don't I already suspect?

No official information will come until tomorrow morning, when we're all scheduled to meet in the dining room for a "debriefing" with Mr. Thornfield.

So, after using the last of the daylight hours to shower and get changed for bed, I climb onto the four-poster and, lying on my back, stare up at the canopy, which is weirdly pleated.

For a long time, I just lie there, replaying my interlude in the hall with the wraith, trying to dissect the conversation. And block out the vision of those eyes . . .

Finally, I give up and message Helen.

You always tell me I come at my problems sideways. Well, apparently, they're coming at me from the same direction.

Send.

Because Rando from the plane came back and you were right. He's not a ghost.

Send.

Something really effed up going on here. This thing acts like he knows me. He *talks* to me like he knows me.

Send.

He knew I was coming. Giovanni, too. Maybe he's been watching all of us. But why does it feel like *I'm* the target?

Send.

No, I don't have $$ to fly back. And this job isn't the kind that required a visa so it's not like I can go get something else.

Send.

Not going back to Lowood don't worry. And not just cuz you made me promise I wouldn't whenever I finally left, too.

Send.

Yeah, I could call Ms. Temple. But she'll ask questions and I'll get a lecture with ur name in it. Plus, I'd have to pay her back and I'm tired of owing people.

Send.

I know. Stop spiraling. Ur right.

Send.

Ok. Fine. Tomorrow. I'll decide what to do then.

Send.

Wish me luck. Afraid to fall asleep here.

Send.

I drop my phone onto the comforter that I don't bother climbing under. Even with the jet lag and the exhaustion, after the creep fest today has been, I'm not actually going to be able to pass out.

Turning on my side, I study the folds of the bed curtains and their loosened ties, my artist's brain mapping the patterns of shadow and light.

Ugh. The way these things are draped—can we say coffin couture?

Also, they've got to be antique. Their fabric is faded and the fringe is scraggly.

Sigh. Me too, curtains. Me too . . .

I peer back toward the door that doesn't lock because this is someone's house and not a hotel. And as I wait for the night to reveal this place for what it really is, Ingrid's bogus card reading replays in my head.

I don't remember the names of the ones she'd pulled, but I do remember the gist of what she'd said about them. About me.

Damaged. Bitter. Broken.

Shutting my eyes tight, I try to force out my surroundings. I try also to tune out the echoing jumble of Ingrid's words. So that I don't have to think about them too hard.

About how right they were . . .

♥ ♥ ♥

Those eyes.

They break through the dark.

Their faraway glow is the only thing that pierces the nothing. Alerts me to the fact that I exist.

They burn two blazing holes in the otherwise vacant void.

For a moment, they are all there is.

But then those seams—all those cracks that map his face and figure—flare once more into being.

And that mouth.

It spreads in a jack-o'-lantern grin.

I want to scream. But I'm caught—and held—by that scorching gaze, unable to blink or look away.

And as the heat envelops me, a dull roar engulfs my mind.

Beyond the low one-note din, though, a far-off voice shouts commands.

And *that voice*.

Something about it summons my soul into the moment—gives me the strength to break free of that monstrous, hypnotic, and unyielding gaze.

And open my eyes.

6

"Wake up!"

I'm on my back, blinking up at a coffered ceiling through a screen of smoke and a frame of flame. Gone is the bed canopy—eaten through.

Sweat soaks my clothes, and fire surrounds me. Flame roars and my skin screams from the heat, the intensity of which dispels any thought I could still be dreaming.

For an instant, I don't know where I am.

I should be at Lowood. In my bunk. I'm not, though.

Fairfax.

"I said, wake up!" comes that snarling voice again, the one that roused me, and I sit bolt upright, searching the smoke-shrouded room for its owner.

There's a tall and lean male figure at the foot of the bed, pulling at the flaming curtains, bringing them down. I gasp, overwhelmed by the realness of what's happening.

Smoke fills my lungs and I start coughing. Then a hand

shoots toward me through the gloom and the gray haze—through the chaos.

I scramble forward, grabbing the arm that grabs mine, and in the next instant, I'm hauled from my pyre, into air that is only degrees cooler, and against someone who is garbed in a thin open robe and pants.

"Get back," he growls as he sweeps me behind him. "Go out into the hall."

I nearly obey, but then . . . *Oh God, my phone.*

Helen. How am I going to talk to her without it?

I'm useless for one more instant as I stand to the side, my skin blazing in the glow of the roasting bed as the stranger yanks down another of the ignited curtains. But when the heavy fabric collapses to his feet with a whoosh that kills the flames, I shake myself into action.

Rushing forward, I catch hold of the last curtain and rip it free. The half-consumed wooden rod supporting it splinters and I yelp, jumping back as hot embers rain over us. But I dash in again and pat down the now-flaming comforter until my fingers find my phone.

Then the stranger draws the burning bedclothes off, using the excess fabric to smother the lines of dancing orange that began to creep over the covers.

While his efforts at last snuff the final flames, they also create more smoke.

"The windows," he says through a cough, "go open the windows."

I'm hesitant to leave him. But the fire is no more, and the air is too thick to see through or try to breathe.

When I reach the casement, I wrench the handles of the

windows and push the panes out. After another round of coughing, I gulp the fresh air, then I whirl back to the bed—but there's no one there.

I hurry past the ruin and out into the darkened hall, where I slam into someone.

I shriek when he—the stranger—catches me by the upper arms.

Harried, he breathes hard from the exertion.

"You're not hurt," he tells me. He doesn't phrase it like a question, but something in his cool tone, colored by its clipped British accent, tells me it is.

I don't answer because I have to fight another cough. Also, there's an open robe and a bare chest in front of me. As well as a lean torso that is a canvas of muscles.

We're so close, and I don't know where to put my gaze. Which results in an involuntary downward flick of my eyes—to the thin trail of fine hair that cuts a vertical path through his navel before vanishing into the waistband of his pants.

My face grows hot again—almost as hot as when I'd been battling the flames.

"I'm okay," I manage, forcing my gaze back to my room. A haze of smoke lives within the doorway, churning from the air that rushes in through the windows I opened.

Or maybe from the movement of something within . . . ?

"What is it?" he asks, like maybe *he* can read my thoughts, too.

Immediately, I take a step back, severing our connection.

The stranger lets me go, and now I can peer up at him.

Shadows envelop a tall and slender frame. His shoulder-length dark hair, wavy, thick, and unruly, curtains his shaded face, obscuring one eye—though it can do little to hide a prominent nose.

"You're here for the job, too." My tone is more accusatory than I mean it to be.

Like me, Giovanni, and Ingrid, he appears to be eighteen. At least he does in this light. Which is almost nonexistent since there are no windows in the corridor.

"What is your name?" he asks.

"Jane," I tell him through teeth that start to chatter because, after being in an inferno, the hall is like a freezer.

"Jane," he repeats, as though he's trying to place me. Or maybe he's simply willing himself to remember the scant syllable. Then he shrugs out of his silken robe before looping it like a cloak around my shoulders. The garment swallows me, and though the fabric is thin, it still carries his warmth. And scent. A tinge of sharp sweetness, like citrus, rises above the acrid odor of smoke. It's mixed with something earthy and oaken.

Something about that aroma quickens my already racing pulse.

Like the whiff of honeysuckle that I'd caught when riding up to the manor, it teases at some backdoor memory. Still, I can't exhume it.

"You're quite shaken, aren't you?" he asks as if I'm a kindergartner who scraped her knee. "Of course, who wouldn't be? You're certain you're not burned? Do you need a doctor?"

I shake my head.

"You should find yourself another room for tonight," he says. "Unless you plan to leave."

He moves to step around me—to go past me.

"Hey," I call after him, and he stalls, peering back with that one eye. "Where are you going?"

"To find the girl who woke me and led me here. Ask her why she's fled after your bed was set afire."

Someone woke him up? Ingrid.

And yeah. I guess it was kind of fishy of her to run off. But maybe she went to get more help . . .

"You know it wasn't an accident," I say.

"I don't, actually. Was it?"

Why does he sound hopeful?

"*No*," I say, a little too forcefully.

By stalling him, I've been trying to figure out his . . . well, for lack of a better word, his power. He said Ingrid had awoken him, so finding me wasn't a psychic event. But . . . if it didn't even cross his mind that I might have accidentally started the fire, doesn't that suggest he has a hunch regarding who—*what*—did?

"I should go find Mr. Thornfield," I say. "He ought to know there's been a fire in his house."

The stranger regards me with an unreadable expression—unreadable partly due to the darkness, and partly due to that obscuring swoop of hair.

"You'll just go knocking about on all the doors, will you?" he challenges. "Say you find our host. What would you have him do? File an incident report with his secretary?"

I start to reply, but my words dry up. This abrupt shift to brusqueness leaves me without a rebuttal.

Still, he lingers, jutting his chin as though he doesn't understand why I'm making him wait so long for an answer.

"I . . . thought he might . . . want to call the police," I say at last.

"The police?" he scoffs. "You think if the police could solve his problem *you'd* be here?"

His words—they do the job of backhanding me awake.

Once more, I'm at a loss for how to reply, and then he starts to go again.

"Wait!" I call.

He stops and turns back like it's the last thing he wants to do. Like he has better places to be, and I'm keeping him from them.

"I'm afraid to be by myself," I admit.

There's a long pause. Then, finally, he speaks.

"Don't worry," he says, his tone bleak, acerbic, "you're not."

He whirls and walks away, hooking a right to take the stairs down to the first floor, leaving me on my own.

Alone with whatever presence he could sense.

A force I can't bring myself to try to read or connect with again since, officially, it nearly succeeded . . . in torching me alive.

7

I don't bother trying to find another room after the fire.

I don't dare venture back into my old one, either. Not even to get my stuff, which probably all reeks of smoke now anyway.

I *do* look up the taxi company I used to get here on my phone. Maybe I could even request Amber—or whatever her name was.

But then there's the issue of not being able to tell her where to take me even if she did come. The last thing I want is to become someone else's problem.

I'd already promised myself I was done with that kind of noise.

So, I go downstairs and sneak back into the room with the worn leather chair. I stay there, tucked in the corner and wrapped in the stranger's robe, stewing in my thoughts as well as the mixed scents of British Boy and smoke while I wait for morning. Or for the wraith to try to off me again. Whichever comes first.

Though I want to message Helen, tell her about the fire, I don't have the heart.

What good would that accomplish when she can't do anything from where she is, either?

I end up studying the wide-cuffed sleeves of the stranger's robe, which I'm pretty sure is silk. The garment is a deep jade, and the design an intricate pattern of interlocking paisleys.

Both of these elements seem to clash with my rescuer's overall temperament. But then, a crisis isn't always a good time to get a feel for someone's personality.

Then again, maybe it's the best time . . .

The stranger, whose name I failed to get, remains an enigma while I, in turn, remain a "creepy little spider," as Ingrid had called me, until the perfume of coffee dislodges me from my haven.

It's still dark as I rove the halls, checking corridors before I enter them. Just in case.

Though I expect the wraith to appear again to threaten, taunt, or attack me, he doesn't, and I make it to the kitchen without incident.

Inside the huge gray-stone room, I *do* find someone.

Stationed between the island counter and the colossal fireplace, which has been converted into a cooking area that houses countertops, a double sink, and an impressive gas range, stands a man with dark, slicked-back hair, neatly trimmed goatee, and horn-rimmed glasses. He wears a snug gray waistcoat and matching tie, and his white shirtsleeves are rolled to the elbow.

He must be in his late thirties or early forties. Which means . . .

"Ah, *Jane*," says the man, lowering his teacup. "*There* you are. Was starting to worry you might flitter off and, after all our scheming, mine and yours, everything would be for naught."

By "scheming" he must mean the job. Weird way to put it, though.

I shift in the open doorway of the kitchen, arms crossed, feet itching to take me elsewhere. Like out the front door.

"He told you about the fire," I say.

"And I gave him a lecture about leaving you on your own like that," says the man as he settles his teacup back into its saucer. "English breakfast? Coffee?"

"I don't know how it happened," I blurt out. Which isn't *entirely* true. I actually have a pretty good idea how the fire came into being.

One word: *retaliation*.

"Mr. Thornfield," I hurry to say, "I hope you don't think that I—"

The man's mouth falls open and out comes a halting laugh. It's the type of laugh that happens without a smile. Like I've said something more preposterous than funny.

"Oh, Miss Reye," chides the man, leveling me with a sober glare, "I'll thank you *never* to call me by that name again. Do that much, and I think we shall get along."

"You're not—?"

"Mr. *Poole*," the man says, "his housekeeper and general do-thy-bidding-er. At your service."

"*You're* Mr. Poole?"

"Fortunately," he says as he pours another cup of tea, which he sets on the countertop before nodding to it. "Because I'd rather be him than anyone else in this manor. No offense."

I tilt my head at him, confused as much as I am shocked. I'm charmed, though, too. There's something about Mr. Poole. Something . . . nice.

Which doesn't jibe with what I know about Poole, because hadn't Giovanni gotten into a tiff with him yesterday?

"Mr. Poole, I—"

"You want to say that a little louder, Jeeves?" comes Giovanni's booming voice from the hall. "And how about to my face?"

A second voice replies, "You heard me well enough. And, honestly, your face is something I'd rather avoid as, like your presence, I find it vexing."

"Says the guy with a literal beak."

I stiffen on my way to the tea, glancing toward the doorway. Because the second voice—it belongs to the stranger, who enters the room scowling.

My breath rushes out of me, stolen by his presence, which is like that of a thundercloud. Dark and broody, but also electrified—an instant away from unleashing something hellacious.

His attire—dark gray slacks and a matching waistcoat layered over a black button-down shirt—only adds to his austerity. The ensemble also seems at odds with his age. Which, now that he's under full lighting, I'm torn on. He could be seventeen for instance. Or he could be twenty.

He has a wide but shapely mouth, and cheekbones high and hollow enough to harbor faint shadows. And that's what he seems to be made up of. Shadows, sharp lines, and limbs.

His sable, chin-length hair is tamer now than last night, too, though it still halfway conceals one eye, which hides more fully behind a small black cloth patch.

That other eye, gray as granite, fastens on me and does not blink.

We stay locked this way as he strides to the counter, our gazes each held by the other's, and the world slows to a crawl as something transmits between us. Whatever that something is, I can't put it into words. There's no language to it. Just a sensation that manifests as an invisible punch to the chest, the echo of almost-pain bringing with it the whisper of a suggestion. That our eyes have met this way sometime and someplace before. Like I know him—and he knows me. Even though we don't.

"You're still here," he says, scanning me, perhaps taking note that I still have his robe on over my T-shirt and pajama pants. "Grayson said you'd left."

"I said she had made herself scarce," Mr. Poole corrects in a monotone that suggests he's used to being misquoted.

The stranger glares at me a moment longer, as if he can't decide whether or not he's sorry I stuck around. Maybe even that he wishes I hadn't.

Then Giovanni enters.

"Finally," says Giovanni, attention shifting to Mr. Poole. "*Please* say you're his boss. Because this ass napkin tried to run me over yesterday with one of your cars."

"You broke into the garage," says the stranger.

Giovanni spreads his arms. "I was just having a look around!" Again, he addresses Mr. Poole. "Look, if I wanted to rob you, I wouldn't have started with the easily traceable vintage vehicles and exotic cars. Nice Lamborghini, by the way."

"Her name is Tilly," says Mr. Poole. "Short for Matilda."

"And the Jag I almost got plastered across?"

"Oh, that would be Gloria," says Mr. Poole.

"Hot names for hot rides," says Giovanni, shoving his hands into his pockets. "You know, if this housekeeper job happens to open up in the next minute or so, you totally already have my résumé."

A beat of awful, horrible silence pulses in which the puzzle pieces snap together.

For me at least.

"You *are* going to fire his ass, right?" Giovanni asks Mr. Poole.

"Giovanni," I say. Because he needs to shut up.

"Hey, Bird," he says. "Nice robe. I didn't know this was going to be a pajama party. Anybody else smell something burning?"

"Boy, do I," mutters Mr. Poole before hiding behind another sip of tea.

"He's talking about you," Giovanni says to the stranger. "Because you're fired."

The stranger's single-eyed gaze, more piercing than ever, shifts to burrow through Giovanni.

"Grayson," says the stranger, his voice dropping into a dangerous drone, "please say there's coffee in the dining room."

"Yes, Mr. Thornfield," says Mr. Poole.

Everything goes quiet, elevating the almost imperceptible hum of the refrigerator to siren status.

Giovanni, still pinned by the stranger's gaze, drains of color.

The moment of tension drags on. And on. Until, at last, the stranger—who has now been identified—passes out of the kitchen and into the adjoining dining room.

More beats of silence elapse in which Giovanni stares after the other boy.

Then he looks to Mr. Poole.

"Wait. So that's . . . ?"

"Mr. Thornfield," repeats Mr. Poole.

"Then you're—?"

"Mr. Poole."

Giovanni points toward the doorway. "So, he's . . ."

"Thornfield."

Giovanni's finger shifts back to the housekeeper.

"Poole," says Mr. Poole, as though coaching a toddler.

"Plot . . . twist," murmurs Giovanni, swallowing hard as he drops his arm to his side.

Then, after a few blinks, he starts toward the dining room. "Hey, Ebert—"

"Elias," corrects Mr. Poole.

"'Lias, my man," says Giovanni, "listen, I take it all back. And you know I was just joshin' about the beak comment, right? It's a noble nose."

Giovanni disappears and I waver in stunned silence until Mr. Poole, after another sip of his tea, speaks.

"Right," says the housekeeper, "one of us—*not* me—should go in there."

I move, because I sense it, too. The boiling of blood—disaster ready to strike.

Ready to strike again.

8

I enter the enormous dining room to find Elias standing at the far end of a long heavy wood table, arms braced against its polished surface, shoulders rigid. Like he's hanging on to his sanity, temper—or *both*—by a thread.

Giovanni, in the meantime, has commandeered the only decanter I see, and is pouring himself a generous mug of coffee.

"Your parents kick it?" asks Giovanni. "Or are they just on vacation?"

Omigod, Giovanni.

I'm mortified for him. Because *someone* needs to be.

But . . . I'm also mortified for me.

Because the entire episode last night has now acquired another layer. One that asks more questions than it answers.

Why, for instance, wasn't Elias up-front about who he is? If he truly owns this manor, why did he not seem to care about the damage wrought by the fire? Why didn't he question me about it? And why did he say what he did about his "problem"?

You think if the police could solve his problem *you'd* be here?

What is wrong with this place? What is wrong with *him*?

"You're going to fire *me* now, aren't you?" says Giovanni, setting the coffee decanter down before taking a noisy, nervous slurp of the steaming liquid. "Does that mean I have to pay for the return flight? In my defense, can we talk about how that last letter made you sound a billion years old? I mean, who uses the word 'expunging'? Let me guess, you're an Oxford brat. Or maybe Eton. Though don't you have to be an earl or something to go there? Hey, Poole!"

Elias's lone visible eye twitches as he stares past Giovanni, past me, and past everything. Like he is both here . . . and not.

"I heard my name," says Mr. Poole, who strides in with a plate of scones, which he deposits on the table.

"Enlighten me," says Giovanni, snagging a pastry. "Don't you have to be a knight or a prince or something to go to Eton? Am I making that up?"

I seize the decanter—and pour a cup of coffee.

"Nonsense," says Mr. Poole. "Though Eton *is* prestigious."

"It's a college, isn't it?"

"Public school," says the housekeeper. "For boys. Old as salt."

"Old as 'expunging,'" mutters Giovanni around another sip.

"Wait a tick," says Mr. Poole as he pauses to regard Giovanni. "By chance, was that *your* apple I found impaled on Lady Athena's spear this morning? It strikes me now as having been a very American apple."

"Hey." Giovanni points at the housekeeper with the scone. "I was coming back for that."

Mr. Poole shoots Giovanni an admonishing glare before bustling out again, back into the kitchen.

I take the steaming mug down to the far end of the table—to Elias. Only when I set it in front of him do I garner his attention, and when that eye flicks to me, he seems to return from whatever secret dimension he'd been waging silent battle in.

"Did you find her?" I ask.

"Her?" His voice is suspicious. "Her who?"

Now that I'm closer, I can't miss the hollowness under his visible eye. Nor the distance in his gaze. It's obvious the person within that stare isn't someone who knows sleep well.

"The girl," I clarify. "The one who woke you."

His attention drops to the coffee, as if he's only just noticed it. "She left. After what happened, I assumed you'd gone with her."

"Ingrid left?" This from Giovanni.

"Mr. Poole told me there was one other guest," says Elias. "And she isn't here."

Though I'm not sorry Ingrid has fled, I'm not certain she doesn't have the right idea.

Because . . . should *any* of us be here? Elias included.

"So, we're it?" asks Giovanni. "I mean, if I'm not fired."

Elias brings the mug of coffee to his lips and takes a small sip. His hand shakes, but the movement is faint, and I'm sure I'm the only one who catches it.

"If I could afford to dismiss you," says Elias, "you would not still be in my line of sight."

"Well, I *am* expensive to get rid of," says Giovanni. "But what they say is true. Everyone has their price. And listen, if it's worth more to you to send me packing, I take cash, card,

Venmo, PayPal, and/or Tilly the Lamborghini. Please, no checks. Not that I don't think you're good for it."

Elias slow blinks, like his eyelids—or at least the one I can see—weigh a thousand pounds.

"You really are *the* Mr. Thornfield?" I ask. "Meaning, there's no—"

"I authored the job listing," says Elias. "And the last letter. Though I'm starting to think I shouldn't have."

The listing. I'd received it in a psychic newsletter I didn't remember subscribing to.

I'd applied without much faith I'd get an answer, or that the job would be legit even if I did. The money involved was kind of outrageous. But all the follow-up correspondence hadn't been kidding about the danger, either.

"You're saying you're disappointed in the turnout?" I fold my arms.

"Hard to be disappointed when no one else would come," says Elias.

"I take it we're out of the loop on something," says Giovanni. "Or, as they call it from where I'm from, suckers."

Elias sets his coffee mug down. "Fairfax Hall has a reputation."

"And apparently," Giovanni interjects, "there's something to that reputation. You said no one else would come. Does that include the big-name pros?"

"Tell me," says Elias, ignoring Giovanni, "which of you has experience clearing spirits?"

The room goes quiet.

"No need to be shy," drones Elias, sarcasm tinting his words. "Humility is no virtue here."

Neither Giovanni nor I utter a sound, and as the silence booms, so does my heart.

I hadn't expected to be unmasked this way. Let alone to find out I wasn't the only person wearing one.

While the emails had questioned me about my abilities, they'd never asked outright about my specific experience in clearing ghosts. They just sort of . . . assumed I could. And had. And because of the number of zeros tacked onto the figure involved, I'd let them.

Elias's coffee cup reclaims his attention. "Just as I thought."

These words from him aren't disappointed so much as they are resigned.

A response that rankles me. Though I don't know why yet.

"You going to clue us in to what's going on here?" asks Giovanni as he pulls out a chair and takes a seat. "Or are you just going to keep emo brooding over your coffee all Tobey Maguire in *Spider-Man 3* except without the cute face and the eyeliner?"

"I need to be rid of this property," says Elias. "In order to sell it, I have to see it clear of what ails it. There is a dark force here. I know at least one of you has already encountered it."

"Yeah," says Giovanni, "Ingrid said she saw it."

"That helps to explain her absence," says Elias.

"Jane drew it," Giovanni adds. "I'll admit, he's not a looker."

Elias's scowl deepens, darkens, as it returns to me. "The entity appeared to you as well?"

"I didn't see it until I drew it," I say. "That's . . . what I do. I draw things that I see. In my head, I mean. Sometimes my drawings can strengthen a spirit."

"The spirit plaguing Fairfax needs no added strength,"

replies Elias. "Only invitation. Which you grant simply by being on this property. If *you* have not seen him yet, Mr. Luchesi, rest assured you will."

I glance to Giovanni. He touches a finger to his lips, passing the gesture off as a scratch.

For half a heartbeat, I'm tempted to rat him out anyway. Confess as well that, like him, I had encountered the entity *before* coming to Fairfax.

But Giovanni must be holding that tidbit close to the vest for some reason. I shouldn't care why. Especially not when he has a habit of spouting nearly every thought in his head. But . . . maybe I'll see how his strategy plays out before pitching him under the bus.

"So, this thing," says Giovanni. "What's it supposed to be? Ain't no run-of-the-mill boggart, that's for sure."

"It is an old thing," replies Elias. "Not of this world."

"You're not suggesting we're dealing with a demon," says Giovanni.

I'm glad someone puts that label on it. I'd been trying not to.

"It is a fitting title if you believe in such things," replies Elias.

"What do you mean 'if we believe in such things'?" challenges Giovanni. "Obviously *you* believe in such things or neither Jane nor I would *be* here."

"I believe in the power of darkness," says Elias, "and the things that inhabit such voids. However, to label my tormenter a 'demon' specifically is to acknowledge the existence of a counterpart. But life, as I have experienced it, has provided little argument for the presence of Providence. Therefore, I cannot ascribe a label to this creature other than 'oppressor.' "

"Soooo," says Giovanni to me, "demon."

"Sorry," I say, cutting in, "but . . . why not just leave?"

Silence again reclaims the room. Now, though, since its resonance is aimed in my direction, I want to shrink.

"I could quit Fairfax," Elias allows, straightening. "Abscond, as you say. Leave my problems where they lie. Pretend as though doing so won't eventually upend someone else's world. That would certainly cut out the need for *your* assistance, wouldn't it? Then you could go back to where you came from. Of course, nothing's stopping you, is there?"

This reaction from him is *almost* vicious. It does the job of shutting me up nearly as well as it does of hitting a nerve. Several.

But his sudden abrasiveness suggests that something about my question hit a nerve with *him* first.

"Okay, so walk me through this," says Giovanni. "You want to clear this property so that you can sell it."

"I assumed that was obvious," replies Elias with another slow blink.

"And you want to clear it before you sell it because you're a nice guy who cares about what happens to other people."

Giovanni offers Elias a smile. The kind that says he doesn't buy that story for one second.

To this, Elias makes no reply. But Giovanni hasn't figured out—I'm guessing in his whole life—when to stop lighting matches near gasoline, and he just keeps talking.

"So that's why you hired some random people to come here and tackle a demon for you. Because of your deep empathy and concern for strangers."

Where Elias's stare had been distant before, it now becomes hyperfocused on Giovanni.

"Believe me or not," snaps Elias after a beat. "It is enough for you to know I need the entity detached from the estate permanently. By any means necessary. If you cannot do that or no longer wish to, you're free to leave through the same door you entered."

"Touchy, touchy," lilts Giovanni. "Did I wander too close to whatever it is you're hiding about this ordeal?"

"It's no secret there is a large sum of money involved in this arrangement," says Elias.

"Which is honestly the only reason I'm still listening to your bullcrap," says Giovanni.

"Why is this thing here?" I ask. *Someone* needs to take the wheel of this conversation. It certainly feels we're headed for some kind of cliff. Or, at the very least, that Elias is.

"The entity—" Elias starts.

But Giovanni raises his hand to interject, and I want to murder him because of course he speaks without being called on.

"For the sake of clarity," he says, "I vote we give this thing a name. Bob feels right. Or Chester. Personally, I'm partial to Bob."

Elias starts again. "Your purpose is to perform a service. Not ask questions. Now that you are here, however, I must warn you of the rules our friend plays by."

"Bob," corrects Giovanni.

"The reason you've begun to see him," continues Elias, "*if* you have seen him, is because you, in turn, have become visible to him. By being here, you've entered into a dance with him. He's well aware, after all, that your aim is to purge him. Due to his nature, however, he cannot initiate interaction. Nor can he encroach upon you in any way unless you first encroach upon him. Ingrid saw the entity because she entered the property.

Basically, if you show up, he shows up. If you go after him, he goes after you."

"You burn him," I murmur, "he burns you."

That lone eye, startled, cuts to me again.

Elias remains silent for a long time, and somehow, I manage to withstand that penetrating gaze. Probably because I find myself searching it in turn. Diving deep to try to locate the source of his pain. Because there *is* pain. Also, I couldn't look away if I wanted. Not with that familiar *something* glinting at me from the very core of that eye.

He looks away, back down to the coffee, a pinch of defeat creasing his brow.

And just like that, without meaning to, I've won a contest (a battle?) I had no idea I'd been locked in.

"This was a terrible mistake," Elias says to his coffee. "Utterly reckless. Look at you. You're both so young."

"Same age as you, Cupcake," says Giovanni. "Or ish. How old *are* you anyway? Gotta be at least eighteen if you're calling the shots around here and throwing tens of thousands of dollars at people you don't know."

Elias closes that eye. He's gone for nearly half a minute. Then, at last, he speaks.

"Thank you for coming," he says, "but you are both now officially dismissed. From the property. From this undertaking." That eye opens and fastens on me. "We're done."

"Wait, what?" Giovanni pipes. "You're firing *both* of us? Me, I get. But not Jane."

"I am correcting a mistake," says Elias. "While I still can. Fret not. Mr. Poole will see to your full and immediate payment. A stipend will be added to cover your travel expenses and lodging, since that was a concern for you, Mr. Luchesi."

"Hooold on there, Zippy," says Giovanni. "I thought we were *in* our lodgings."

"Accommodations can be found in Bakewell," continues Elias in that careless monotone, "which is the nearest village. Though you are welcome to remain at Fairfax until morning, after last night, I do not advise it."

"Last night?" asks Giovanni. "What happened last night?"

"You're calling this off because of the fire?" I ask.

Because of me?

"Fire?" prompts Giovanni. "What fire? What are you talking about?"

"Jane," says Elias, "I won't ask what you did to provoke him, but the fallout of your actions, whatever they might have been, has put into stark relief the sheer heedlessness of this endeavor. Mr. Luchesi makes a point as well. I should never have asked anyone, least of all strangers, to put themselves at such risk."

"Dude," says Giovanni, "you're not supposed to agree with me. You're making me look bad."

"You knew last night the entity started the fire," I argue.

"*Bob* started a fire?" asks Giovanni.

"Yes," says Elias, answering me, "which was why I'd hoped you'd left. I don't want to have to hope for that anymore, though. And that is why I now desire for you both to leave. By daybreak at latest—preferably immediately."

I don't get a chance to argue. Because someone enters to stand in the archway leading into the hall.

"*So* sorry I'm late," says the girl.

Ingrid.

9

"I run a YouTube channel," Ingrid announces as she breezes into the room. "Ingrid with an Eye?" She pauses to point at the center of her forehead. Like she's sure we're too dense to get the pun. "Anyway, I had to finish posting my weekly readings for Aries, Leo, and Sagittarius, but the internet here is spotty, and I had to go hunting for a place to upload."

"*I'm* a Leo," says Giovanni.

"Oh, that does *not* surprise me." Ingrid laughs as she sinks into one of the chairs, looking well rested and put together. Which, even more than her lateness *or* obliviousness, makes me want to slap her. But then again, I guess she did help save my life last night. Right?

"Taking that as a compliment," says Giovanni. "How many followers you got?"

"I *have*," Ingrid says, selecting a scone and a small plate, "nearly a hundred thousand subscribers."

"Impressive," says Giovanni. "So, care to share what's in the stars for me today? Let me guess. Encounter with a shady truth-leaver-outer and I get fired."

"Mm," says Ingrid as she chews a bite, then swallows. "No. The Tower and The Chariot. Beware of collisions with cars."

"I almost got ran over *yesterday*, Ingrid," drones Giovanni.

"Well, it's a weekly reading," she says. "Energies are fluid."

"Bullshit's not," says Giovanni, "and, in case you were wondering, there've been piles of it stinking up this dining room for the past ten minutes."

"Your hair is pink," says Elias as he continues to frown at Ingrid, whose attention shifts to him.

"And you, sir," she replies, "appear to be lacking an eye."

"Wooow," says Giovanni. "So, who else wants to play Obvious Observations? I'm uncomfortable, *you're* uncomfortable—it's horrible awkwardness for the whole family."

"The patch is actually quite dashing," says Ingrid. "I'm assuming you're a psychic as well? *Also* enticing. Are you local? Or a Londoner, like me? Single? My cards say I'm to meet a mysterious gentleman, and *you* certainly fit that description."

Elias doesn't reply to Ingrid, and he doesn't press the issue of her hair again. I can tell, though, that something about her stirs his concern. Could it be Ingrid *wasn't* the one who awakened him last night? But then that would mean there's still someone else. Or, at least, there was . . .

"Has anyone encountered our host yet?" asks Ingrid.

"Oooh, ooh," says Giovanni, "allow me. Elias, this is Ingrid. Ingrid? Meet Elias. Cue shocking revelation sound riff."

"I'm sorry," says Ingrid, blinking wide, "what?"

"The demon," I say. "Can we please get back to the demon?"

"Demon?" pipes Ingrid. "Is *that* what that thing was last night? Please, someone, tell me what on earth is happening. My cards said it was a lost soul. But that hardly seems right."

"It no longer matters," Elias cuts in. "As I was saying before you entered, you are *all* dismissed. Please accept my apology for wasting your time. Mr. Poole will issue your checks. Good day."

Abandoning his coffee, Elias sweeps into the hall.

I gape after him, then spare a glance for the others.

"Was it something I said?" asks Ingrid.

"Beats me," says Giovanni, "but I do *not* volunteer as tribute."

"Was that *really* Elias Thornfield?" she presses. "The same who hired us?"

"Apparently," I answer.

"You're fired, by the way," adds Giovanni. "I'm fired." He points to me. "She's fired. Actually, thanks to Bob—we named the demon Bob—Jane is extra fired, though we're still waiting for the deets on *that*."

He arches his brows at me. I glare back. But Giovanni is the last person on my mind.

Another four seconds elapse, and then I move, rushing out into the hall before Elias can get away.

"Elias!" I call as he rounds a corner. When he doesn't stop, I jog after him. "*Elias.*"

Still, he doesn't respond.

So, I strip off the robe, ball it up, and toss it at him. Only when the garment nails him in the back of the head does he halt.

"What is your major malfunction?" I ask.

Ironic to have those particular words coming out of my mouth since that's what everyone at Lowood always asked *me.*

"You go through the trouble of bringing us all the way here," I challenge, "make a huge deal about how dangerous the job is, and then flake over a fire? Just because the help that shows up doesn't look like what you had in mind, that doesn't automatically mean we're a lost cause."

It doesn't mean *I* am.

"I am so *tired* of being jerked around by people who take one look at me and just assume whatever the hell they want. Did you ever stop to think, for instance, that maybe this thing set my bed on fire for a *reason*?" Reaching him, I stoop to collect the robe, which I again ball up before rounding on him. "*No.* You didn't." I shove his robe hard against his chest. "You prefer to write us all off, cut your checks because you can, and tell us to get lost because you want to assume we're worthless."

Elias doesn't move to accept the robe. He doesn't move at all.

And when I peer up at him, I'm rocked.

Tears streak his otherwise stoic face—though only on one side. The right. Beneath that lone visible eye.

A horrible stretch of silence, during which I don't know what to do or say, ticks by, my confusion festering until it becomes a living and devouring thing.

My insides turn over, too, the sensation bringing with it the impulse to take back everything I just said, even despite his previous coldness—his apathy.

An eon passes in which neither of us move.

And then, without warning, he takes the robe with one hand . . . and touches my cheek with the other.

"No one ever said *you* were the lost cause."

His voice is soft. Gentle enough to give me mental whiplash. Because what just happened to the sullen, chickenshit fail-boy I berated two seconds ago?

And why am I letting him touch me? Maybe it's the faint play of static that passes between us when his thumb grazes my cheekbone that keeps me frozen. And speechless.

Or maybe it's that damn *eye*.

Brimming with a sadness I can't help but recognize—and resonate with—it searches me. Reels me in even while it locks me out, all while that glint of the real him winks at me from its depths.

"Go home, Jane," he says at last.

Then, dropping his arm, he steps around me—and passes on, that scent of citrus and cinders swirling in his wake.

"You mean go back to where I came from," I correct, calling after him even as he rounds the corner, vanishing. "Can't. But just so you know, your little problem was there, too. Has been ever since I signed your sketchy waiver. Which is why I *know* you're lying about this place, yourself, *and* this thing. If he followed me here, who's to say he won't follow me back? You obviously don't care."

Though I wait—and wait—I do so in vain.

Because Elias never reappears.

Fine. I should have left long before now anyway.

Would have, too. If not for the money.

Problem solved, though, since he's paying us anyway. Which means I am free to go.

Correction: I am free.

And hopefully, my bailing out will be enough to get this demon thing off my back.

Mind made up, I give the finger to the corner Elias disappeared behind, holding the gesture as I back up through an archway. But then I start—someone is standing there, form rigid and spine flush with the wall.

"Uhhh," says a thoroughly caught Giovanni. "Nice bird . . . Bird."

10

I drop my arm, putting my hand on my hip instead. Somehow, Giovanni has managed *again* to surprise me.

And not in a good way.

"Were you seriously eavesdropping?" I ask.

"That's rich coming from you," he says.

"I wasn't eavesdropping in the study. I was there first. And can you stop tailing me?"

"C'mon," he scoffs, mimicking my pose. "That guy's a total shade parade. *Someone* had to make sure you were okay."

I level him with an I'm-not-buying-it glare. "You weren't looking out for me, you just wanted to listen in because you like to meddle. And for the record, I don't need anyone to look out for me."

I turn in the direction of the front of the manor. Because from there at least, I know how to get to my room. What's left of my room.

Of course, Giovanni follows.

"Hey, what's this jazz about a fire?" he asks.

"Elias's buddy torched my bed last night," I tell him.

"Whoa. Are you shitting me right now?"

"Elias put out the fire," I say.

After pulling me from the flames. Of course, he'd also been the one to put me into them—indirectly speaking. Like he had all of us. He'd pitched us into the blaze for a reason, obviously. Even if he's going to insist on being cagey about what that reason was. Along with what about this whole situation is bad enough to make him . . . cry.

"Where are you going now?" Giovanni asks.

"To get my stuff."

"What? You're bailing?" He's genuinely floored.

But not as floored as me.

Halting, I face him. "You *aren't?*"

"Can't." He rubs the back of his neck.

"Can't," I repeat.

"Yeeaah," he says. "Ingrid and I made a paranormal Hunger Games–style bet." He aims his thumb over his shoulder. "Just now."

"A bet? What kind of bet?"

"Over which one of our group is going to give Bob the boot tonight."

"You're serious."

"Thornface said we could stay." He says this like my concern has anything to do with Elias. And his comment. Does it mean that Ingrid has decided to stick around, too? *Why?*

I fold my arms. "Who did Ingrid bet on?" I have to ask.

"Me?"

Flummoxed, I spread my arms and let them flop to my sides again. "Then who did *you* bet on?"

"You."

I shut my eyes.

"You said you were here because of the money," I remind him.

"And I still am. I just . . . uh. Need more."

Need? And *more*?

"My bed was on fire," I remind him.

"Yeah," he says with downward inflection, like I'd told him I found a roach in the sink. "That's intense."

Intense? Is he hearing himself?

No. He isn't. Because he's Giovanni.

So, because I don't have the tools to reason with irrationality, I give him a nod—and resume walking.

"There's an old Italian proverb," he calls, hurrying after. " 'Since the house is on fire, let us warm ourselves.' "

I don't dignify that with a response. First of all, what does that even *mean*? Secondly, having been *in* the fire was warm enough for me. Besides, if *Elias* is tapping out, then why should I—or any of us—continue to put our keisters on the line?

"I'll split the winnings with you," Giovanni says when we arrive in the foyer. "Eighty-twenty."

Now I give *him* the finger.

"Seventy-thirty."

Two fingers.

"Fine," he says. "Fifty-fifty. I get fifty, you get fifty . . . minus a small processing fee since I'm the broker for the bet."

I mount the stairs.

"Bird."

I stop. "Do you have to call me that?"

"You got something against birds?"

"I'm not a bird."

"You look like you're flyin' to me."

I glower at him, detesting him even more than before but now for a far more infuriating reason. Mainly because, well, despite my sincere wish he weren't, he happens to be . . . ugh, likable.

Beyond the bravado, the rock star looks, the nonstop chicanery, the swagger, not to mention all that piss and vinegar, there's someone genuine there. But isn't my growing affinity for him all the more reason for me to, as he said, bail?

I didn't come here to make friends. I don't *want* friends.

They cost too much.

"Goodbye, Giovanni," I say.

"Jane."

I glare back at him.

"Food for thought," he says, "but you *did* kind of make a point just now. When you called out Lurch."

Lurch?

"You know," continues Giovanni, "about you being a target for a reason."

"You said this thing's been hassling you, too."

"Just the one time. But I heard *you* tell Tim Burton Bob's been creeping on you since you signed on. Don't you think that's sus? I mean, if *I* was Bob, I'd want to target the biggest threat first. Try to cut her off at the pass. Undermine her right from the start."

"I think his plan worked," I say. "Because I'm done. Extra-crispy done."

"Want to make a bet you're not?"

And *there* we go. Officially, and finally, I want to strangle him more than make out with him. Which is kind of a relief.

"Ten minutes ago, you were Elias's worst enemy. Now you're arguing for him?"

"Strategy, Jane," says Giovanni. "Think Peeta and Katniss." He swivels a hand between us like we're their counterparts. "How by working together, they outwitted the Gamemakers and won. Well, *kinda*. Spoiler alert if you haven't seen the movies."

"I read the books."

"There you go." He spreads his arms. "So, you know what I'm talking about even better than *I* do."

I roll my eyes and resume my climb.

"When you change your mind, Bird," he says, "my offer to form an alliance stands."

"You'll have better luck teaming up with your betting partner, Ingrid."

"She's not the girl on fire."

Again, I stop and turn back. But Giovanni's already walking away.

And then he's gone. Which leaves me with one option.

And that's to get gone, too.

Except . . . I drag my feet all the way up the rest of the stairs. Then, when I reach the second floor, I dither around, pulling out my phone and bringing up Messenger. My thumbs hover over letters, but they never land. I want Helen to tell me what to do. But . . . don't I already know what that would be?

Deep down, I do.

And that's why, by the time I reach the Red Room, my heart is the pyre.

Along the way, I told myself I would walk in, pack my stuff, find Poole, get my money, and then summon the tatted taxi girl.

Because anywhere has to be better than here.

The bed, burnt and charred, reeking of ruin, screams that truth at me.

And yet, here I stand, making no move toward my latest plans.

Probably because Elias's face parades through my head—the pain behind that eye and the resignation in his voice beckoning me to reconsider.

Damnit. *Why* did I go after him like that? Just had to tell him off, didn't I?

I broke my own hands-off rule when it comes to dealing with other people. And now here I am, paying the price. One I can't afford.

"He's in a bad way, there's no denying it."

Mr. Poole leans against the doorjamb.

"Let me guess," I say, "he sent you to escort me out."

Not the first time. Won't be the last. Wish I could say I've been kicked out of nicer joints but . . .

"*I* sent me to see if you needed transportation. We can even take Gloria if you like. She's a bit more stylish than Penelope, the Fiesta."

I'm dubious.

"He has a Ford Fiesta?"

"No, but *I* do."

I laugh. I can't help it. And Mr. Poole, hands in his pockets, strolls into the room.

"Out of curiosity, though, can you be talked out of leaving?" he asks. "Persuaded by my cooking? Bribed with homemade biscotti? I won't hesitate to make him buy an espresso machine. Can have it delivered by the afternoon. Just you say the word."

"You care about him," I say.

Mr. Poole sighs, big and heavy.

"It's my job to care." His tone loses all inflection as it drops several octaves.

"Where are his parents?" I ask.

"No relations. Everyone is dead."

The flames consuming my heart roar higher, hotter. I grit my teeth and, taking a deep breath, one that tastes of ash and charcoal and bitterness, I hold it.

One one-thousand, two one-thousand, three's a charm . . .

I let go of the breath and it rushes out of me like it contains my soul.

But nope. Still not ready to grab my stuff and blow this haunted-house ride.

Not *yet*.

"Can I ask . . . what happened to his eye?"

Mr. Poole deliberates, like he's searching for the right words. Or maybe sorting through what he can say that won't get him fired.

"*Damaged*, I think, is the best word for it," he replies at last. "And trust me, you wouldn't want to see it."

A response that implies *he* has.

"Something tells me it wasn't an accident," I press.

"Something tells *me* you might be good at this psychic thing."

I shift my weight to one foot and prop my hand on my hip. "What is going on here? The truth."

Mr. Poole stares at the charred bed, holding his silence for long enough that I almost repeat myself.

"Mr. Thornfield is the target of a very dark force," he finally says. "One that seeks to undo him. You might think of him as a drowning man. Or, perhaps"—he gestures to the bed—"a burning one."

"This entity," I say, "what does it want from him? And what's the *real* reason Elias doesn't just leave?"

"Mr. Thornfield can leave," Mr. Poole allows. "But, like most people, that won't stop him from taking his *true* troubles with him."

I scowl. And fold my arms. But only because I'm low-key guilty of doing some recent problem-dodging myself.

I left Lowood, sure. Maybe punched a face that needed punching on my way out . . .

But *this* time, when I dip, it'll be with enough green to get my own place, so *still* no regrets.

Except that eye. Will I *ever* get that eye out of my head?

Or forgive myself.

Now it's my turn to sigh. Short, sharp, and shallow.

"I don't get it," I say. "Are you trying to tell me he's cursed or something?"

"Or something," allows Mr. Poole as he frowns at the bed.

So, he's going to be cagey, too. Though I want to blame him for that, I can't quite make myself. Probably, his job is on the line.

Fair enough.

But this is not my circus. And these "dark forces" of Elias's are not my monkeys.

"I have a confession," says Mr. Poole.

Great. Because this place needs another shady character. I side-eye Poole, half expecting him to peel his face off and reveal Scooby Doo–style that he's the villain.

"This . . . plan," says Mr. Poole, "to invite sensitives to the estate in an effort to liberate Mr. Thornfield. It was . . . partly *my* idea."

I should be shocked but, for some reason, I'm not.

"Elias said he wrote the listing."

"He did," says Mr. Poole. "But only at my behest. *I* was the one to send it out. And to select, email interview, and hire the three of you. Truly, he didn't think anyone would come. And you lot were the only ones to answer the call. When I told him people *were* coming, he didn't seem to believe me. Then, yesterday, you all began to show up, and he experienced somewhat of a . . . crisis. Which is why he retreated to the garage. Mr. Luchesi encountered him there and Mr. Thornfield, rather adverse to being indebted to or dependent upon anyone, reacted . . . Well, we'll just say he *over*reacted."

"What you're saying is that he needs help," I murmur, "but doesn't want it."

"A walking, talking paradox if ever there was one," Mr. Poole mumbles in return.

"So then," I say, "you know all about Bob."

"Bob?"

I roll my eyes at Giovanni's selected name. Which *does* kind of simplify things since calling the demon "the entity" or even "the demon" isn't as streamlined. Also, something about calling him "Bob" *does* let some steam out of the fear he invokes. Not a lot. But some.

"That's what Giovanni calls the demon," I say.

"Ah," says Mr. Poole. "Bobby. What shall I say of him other than that . . . we've met?"

I nod. And nod. Lots of nodding.

Until I start shaking my head instead.

"*Damnit*, Giovanni," I grumble as I stalk toward the chair where I stowed my suitcase. It, too, stinks of smoke. Probably just like everything inside.

"Is there something the matter?" asks Mr. Poole. "Something Mr. Luchesi has said?"

"He got in my head," I snap. "You too. *Punks*."

"I beg your pardon?"

"Just . . . I need another room, okay? This one sucked anyway—no offense."

As I draw the zippers on the suitcase shut, the permeating odor of stale smoke and flambéed fabric carries me back to last night.

A flash of that hand shooting to me through the dark, the dancing flames, and the obscuring haze flicker in my mind. That one-eyed stare is a ghost in my memory, too. As well as that echo of . . . *whatever* I felt when he came into the kitchen this morning, our souls seeming to flare with our proximity to each other. Like they knew something about us we didn't.

"I *knew* you would stay," says Mr. Poole as I lift the strap of my knapsack from the ear of the chair. But . . . it comes away in my grasp too loose and empty feeling. Too light. "Truly, I never doubted it for a moment. Despite what Mr. Thornfield might say about it, I know he *will* be pleased."

Even before I bother opening the bag, I'm all too aware of what has gone missing.

Right along with who must have taken it.

"Where is that asshole?" I demand. "So that I can kill him before I save him."

11

I pretend to simmer down with the fourfold breathing that doesn't work while I let Mr. Poole put me in the "Moroccan Room." I also allow him to take a few of my clothes to clean so I'll have something to wear, but *only* after he promises to let me do the rest myself later.

If I survive long enough for there to *be* a later.

Though there is a fireplace in this room, I'm relieved the bed has no curtains. Instead, crafted from dark chocolatey wood, it's built into a nook, its mattress swamped by fancy pillows.

Pendant lamps hang from the raftered ceiling, some crafted from brass and others jewel-toned glass. Matching floor lamps cozy up to colorful ottomans and low-lying sofas. While the metal lamps cast intricate light patterns across wood-paneled walls, Oriental carpets, and parquet floor, the stained glass ones tint the space in parti-colored tones.

Unlike the Red Room, there are no corners for anything to hide behind and the middle of the space is open and more inviting.

Still, I wouldn't call it homey. There's something . . . ominous about this room and all the others. A pervading sense of foreboding that doesn't have anything to do with the decor. And despite its initial charm, the longer I spend in Fairfax, the more I get the sense this place once had a soul but that, somewhere along the way . . . that soul packed up and left.

Doesn't matter. I don't need to get too comfortable here anyway.

Even if Mr. Poole seems confident that I'll be staying, I'm not.

I'm just giving this ordeal—*Elias*—another chance.

I don't go searching for him, though, until the evening hours. According to Mr. Poole, Elias "took Tilly for a jaunt" right after I upbraided him for being a coward.

Well, right after he subsequently nicked my sketchbook.

Has my work been out there riding shotgun with him through the countryside? Probably.

The fact that he snagged it at all suggests that *something* I said got through to him. Prompted him to take the passive-aggressive route of kidnapping my originals and holding them hostage. Because approaching me like a grown-ass man and using his damn words to ask me to stay presented too much of a hurdle for his rich-boy pride. Or something.

After dinner, which Mr. Poole brings to me since I'm not up for rejoining the group until I talk to Elias, I go down to the first floor.

My heart keeps time with my quickened steps as I wend through the darkening halls. And then I arrive at the room with the lit candles. The room Mr. Poole had referred to as Elias's "preferred haunt" when I'd asked the housekeeper where I might find him.

My breath catches when I drift to hover in the open doorway. Because the large bank-style desk Ingrid used for her tarot reading now has my work strewn across it. The seats of several of the surrounding chairs support more of my sketches.

My first impulse is to start snatching everything up—stuff the drawings all back into the sketchpad I no longer possess. Instead, I go to face the source of the problem.

The source of *my* problem.

Of course, I find him behind the folding screen, looking like a true spider with those long thin legs and sharp elbows.

Though the candlelight splashes him in my shadow, he doesn't look up from the sketchpad, which he holds between both hands.

"The drawing of Melekd'mot isn't here," he says.

"*What?*"

"That's his name," replies Elias as he continues to study whatever drawing he's flipped to. "I wouldn't use it too freely. Speak of the devil . . . and all that."

All the more reason just to stick with "Bob."

Of course, the whole he-actually-has-a-name thing *is* interesting intel. After all, if Elias knows Bob's real name, that means he's also had a conversation or two with him. But hadn't I suspected as much already?

"I burned that drawing," I say. "Last night. Before bed."

At last, Elias dignifies me with his attention, that eye flicking up to regard me with grim irony.

"Ah," he says, like someone getting the punch line to a joke way too late for it to be funny anymore.

"Yeah." I put my hands on my hips. And I wait for an apology.

It never comes.

Another beat passes. And then Elias turns the sketchpad around to reveal my newest drawing—the one I started yesterday but have yet to finish.

"Who is this?"

I fold my arms. "Helen."

"A friend of yours?"

"My best friend."

"Her hair," he says. "What color is it?"

For a long time, I don't say anything. But then, I give in.

"Her hair *was* . . . red."

The mottled hue of a bed of burning embers to be precise, brilliant where lit, and almost black in the hands of shadows.

No one had hair like Helen.

That eye flicks to the paper again.

"I thought it might be," he replies in an almost inaudible mutter.

"It's a charcoal drawing," I argue.

"Yes, but there's something between—or perhaps even within—the layered tones of gray. Perchance it's the texture of the curls. Or maybe it's the depth of the shadows in between that suggests the contrast of a vivid shade."

My face begins to burn. Because these are compliments masquerading as observations.

"Why did you want the drawing of your homeboy?" I ask.

"I didn't really want the drawing," he says. "I wanted answers. But I wasn't ready to ask you for them. Or, frankly, to believe you had them."

"I probably don't."

"Maybe you *are* the answer," he replies.

Now *I* get quiet. Because, coming from him, that statement is both encouraging . . . and terrifying.

"I draw things," I say. "Not sure how that's going to help. But I'm here. And maybe my shtick will help one of the others do their thing. I dunno."

A beat passes. And then he changes the subject—or, rather, reverts it.

"Grayson advised me to apologize for absconding with your renderings," he says.

"Which *isn't* an apology."

"I am not sorry. But . . . I *am* indebted to you."

I stiffen, my throat tightening as I lower my arms to my sides again. "I haven't done anything."

"You stayed," he replies, his voice so soft it's almost not there. As though his throat is closing up on him, too, if for different reasons.

"I might still go—"

"I know," he says, "but by now you are well aware that every hour spent within these walls is a gamble. And clearly, you're not still here because of the money. Rather, you must have remained because, erstwhile, Grayson lied to you well enough to convince you I *am* worthy of your efforts. For your willingness to believe him, I am . . . obliged."

Obliged. Absconding. Perchance. *Erstwhile?*

Again, Giovanni was right. This guy talks like he clawed his way out of a Regency-era film remake with gothic undertones. Mr. Darcy with a splash of Dr. Frankenstein.

"This demon," I say, cutting to the chase. "How did you get involved with him?"

"A capital error on my part led to my current entanglement," he says. "Which leads me to ask how, exactly, you encountered the demon before arriving at Fairfax. Given that you had not yet encroached upon his territory, he should not have been able to interact with you."

"It doesn't take a genius to figure out *you're* the territory. Not Fairfax."

He goes silent. A wrestling-ring bell dings in my head and I award myself a point.

I shrug. "Just don't know why you'd lie about that."

Quiet booms from him. Because I'm saying things he doesn't like. Poking holes in his half-assed story. But if I'm going to have any luck helping him, if any of us are, then at the very least, don't I need him to start being straight with us?

"So," I continue, "taking that into consideration, my guess is that Bob started blipping on my radar because he knew you were calling me in. And something about that ruffled his fire and brimstone."

"Yes," he says, "I've been ruminating on what you said."

"Well, there's that," I say. "Wish I had a cookie to give you."

"There *is* something afoot, Jane," he says.

"Yeah. It's called the diabolical. And didn't *you* say Bob couldn't come near someone unless they came near him first? Which, logic would imply, means that you are leaving a big fat Elias-shaped hole out of your story since you just so happen to be the belle of the proverbial ball."

"You don't understand," he says, still deflecting. "Until last night, you and I had never met. So, he should not have been able to reach you until your arrival. Because you never would have been a threat until you officially answered my summons. Showed up. Became *invested*. Even then, he should only have been able to appear before you or, as you say, trip your senses."

"Well, I'm apparently the exception to the rule." Me and possibly Giovanni.

"Apparently, you are," he says, surprising me by agreeing.

Then we subject hop again. Because that's apparently how this guy operates.

"In the hall, you said you can't go home," Elias says. "Why?"

"I said I can't go back to where I came from," I correct. "My address was on the letter you sent, but Mr. Poole told me *he* was the one to send them out. So, I guess you don't know Lowood is a girls' school."

"You cannot return there," he guesses.

"I aged out of the system last month," I tell him. "And maybe lit a few fires of my own on the way out. So, basically, no. Pretty much *anywhere* I go that isn't my own place is going to be a short-term fix. One of the reasons why I took this job. So that I wouldn't *have* to go back there."

"You've no family." He states this like he's looking to abbreviate my issue—encapsulate it in an easy-to-swallow pill to aid his understanding.

"Looks like we have at least one thing in common," I say.

He blinks at me, and several seconds drain away, lost to silence.

Then, without warning, he stands.

"I have questions." He brushes past me to the desk, and I have to resist the urge to snatch my sketchbook away, which he's tucked under one arm. "Ones I think you *can* answer. This drawing. Tell me what is happening here."

He gestures to one of the sketches he's unearthed from my collection.

Hands curling into fists, jaw jutting, I drift to stand at his side.

The drawing is another one of my surrealist pieces. In fact, all the drawings on the desk are. Because, apparently, he was able to pick them out from the spirit sketches.

This one, which I'd spent hours on and still wasn't happy with, features the heads of a young man and a young woman—each in profile with their faces turned away from the other. Both their skulls are split open at the top to reveal figures standing within. A replica of the girl in the boy's head reaches for a replica of the boy in the girl's head, though their hands fall just short of touching. But lush rose vines spill from the skull of the girl while rambling briars wind out from that of the boy. The vines swirl around their corresponding figures, providing key coverage to their nude frames before spiraling up to intertwine in a traditional lover's knot.

"If I could tell you what's happening," I say, "then I wouldn't have to draw it, would I?"

That eye snaps to mine, scrutinizing. "These are not spirits?"

"Not everything I do is spirit related." I go to grab the drawing, but he lifts it away, holding it up to the light for further scrutiny.

"You mean not everything you draw is related to the spirits outside of your own."

Why do I suddenly feel like *I'm* the naked one here?

"Some of these are kind of personal, you know." I reach across him and take the drawing, which he releases to me. The one I hope to snatch up next, though, is the one he then seizes.

"Who is this?" he asks.

The figure in question is a young man—maybe the same from the first drawing. I'm never sure. Whoever he is, his expression is distraught, his clockface irises focused on the viewer while the crown of his head is depicted as a lit candle—one that's been left to burn. Wax drips from the resulting bowl in his skull. The streams streak his cheeks and trail from his chin like tears.

"That's no one," I say, and take that drawing from him, too.

He goes for a third sketch, featuring a sleeping woman in profile, her face cast skyward. Glass bottles with rolled-up messages inside bob in her turbulent and white-capped ocean-wave hair, which is webbed with sea froth.

I get this last one, along with the girl with the flower-filled rib cage, away from him before he can examine them more closely, an action that elicits from him an exasperated huff.

Because *of course* my work should be at his disposal.

He snatches up the last one, which is of a girl embracing a boy, whose body, like a clay pot, is fractured and breaking. Her crushing embrace is the only thing holding him together.

"Are there more drawings of these two in existence?"

I'd never said they were the same couple populating my drawings. Not even to myself. His observation, though, leads me to believe that maybe they are, and always have been.

"No."

"The inside of your head," he says, "does this couple occupy more of its furniture?"

"I guess." I take that drawing from him, too.

"And this one." Finally, he extends the sketchpad back to me. "Do you plan to finish it? I should like to see her face when you do."

"That's not going to help you with your demon infestation."

"Won't it?"

Slowly, I take the sketchpad from him. I don't reply, though, because the question strikes me as rhetorical. Or maybe I just don't want to answer.

"Your gift holds power, Jane," says Elias. "It might lack the mastery of one with more years," he goes on to say, "but it is . . . real."

His words shouldn't burn. Who is he, after all, to judge my work?

"I taught myself how to draw," I snip. "And what do you think I plan to do with the money anyway? I want to go to art school. But everybody has to start somewhere. And . . . I'm better than I was a year ago."

Two years ago. Because Helen also made me promise never to give up . . .

"How interesting," Elias muses. "You think I mean your drawings."

My gaze snaps up to his. He smirks like he set that trap on purpose.

"And so, I have learned something true about you," he says. "That you possess a woundable pride in regard to your art. Which means you care deeply about it. And to care for something is to live. You'll forgive me my ennui. For *I* have not cared for much of anything in a very long time."

Once again, the silence between us swells and I can't look away from that eye. The one that holds all the secrets, all the truth—everything he's not telling me with his words.

His last statement also contains a paradox that I'm all too willing to point out.

"*I* haven't cried since Helen," I confess. "Not once. And that was two years ago. Earlier, though, you—"

"I only mourn what is already lost," he says, "which is . . . everything."

"If that were true," I say, "I wouldn't be here and you wouldn't have stolen my crap."

That fleeting smile appears again, a faint curl of his lips that falls away the next instant.

"Let us see how tonight goes, shall we?" asks Elias.

And then he's gone. Leaving me in a sea of my own work, the silent screams of all my dark and twisted spirit drawings echoing the growing turmoil within.

Wanting to seal my drawings away again so that no one else will get a glimpse into the refuge of my mind, I start to gather them.

I stop, though, when my hand encounters one that *isn't* mine. At least . . . I have no recollection of drawing it.

At the same time, when I pick up the rendering to study it more closely, I find my style, habits, and hallmarks are infused in the sketch, which features a girl. She stands facing away from the viewer, her long and straight black hair hanging sleek down her back.

Her slight and willowy frame is familiar as well. Too familiar.

What's more, she's in a room identical to the one I'm in—except ruined and blasted through, with fallen walls, a toppled burnt desk, and a haze of smoke.

And the girl. She's holding a drawing.

Just like this one.

12

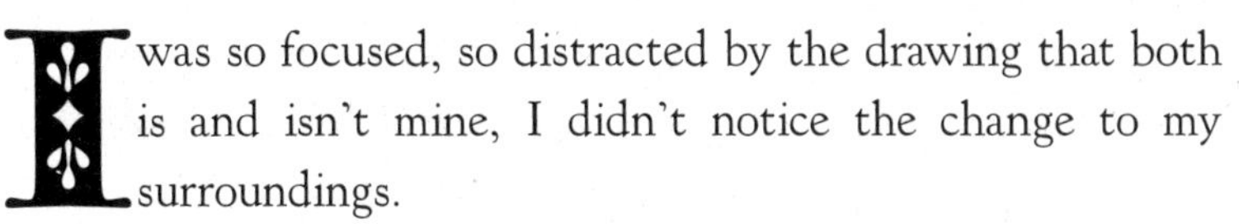

I was so focused, so distracted by the drawing that both is and isn't mine, I didn't notice the change to my surroundings.

Lowering the paper, I find myself transported—to a room identical to the one in the picture, one filled with scorched rubble and, just as before, a torrent of flaring, flying embers.

I'm back. Back in that bleak version of Fairfax, the red-orange horizon transforming the holes in walls into angry wounds.

Spinning toward the hall, I almost call out for Elias. But my voice catches when an ebony-robed figure passes by the doorway, which, along with the surrounding interior walls, still stands.

The moment strikes me as something of a replay of what Ingrid must have seen yesterday. Except now I'm in the demon's realm, and he doesn't glance my way as he had with her.

Hands shaking, heart slamming, I deliberate.

Because, this time, I *don't* want to go after him. Obviously, that's the response he's after.

And I talked a big game yesterday, but that was before I learned *this* little parlor trick of his. Or that his favorite game happens to be tag.

With that thought, all of Elias's warnings come back to haunt me. What, for instance, will I empower this thing to do if I engage?

But. Is there any way out of a head-to-head battle no matter what I do?

Not at this point. No.

Dropping the drawing, which burns away, dissolving into still more ash, I march through the door and hang a left into the wrecked corridor.

I wade through more floating embers that flow up from the burnt and eaten-through carpeting toward the same roiling cinnabar sky, which the blackened and crumbling ruins of Fairfax again open to.

"Where are you?"

There's no answer—no response. Just that hollow wind that whips through the gutted passage, stirring the firelit sparks into luminous eddies. So, I stalk farther down the hall, fueled by the knowledge that this demon wouldn't invite me to his playground if he wasn't nervous, on some level, that I packed a punch.

"Do you know what a demon is?"

I whirl with a short cry I can't help. And of course, he stands at the far end of the hall—*opposite* the direction I'd seen him go.

"It's a soul," he says, answering his own question, ". . . without a soul."

"You know," I say, "that really clears things up."

A pause. And then he starts toward me, steps slow and measured, the hem of his cloak dragging, sending a flare of embers up behind him. Like that's all this world is made up of—smoldering ash.

"I used to be like you," he says, pale cracked hands lowering the hood of his cloak, revealing the curled obsidian ram's horns that, until this moment, had remained hidden. Now loose, his hair, white as his skin, spills around his black-clad shoulders. The hollow wind lifts strands into a dance, and those eyes beam at me—the same two from last night's dream. "Long ago."

"We're nothing alike," I say, fighting the gut-level urge to turn tail and haul ass through this house of horrors. "*I* keep my dental appointments."

He doesn't stop until he's within arm's reach of me. His nearness keeps kicking my already screaming instinct. Even as he towers over me, I manage to hold my ground.

It's not because I'm brave. I'm just a realist.

Outrunning him is a fool's errand. Outwitting him, though? That's still a toss-up.

An acrid odor rolls off him—like burning tar, smoke, and old blood.

I should avoid meeting his gaze again, but I can't. His eyes take their hypnotic hold of me. Or maybe I'm just afraid to look away, even for a second.

I haven't touched this thing. So, doesn't that mean he can't touch me?

Except he already did, on the plane. Though that had been a dream. Is this?

"We are, in fact, the same," argues the demon. "With only a

single trait—one shining difference—separating us. And that is hope. I thought I ripped that out of you last time. But I didn't get all of it, did I? Or else you wouldn't be here."

"There *is* no last time," I insist, taking a step back from him, and another. "Bad as you want to fool yourself into thinking we have a history, we don't."

"Where are you going, Jane?"

I don't answer. Instead, I whirl—and slam straight into someone.

Not someone. *Him.*

And he's solid enough, *real* enough, to send me scampering back. Except an arm lashes out, a craggy hand catching me by the throat.

A scream surges up from my gut, but in his wrenching grasp, I can only gasp.

"What's that?" He tilts his head at me as he strides forward, backing me through the decimated hall, those cadaverous eyes brightening in their sunken sockets. "You want to know if I can kill you? Alas, no. At least, I can't take my shot until you take yours. But I *can* touch you. Torment you. Teach you. *Remind* you. Don't worry, though. Soon enough, I promise I *shall* return you to Helen's company."

Helen? *Helen.*

He's invoking her name as a way to scare me—break me.

But that's where he's gone wrong.

Because as frightened as I am now of him, this fear—this moment? That terror can't compete with the horror of my past.

With that day.

That morning.

When I woke up next to a cold friend.

When I awoke to find myself in this brutal world truly and utterly alone.

Helen died. She's gone. But everything she ever said and everything she ever was still fumes inside me. And the flame of her, that roaring part of her that survives within me, sparks to life with his utterance of her name.

And just like that, *I'm* the one burning.

I lash out at him, fingers catching hold of the black-bead necklace he wears. My nails scrape brittle-clay skin, which flakes at my touch, sending up a stream of dancing cinders.

Like the demon himself, the leather twine and its lone bead are real, and my hold on them prompts the demon to release my throat and grab the hand that clasps the necklace.

"You don't get to say her name," I snarl at him, yanking him down as I put my face in his.

For the span of a single heartbeat, there's something in those molten eyes that pleads.

And that's when he tears the necklace free.

He releases me the instant the string breaks—and the necklace comes away in my hand.

I don't think to drop the token. Instead, as he bares those shark's teeth, I take my chance and bolt down the hall, half tumbling, half charging into the foyer, which is restored—flush with color and void of embers. Walls meet and, above me, the ceiling seals the night from view. Underfoot, the flawless carpet hides the pale and polished stone floor. Though it also sports sooty footprints—*mine.*

Back now in the true Fairfax, I wheel around to scan the direction I came.

The hall leading to the study is normal. Everything is normal.

Breath ragged, my pulse still racing, my panic palpable, I scan for anomalies.

There's none. Everything is too quiet. And from next to the stairs, the portrait of that young woman judges me.

"Elias!" I shout. I don't know who else to call for. Until, suddenly, I do. "Giovanni!"

Neither one of them answers me. No one does. But there's got to be *someone* on the ground floor. Maybe Mr. Poole.

I veer into the dining room, the site of that morning's meeting.

The space is empty, so I stream through it and into the kitchen. My surroundings don't change. But can't I still feel him? The demon's here with me. Just like he was on the plane. Except it's harder to pinpoint him now. He's everywhere. In the doorway behind me. On the ceiling.

Beside me.

There. A flash of him in the darkened glass of the kitchen windows.

"Go away!" I command, and veer into the adjoining hall, which feeds me into another until I'm back to where I started, standing outside of that study.

All the candles within snuff at once, plunging the room into pitch-darkness.

Within the gloom, those eyes ignite, their piercing glow prompting my hands, already balled into fists, to tighten.

"Leave me alone!" I screech into the void—into that firelit gaze. Which then snaps out of sight—out of being.

But I'm not gullible enough to think this thing is that easy to shake.

I back up, ready to start running again, but my spine slams into something—*someone.*

Without thinking, I swing around with a roar, launching my fist into the air.

My knuckles connect with flesh—*warm* flesh—and my target's head jerks to the side. He even staggers a step, his expression astonished.

"Son of a *foxtrot*!"

I gasp as he straightens.

"Friggin' *uncle*, man," he says, extending a palm toward me as if to ward off another strike.

"Oh my God," I say. "Giovanni."

13

"Where'd you even learn to hit like that anyway?"

Giovanni and I sit opposite one another at the small kitchen table near the big windows that overlook the enormous stone porch, which is blocked from view due to the darkness without. Instead, it's our reflections in the glass that keep us company.

I'm grateful ours are the only ones. Though I keep waiting for *his* to show back up.

Giovanni has a makeshift plastic baggie ice pack pressed to his face.

Mr. Poole wasn't around, so we had to hunt through some drawers and improvise.

"Seriously," says Giovanni, "you're like the size of a canary but I feel like I've made out with a Mack truck. You got a cage-fighting brother or something?"

I chew on my bottom lip. Because despite Giovanni's . . . Giovanni-ness, he didn't deserve to be slugged.

"I'm surprised you didn't pick up on who taught me," I say. My way of trying to determine if he did, since there'd been skin-to-skin contact.

"Well, you see," he replies, "my tactile talent requires concentration and I guess I forgot to focus with your knuckles lodged in my skull."

"Don't you think you're being a little dramatic?" Maybe I ask because I'm ready for the barrage of guilt-tripping to stop already. Also, I need to talk to him.

"Oh, I'm sorry," he says, "my face has only been tenderized to a pulp. You're right, though. I should realize I deserved Jane Smash and stop being so theatrical, except, oh yeah, I wasn't who you meant to clock and you mistook me for a horned demon of the underworld and that's a likely story."

"You don't believe me."

"I believe you," he says, "I'm just laying it on thick because it makes me feel better about your kicking my ass."

"I didn't kick your ass."

"Maybe not," he says, "but clearly, you could."

I roll my eyes. "The ice is kind of melted. Do you need some more?"

"No," he snipes. Then, "Yeah, kinda."

I rise and go to the enormous fridge. I'm back seconds later with a coffee mug of cubes.

Giovanni doesn't say anything as I reclaim my seat across from him. I don't say anything either and, for a moment, he's absorbed in reloading his plastic baggie.

"No one can know about this," he mumbles to himself. "Gotta tell 'em I walked into a rake. Mauled by tigers. Fell down the stairs. Bird flew into my face. There we go. That one's not a lie."

"Helen," I say.

"Hm?"

"Helen," I repeat. "She's the one who taught me. How to punch."

"Older sister or something?"

Wow. He doesn't remember picking her name up off me. Which means he must not know what happened to her, either.

"Or something . . ." I mutter, borrowing Mr. Poole's vague response from earlier.

"Well, my compliments to Sensei Helen," he grumbles. "She's armed you well."

I cringe-smile, because he's not wrong. Helen had shown me how to make a fist by tucking my first two fingers around my thumb to form a striking point with the knuckles. And how to put weight behind my punches rather than just slinging a loose arm. "Say no to noodle arm," she'd remind me. And like most everything she'd ever said to me . . . the advice had stuck.

"So, you're telling me you had another run-in with Bob," says Giovanni. "*After*, I notice, you decided to stay. Didn't we have a bet about that?"

"Saw him," I admit, ignoring the bet remark. "Had a chat. Ticked him off."

"Hmph," he says. "Got a few questions about Bob, but first, why *did* you decide to stay? Not that I'm sorry. Even if you did pulverize my face-slash-pride."

I shrug. "I'm like you. Can't go back."

"You were about to go back. *Something* must have changed your mind. Or . . . someone. Like maybe a hunky Italian guy."

"Wait. There's another guy who showed up?"

"Woooooooow." He slouches in his seat, cheek turned like I just walloped him a second time.

In spite of my frazzled nerves, a grin fights hard to break onto my face. It's a war I'm destined to lose.

"At last, she smiles," says Giovanni. "Granted, it's at my expense, but in this instance, I gladly pay the bill. Soon as I get out of the burn unit, that is . . ."

I snicker, unable to help it. And I let the moment linger. Until the weight of all the ones that have come before tempers the levity.

"I don't think I'm going to win your bet for you," I say, my smile falling, my mirth wilting.

"Maybe not *tonight*," he says. "But it looks like we've got more time now. What'd you say to Thornfart to dislodge that broomstick anyway?"

"You heard what I said to him."

"Okay. Fine. Then what'd he say to *you*?"

"It wasn't anything he said."

"He did something," Giovanni guesses.

"More like . . . he *is* something," I say. Trapped, lost. Hopeless . . .

The demon's words from earlier return to me. About how, according to him, the only thing separating us, me from him, is hope.

In so many words, Elias himself had said *he* is out of hope.

"Obviously, he needs help," I murmur.

"I guess it's going to stay a mystery then—whatever passed between you two."

"I guess so," I say, "but . . . not just a mystery to you."

His smirk returns. "Just something about him, huh?"

I frown at Giovanni. Because he's trying to pry me open like an oyster—glimpse the grit inside, determine whether or not it's some kind of juicy pearl.

But it's just grit.

"I need you to do something for me," I say, my hand tightening around the leather strap of the necklace I still hold. *Bob's* necklace.

"A favor, eh?" he asks. "Does that mean you're up for forming that alliance?"

I don't answer. Instead, I hover my fist over the table and then relinquish the necklace.

My already thudding heart booms extra hard with the quiet *thunk* its lone bead makes against the polished wood. Then, swallowing hard, I pull my hand away.

"Um," I say. "Can you . . . get a read on that?"

For a long time, neither of us moves. Or says anything.

"Huh," Giovanni murmurs at last, tilting his head at the artifact. "Where'd ya get . . . that?"

The way he asks . . . Well, it's not like he really wants to know the answer.

I clear my throat and go over my options for responding.

For now, until I get his thoughts on this necklace, I'll hold back on telling him about the alternate hell-world Fairfax.

"Um, that's Bob's," I say. Because, at the very least, he should know that much before touching it, right?

Giovanni blinks. Lowering his ice pack to the table, he nods, letting that tidbit sink in, all while never looking away from the bead.

"That's, uh . . ." he says at last, "a little more corporeal than I want it to be."

"Right?" I ask, breathless, my nerves winding tighter once again. Because spirits aren't supposed to be tangible.

"Yesterday, you told Thornfield you encountered this thing before," he says. "That it was tagging you. Was Bob, uh, this amount of real then, too?"

"N-no," I say, mind flitting back to the incident on the plane. "I don't think so. He wasn't . . . until I got here."

"You know," says Giovanni, "there *is* something up with the energy in this place. That door I touched yesterday. I'm starting to realize that kind of static is everywhere. It got stronger after Thornfield showed up, too. Jane. There's something going *on* here."

I lean forward over the table, eyes boring into his. "I *concur.*"

"No wonder you tried to punch him," he mutters, his expression turning queasy as his gaze flicks back down to the necklace that *shouldn't* be there. Because spirits, at least all the ones I've ever encountered, don't have bodies. *Or* possessions.

Giovanni takes in a deep breath and holds it. Still, he trains his gaze on that lone bead.

"Guessing he didn't lend this to you for safekeeping," he mumbles, stalling.

At least my impression is that he's stalling. Can't say I blame him. On the plane, I hadn't wanted to peer too closely, either. And look where doing so has gotten me.

"Listen," I say. "Forget it. I get it if you don't—"

Giovanni hovers his free hand over the bead and his eyes go to one side, like he's listening for something, trying to decipher whispers or excavate some far-off memory. Then, between finger and thumb, he plucks up the black bead pendant.

Straightaway he drops it, scoots back his chair, and stands.

His hands go to his hips and he starts pacing. He's angry, and I'm sure I'm about to get reamed. He shakes his head.

"What?" I say. "What is it?"

"That is . . . really, really old. Like, borderline ancient."

"I used to be like you," the demon had said. "Long ago."

Well. Now, thanks to Giovanni, I have an idea of just *how* long.

"And?" I prompt, glad his anger doesn't seem to be aimed at me. Instead, it just seems . . . to be. Or like maybe . . . it isn't even his.

"Belonged to some ancient chick the demon used to know," he says, still pacing. "Murdered."

"Oh my God."

"He, the demon, uh . . ." Giovanni trails off, hand going to cover his mouth.

"He killed her?"

Giovanni shuts his eyes. His brow pinches with pain. Once again, he shakes his head, and this time, he means it as an answer.

"No," he says at last, voice uncharacteristically thin. "He didn't. He . . . wanted revenge for her death."

We both go silent for a long time after that, our stares again reclaimed by the necklace.

"And, in case you were wondering," Giovanni says at last, "he got it. And that's why he is . . . what he is. But that's all I know. That's all I got. And just so *you* know." He points to the necklace. "I'm never touching that thing again and you should probably get rid of it."

He's upset. Bothered enough by whatever energies—

memories—he picked up from the necklace that his eyes have gone red.

He even sniffs as I stand.

Maybe I shouldn't have asked for him to read the necklace.

I start to stammer an apology, but he's already walking away.

"Giovanni, wait," I call after him.

"I'll catch you tomorrow," he says.

"Tomorrow when?"

"I don't know," he says. But then he adds, "Noon," over his shoulder before leaving.

And this time, even though the last thing I want is to be alone again . . . I let him go.

14

I don't do what Giovanni told me to. Meaning, I don't "get rid of" the necklace.

No need to make things worse and tick this demon off further by chucking his bling into the toilet or burning it. Already learned my lesson there. And now that, through the avenue of Giovanni, the necklace has revealed something about my enemy—roughly—I don't need it anyway.

I certainly don't want it.

I do, however, want what's mine.

So, I return with the necklace to the study.

I flick the lights on, bracing myself for a sketchpad massacre. Or worse.

The room is empty, though, and my drawings are all intact.

I swap the necklace out for my work, trusting (hoping) that Bob will find it so that he doesn't come *asking* for it. Then I hurry back to the Moroccan Room—like it's home base in some twisted game of hide-and-seek and I'll be "safe" there.

After I set the sketchpad on the low-lying coffee table, I pace, sparing glances at it while replaying my conversations with Mr. Poole, Giovanni, Elias . . .

I *need* to go to bed. I need to rest. I need to have my wits about me.

I'm alone, though, and inside a sprawling manor that contains something that wants me dead.

Or, at the very least, out of the picture.

The picture.

I return to the sketchbook and flip it open to my unfinished drawing of Helen.

The guidelines I made yesterday are still present, providing the barest impression of where everything is supposed to go: Helen's nose, mouth, eyes.

Though still sore from their collision with Giovanni's cheekbone, the fingers of my right hand twitch with the instinct to fill in the drawing's missing parts.

So, I settle onto my knees in front of the coffee table and dig through my bag for my charcoals. Clasping a broken piece from one of the raw sticks between three fingers, I hover the bit of black over the white, calculating where to start, and even if I should.

Previously, I'd been so afraid I wouldn't get Helen right.

That face that had been in front of mine every damn day until . . . it wasn't.

Making myself again be brave, I give Helen the impression of eyes. I outline her slightly upturned nose next. Full lips come after that, conveying the faintest of smiles because—wasn't she always up to something?

Her freckles go everywhere—gamboling across the bridge

of her nose and along the bones of her cheeks, plentiful as wildflowers. I trade the black charcoal bit for a white one, adding highlights that give the drawing depth and—*almost*—life. And suddenly, my best friend, Helen Burns, rises through the paper, burning indeed. As she'd always done.

She's not finished. Aside from her hair, she's just a wisp of herself. A suggestion of a memory—a mirage of uncertain lines rendered by an uncertain hand.

Still, I have to shut my eyes to block her out. Because the twisted knife of sorrow corkscrewing its way through my heart is too painful. That, and my relief that I *haven't* forgotten her face, is too potent to process or contain.

The rupture of bittersweet emotions sends the charcoal bit tumbling to the carpet.

Oh, Helen.

"I should like to see her face." Elias's words from earlier echo unbidden from the corners of the day's memory, eliciting from me a sharp hitch.

And now, because it hurts worse to keep my eyes closed since doing so seals me in a world where Helen is no more, I open them again to peer down on that face that, even though it's just a facsimile, still . . . *exists*.

I trace the air just above one of Helen's paper cheeks, too afraid of smudging the work with charcoaled fingertips to actually touch her. As I do, I can't help the audible response that bubbles from deep within me, dislodged like a shell shard from so many layers of sucking silt.

"Yeah," I whisper, managing to swallow the tears I thought had all dried up, "I should like to see her face, too . . ."

♥ ♥ ♥

A LOW REPETITIVE beep, along with the scent of fresh-brewed coffee, summons me out of sleep.

Lying on my side, I open my eyes to a blank white wall. A *familiar* blank white wall.

I frown at the nearby overlarge window with its miniblinds, trying to place my surroundings—or rather, dismiss them as impossible. But then a man garbed in pale gray scrubs, the same hue of the diffuse light slanting in through the blinds, drifts into view.

He has a clipboard in one hand—and a paper cup in the other. The aroma of coffee follows him as he checks the beeping heart monitor. Then, after taking a sip, he glances down at me through a pair of horn-rimmed glasses.

Wait. *Mr. Poole?*

He gives me a tight worried smile, and then, without a word, he reroutes the way he came.

I turn over in the bed to watch him go, but I gasp to find a face in front of mine.

And not just any face.

"Hey," Helen says. And it *is* Helen.

Even though she's older now, the same age as me, it's her. Her face might be less cherubic than it once was, with fuller lips and narrower cheeks, but her nose is as button-y as ever.

Medieval-princess-long, her fiery curls spill everywhere.

Last time I saw Helen, she didn't have any hair at all. Her skin was ashen, her bright bottle-green eyes bereft of their shine and dulled from weariness.

She's not sick now. In fact, a faint glow haloes her—as

well as that lilac essence that's somehow less acidic, as if she's stuffed actual flower petals into the pockets of her jeans rather than just misting herself down in her off-brand Walgreens body spray.

"*Helen*," I whisper, and seize her hand, which is warm, soft, and *real*. Her name is all I can say as my heart kicks to life in my chest, banging a Morse code message to my brain.

Dream.

This must be a dream. Otherwise, how could we be back in that same hospital bed together, face-to-face with our knees tucked up between us?

Instead of a hospital gown, though, Helen has on her usual—T-shirt, jeans, and hoodie.

The room, cold, sterile, and deserted, is dark like it had been the night she died. Now, though, that fuzzy gray light that sneaks in through the blinds turns everything hazy, like in a movie flashback sequence.

"I got your message," Helen says, squeezing my hand.

"Which one?"

She blinks, and slow smiles. "All of them."

"Yeah?" I swallow, tormented by the idea that, despite how vivid this moment is, it might not be—probably isn't—real. Any second, I'll wake up and not be able to remember a thing about seeing her. "How . . . how come you never write back?"

Even as her smile falls, I'm struck with how beautiful she's become. Which compounds my sadness. Because I'm reminded of how much the world is missing out. Who knows what she might have grown up to be? She could have been a bakery owner like she always wanted. Maybe even a movie star. I could see her in one of the new superhero films, decked out in armor, and kicking everyone's ass.

"I had to wait," says Helen. "I needed to wait."

"Wait for what?"

"Things are thin here," she says, eyes scouring mine. "And getting thinner."

Even though in the back of my mind I'm aware that this conversation, this *dream*, makes no sense, I want it to. Because if I can make it make sense, then I'll be able to believe when I wake up that it *was* real. That *she* was real. That she's still out there. *Somewhere.*

"Helen, I'm afraid this is a dream," I say, because it was never hard to tell Helen when I was scared. Could never keep it from her anyway. "I'm afraid *you're* just a dream."

"*Everything* is a dream," she whispers.

I let that sit. But the longer her words stew in my head, the less I like what she's implying. Not that her meaning is clear to begin with.

"Come with me," Helen says, and rolling away from me, she climbs out of bed. "Time is running out. And there's something you need to see."

Her motions unfold too easily, not at all like they had during her last days, when every shift of her emaciated body, every word uttered by cracked lips, every *breath*, had been a fight.

I'm so stunned by her rejuvenation, her return to health, that I can only stare after her as she heads to the door. As she moves through the room, though, my surroundings begin to change, as if her steps burn away some invisible curtain, or as if her stride erases some filter.

The hospital room dissolves, its nondescript walls replaced

by light-mottled wood, the stark linoleum becoming parquet populated by lush and colorful carpets. The door, left ajar by the nurse who my mind had cast as Mr. Poole, is the last thing to transform as Helen opens it to slip into the hall without a single backward glance, her hair trailing after, bright as a beacon.

The instant she's gone, I sit up. As the room rights itself, I'm keenly aware of being wide awake. Almost as if I hadn't been asleep at all . . .

Like, instead of a dream, I'd simply been inside a vision. *Another* vision.

Except the pillow next to mine still holds the indentation of a head.

Along with that pervading aroma of lilac.

Also, the door to my room now hangs wide open—to the same degree Helen had pulled it as it transformed from the heavy hospital door to the carved dark wood one.

Almost like . . .

If I hurry . . . I might still catch her.

15

"Helen?"

The darkened hall swallows my whisper.

"Helen!" I rasp, checking left and right, but she doesn't reappear.

For a moment, I'm torn. Because, in this house, leaving the sanctity of my room feels like abandoning a foxhole for a field of landmines.

But then, it's not like my room is truly any safer.

I pad barefooted out into the corridor, my phone clenched in one fist, its flashlight activated.

With no clues to go on, I pick a direction, moving with my bubble of light toward the stairs leading down to the first floor. But then I halt at the whisper of my name.

"*Jane.*"

I spin and peer back the way I came.

Still, there's no one.

I start in that direction anyway, ears tuned for any other

noise, any other indication I'm not imagining things, or being tricked into seeing and hearing them.

Hooking a corner, I find myself in a long blue-tinted corridor lined on one side with windows. The sashes of a few have been opened to allow in the cool night air, and the gauzy white curtains that frame them lift and float like specters.

I raise my phone, but the moonlight washes out the artificial glow, painting everything that's not deep blue or black in tones of pale silver.

With no sign or sound from Helen, I'm stalled yet again.

Until the breath of the wind fails and the curtains fall to reveal the flip of flowing red hair as it vanishes around the next bend.

"Helen!" I call, no longer bothering to whisper. "Helen, wait!"

I run, my breath fast and loud, my feet not quick enough.

Swinging around the bend, I keep running, but again there's no sign of her. She's getting away. She's leaving me. Again.

My chest tightens, and in my rib cage, my laboring heart starts to crack along the old seam her death ripped—bleeding afresh.

What's worse, this hall terminates in a dead end. There are no more hallways to turn down, but there *are* doors. I trade my gaze between all of them. Because she has to be behind one.

But it's the squeak of hinges that halts me and draws my attention to a set of darkened steps I nearly pass by.

I aim my phone's light into the open archway, and the glow illuminates the stone steps that curve up to some unknown area.

The creak of hinges—it had come from up there. And so, that's where I go.

There's no banister to hold on to as I ascend and round the climb, just cold and unadorned stone walls that I press my hand against to keep steady.

At the summit of the steps there waits a door that hangs ajar.

I peer through the crack into a chamber populated by the silhouettes of furniture and bric-a-brac.

When I press on the door, the hinges whine, and the source of the noise that had brought me here cannot now be denied. I push a little more, and the door yields, opening to allow my light to invade the space within.

Darkened pendant lights hang from a vaulted ceiling that, in the center, supports a circular, crosshatched skylight.

Moonlight pours through, creating a wide spotlight on the naked floorboards of the sprawling attic suite. I drift to stand in its glow, and turn to survey the room's adornments.

Against the far wall dwells another four-poster bed. Its heavy dark green curtains hang loose around the rumpled bedclothes. Closer to me, a beaten and studded leather couch plays host to a large pillow that has also seen better days. The couch is paired with a coffee table, its surface swamped by tattered books. There's a vintage turntable stereo in one corner, bins of vinyl records stacked on either side. Steamer trunks serve as more desk-like surfaces, supporting trays of candles and still more books, both modern paperbacks and ancient-looking cracked-spined hardbacks. Exotic car magazines are layered with folded and aged newspapers as well, the crossword puzzles of which are jammed with answers.

Though there's no artificial light to be had aside from my phone flashlight, floor lamps—as mismatched as everything else—stand here and there, placed strategically near armchairs, as though the room's restless inhabitant can cope only with so much light at one time.

Clothes—*nice* clothes—litter the floor near a large wardrobe, the door of which hangs open. Dark garments make their home inside, shadows waiting to be donned.

Someone's scent hangs in the air, as though this enormous room knows its occupant well enough to be soaked in his essence.

That scent is citrus and smoke, wood dust, and ash.

And now I really *am* a creepy spider. For walking straight up and into Elias's bedroom.

Aside from being fascinated by all his private quarters convey about him, I'm beyond thankful he's not here. Now that I've had my fun, now that Helen's had hers, everything within me screams to beat a hasty retreat.

Because I can't just—

There comes a rattling from the far wall. My eyes fly to the source—a narrow door. One secured with an aged deadbolt.

Making a horrible racket, the door clatters in its frame as if possessed. Or as if whoever—whatever—happens to reside on the other side has perceived the presence of an intruder and wants free. Either to escape, or to devour.

My instincts scream at me to *go*. To rush back down the way I'd come and pray never to find out just how close I got to facing that room's occupant.

I swallow hard, but the lump in my throat doesn't go down, and my feet refuse to move.

For some reason, I can't will myself into motion. I'm frozen by the question of what will happen next, and what Elias will say—what he'll think of me—if *he's* the one who comes bursting out that door to find me lurking in his bedroom.

The thumb turn flicks with a *clack*, the knob twists, and the door bursts open with a high-pitched *scrreeeeeee.*

I stifle a yip with my hand, but still I stay put, every part of me tensed and coiled.

But no matter how long I stand here waiting, no one emerges from the room within a room. The door just . . . hangs open.

"Hello?" I call, my voice weak, soft, and un-Jane-like. "E-Elias?"

Nothing.

"Helen?" I try again, forcing bravery into my tone.

No answer.

But something *does* call to me. There, just within the second doorway, dwell stacks of notebooks, their edges awash in a shaft of moonlight. They're old, some even bound together by frayed twine, the pages between the binding brittle and yellowed.

I cast my light behind me, toward the curving stairs, again tuning my ear to any disturbances.

Stillness reigns. No one enters from either direction.

I waffle while both doorways pull at me, each enticing me for different reasons. I take a step back toward the stairwell but then stop, glancing once more to the interior door.

Helen said there was something she needed me to see.

I let out a breath and the floorboards complain as I cross through the cage of moonlight mapping them. Dust motes swirl in the disturbed air while my discomfort at encroaching on Elias's territory magnifies with each step.

But no matter what, Helen had been the one person I could never disappoint. Or say no to. She'd been the one to push me into getting on my first roller coaster. And this moment—it is hitting my system like that one. Except the stress level is times a million.

On my way to the second room, I pause next to the bed, unable to help surveying the twisted state of the bedclothes and the collection of coffee cups and over-the-counter sleeping pill bottles populating the bedside table.

I'd been right to assume sleep is no friend to Elias Thornfield.

Leaving the contradictory items where they lie, I pass into the second room, which, though much smaller than the adjoining attic suite, is still large by my standards.

The room's lone window sheds light on two solitary pieces of furniture: a small antique writing desk, its surface strewn with pens, paper, and more notebooks (these modern), and a simple chair—identical to those in the downstairs foyer and the one from that portrait of the young woman.

Elias's robe—the same one he'd looped around my shoulders after the fire, the one I'd chucked at him—drapes the backrest of the chair.

Does this mean he'd come straight here after that interlude? Or, the moment after my words had sunk in, had he instead made a beeline for my room to retrieve my sketches?

The sketches he then invited himself to peruse.

Suddenly, I'm less worried about trespassing, and I pivot to survey the stacks and stacks of journals that surround me.

The same aroma that first hit me when I entered the manor

invades my nostrils. The odor doesn't belong to books this time. Instead, it's the ancient journals that waft this distinct and unmistakable perfume of ink and age.

The stacks of journals, hip high in some places and as tall as me in others, line the stone walls and stuff the mouth of a fireplace. The pages fade in an ombre pattern from one side of the room to the other, going from dingy yellow to clean white.

I hesitate before I start my inspection. Are these journals really what Helen means for me to see? Since there's no one in the room, I can only assume it *was* Helen who opened the door. *Both* doors.

Hopefully, since she's not here, she's somewhere keeping a lookout for me.

Deciding to trust her, as I had yet to regret doing, I select a waist-high stack of older journals and flip open the top book, a traditional hardbound journal, to a page somewhere in the middle.

I find a diary entry. Or . . . is it a letter?

12 June 1925

Dearest Thea,

There are words and then there is silence. I grant the former to you within these pages and all those that have come before. Ever, though, do you reserve the latter for me.

I remember the days, however, when your laughter cloaked my heart in its wind. In the night would you then sweep me away with promises that, though unspoken, were still bestowed by your lips. Would that you were here. Would that you had never left. Would that I had been all I am now that fateful day we first spoke—but without the travesty of my mistake.

Would that have changed anything?

The gods are cruel.

Your very breath was kindness.

And that is why I've come to assume you must have been a dream. Conjured from the vaults of my own being. Or else the heavens masquerade in light, and you were just a phantom sent to convince me angels were real.

Eternally yours,

Elias

I shut the journal, my cheeks pinkened by the wording.

That one part—does it mean what I think?

Some kind of twisty sensation that is utterly foreign to me ties my insides in knots when the image of Elias kissing someone flits into my mind. I push the visual aside, because this *can't* be Elias's journal—even if the language does seem to echo his own weird and archaic way of speaking. And sound eerily like his letter to us . . .

The date forbids it. The *math* forbids it.

Flummoxed, and even more curious, I move down the line of notebooks toward another stack. This time, with care, I tug one out from the middle and, opening it, I let it fall to the page it wants.

25 September 1940

My Loveliest Thea,

Again, the world fumes war. It acts out echoes of what, in your absence, I have become within.

Man tears apart his fellows, and I am no better.

Who, though, have I to rend to shreds but myself?

What is left, at least.

My love, I am wrecked without you—a shell of that boy who, with a daring kiss, answered the pitch of your fever with his own and, in so doing, contaminated <u>*both*</u> *our fates.*

Like the bombed buildings in London that the papers show, I am half-collapsed and blasted through where still standing. Cruelly, I am left to teeter on the precipice of total destruction, never permitted to crumble one way or the other.

One day, though, I shall fall. But never again into your arms.

I am grateful you're not here to see me this way. Nor this greater chapter of darkness in human history.

Even so, I tell myself I <u>*would*</u> *be happy just to behold you one last time.*

I would not be. One glance, one touch, one kiss—it was never enough even when you were here.

Without you, though, lies like this have become my new bedfellows.

They seduce and sustain me the way nothing else of this world can.

All the same, it is a small consolation to tell myself the remnants of my soul could be sated with the gift of a final farewell.

Nightly, it is what I barter and beg your wardens for.

And mine.

Dream of me while you sleep. If you are even there.

Officially, I don't have a good feeling about being in this room, this house, this . . . job.

My mind tells me to turn around and get out of the attic, the manor, the country. My gut, though, urges me on. And so, I abandon this journal as well and shift down yet again, this time finding my way to the desk.

There's a notebook set apart from the others; black spiral-bound college rule—the kind you might get at the drugstore for under a dollar.

I flip its cover open to find it bookmarked by a black pen. The date heading the entry is yesterday's, and the letter below is the simplest yet.

My Beloved Thea,

This situation. It has reduced me to the role of petty thief. And what, you ask, is so dear that I would stoop to steal?

A glimmer of hope—the only currency still precious to me.

How do I explain?

An hour ago, all was lost. He had won. And I was more certain than ever I would never see you again.

But then . . .

Could it be, is it possible, that you have forgiven me after all?

Either way, I am and always shall be yours,

Okay. *What.*

He's talking about me in this last one. My drawings, at least.

While I scan yesterday's entry again, the back of my brain works double time to try to make sense of these letters, and all the writing that surrounds me.

Is *every* entry addressed to Thea? And are they *all* written this way?

Devastatingly and gut-wrenchingly beautiful? With words simultaneously as pure as they are pitiful?

My stomach untwists and retwists as my glowing phone draws my attention, and I'm reminded instantly of my own one-sided correspondences with Helen—a million times less eloquent, but equally as heartfelt. As bereft.

But . . . that can't be what's going on here.

This simply has to be some kind of . . . poetry project. Or ongoing creative writing venture.

But then, how many books would these legions of journals equate to? And how come I'm sort of alluded to in the most recent?

You know what? None of my damn business.

I've seen enough. Time to bounce.

But . . . my hand, as it goes to tug open the simple desk's lone drawer, argues otherwise.

There are more pens within, as well as a stack of photos bound by string. I brush the pens aside, unearth the photos, and untie their twine.

The first photo depicts a young woman—the same from the portrait downstairs. She sits at the wheel of an old-fashioned motorcar shown in sideview. It's an open-air two-seater buggy kind with huge thin tires and bug-eyed headlights. The woman has on a long plaid skirt and wide-brimmed, ribbon-wrapped hat. Behind her looms the portico of Fairfax Hall.

The next photo is a full-body portrait. Again, the subject is the same girl from the painting in the foyer, though her face is in profile here. Resplendent in a stunning lace-trimmed gown, hair bundled at the nape of her neck, she leans an elbow on the mantel of a fireplace I recognize from the downstairs drawing room.

I flip to the last black-and-white image—the most jarring of all.

Because there is *Elias*, garbed in a suit of black and a white dress shirt paired with matching bow tie. Seated in a chair that is twin to the one accompanying the desk in front of me, he watches the photographer with that one eye, because he still has on the patch.

Elias, though, isn't the oddest thing about this photo.

Next to him stands the same girl. And this time, she's arrayed from head to foot in white.

Yards of lace cascade from her crown of fresh roses, the bridal veil brushing Elias's shoulder as it tumbles to pool about the hem of an epic wedding gown. And the dress's high collar, cinched waist, and poufed sleeves place the photo's subjects, just like the other two, firmly in the Edwardian era.

The couple in the photo can't be much older than eighteen, though. Approximately the age Elias is now.

But that's . . . impossible.

While the girl shares a slight and candid smile with the viewer, a spray of lilies, roses, snapdragons, and sweet peas spilling from her hands, Elias—or *whoever* this photo depicts—is all seriousness and somber attitude. There's an edge of anxiety to him as well, suggested in the stiffness of his pose and the pinch in his brow.

Scanning the photo, bringing it closer, I search for any clues that this image has been staged.

I find something far more ominous.

There, at the place where the woman's elbow meets with Elias's shoulder, *just* visible through the gauze of the veil, watches an eye.

To the casual viewer, the anomaly might seem just that. An odd pattern of light, or even a splotch from age.

To me, however, the eye's slit pupil, as well as the curve of a flaking white cheek, is unmistakable.

The demon is there.

With shaking hands, I flip the photo over and discover a date on the yellowed and time-tattered reverse side—dashed off in the same tight cursive I found inside the journals.

Elias and Thea Thornfield—11 May 1904

Terror swells from my depths, mixing with an overwhelming confusion.

This makes no sense. At the same time, the clues *want* to fit together, and yet I can't bring myself to let them.

The only thing I can agree with myself on is that I *really* shouldn't be rifling through Elias's personal things like this. Even if this discovery *does* involve the demon.

With tremoring hands and breath, I secure the photos back in their string. Then I shove them into the drawer and scoot pens overtop of them once more.

The journals—will he notice they've been disturbed?

I close the cover of the one on the desk, hiding yesterday's entry. The rest, I'm going to leave as is. Because I need to get out of here—*now*.

When I turn, though, I find the exit blocked.

And myself the target of a familiar one-eyed stare.

16

"E-Elias," I stammer, "I-I'm . . . I was just . . ." I take a step back, colliding with the desk to send pens spilling. "I . . . know I shouldn't be in here."

He casts his gaze to the floor, his stare going sightless like it had yesterday in the dining room.

"And yet . . . here you are."

Anger rolls off him, making me want to run. With him standing in the doorway, though, there's nowhere to go.

"I . . . It was . . ."

It was what, Jane? Helen?

It *was* Helen, though.

"I'm sorry," I whisper. "I'm not . . . If you think I'm going to tell someone . . . I—I swear I won't say anything."

My words jumble in my mouth. They leave my lips half-formed and almost without enough breath to support them. I'm just talking to talk, because the pulsating silence threatens to kill me—as does that expression on his face. One of inner confliction, and simmering, barely contained fury.

"What?" he asks in a growl. "You're not going to tell anyone *what* exactly?"

I wait—stalling. My hope is that he doesn't really want a reply, and that his wrath is something that will pass. That I'm actually *not* about to become another ghost of Fairfax Hall.

"Answer me!" he shouts.

With so much volume added, that normally quiet voice strikes my spine like a bolt of lightning. And suddenly, the gravity of what I've done begins to sink in.

At the same time, I can't bring myself to speak again, not even to stammer another apology. Because anything I utter can only incriminate me further. When the seconds wear on too long, though, and time itself seems to fray, I force myself to speak.

"I can leave."

Finally, Elias moves. But, instead of stepping aside to let me out, he crosses into the room—and slams the door behind him with a shattering *bang* that makes me hitch and jump.

"Are you satisfied?" he asks, his voice quiet again—dangerously so. "Did your findings quell whatever curiosity led you here? Or are you disturbed by what you discovered?"

I swallow against the knot in my throat, and curl my hands around the hem of my T-shirt.

Head bowed so that his hair hangs to hide half of his face—the half with the patch—Elias sneers. And then he speaks. "Tell me how much you know."

"I don't know anything," I insist, shaking my head.

That eye flicks up to me. Filled now with ice and ire, it forbids me from patronizing him.

Moving away from the door, he snatches the last journal I'd left open and holds it up.

"You've read the letters!" He flings the book to my feet, its open pages a testament to my sin. An apparently unforgivable one. "I don't know which you've read, or how much, but, *yes*, Jane, they *do* all say the same thing."

"I don't know what I read."

"Thea, Thea, Thea," he says, ripping free another journal from a stack. He opens it and tosses it to the floor before repeating this action with another journal, and another.

As they land, I can't help glancing down. While the handwritten words are now a scramble to my addled brain, the name in every salutation is unmistakable, unavoidable. Echoes of his last repeated word.

"I know you know enough," he snarls.

But . . . what does he mean by *enough*?

"And what *do* I know?" I ask, my voice going defensive. Because I'm scared. Of being sealed in this room with him. Of being alone with him. This person who can't be what I think he is. Not that my napalmed mind has a name for it.

"That I love a dead woman," he says, "and have for the span of what many would consider multiple lifetimes. That I am consumed near to the point of madness by the loss of her, which time has done nothing to heal. That, though I am as old as you are, I am also . . . not."

"That can't be you in the photo," I say.

"Very well, Jane!" he shouts, flinging the next journal clear across the room. "It isn't! The photo is a fake. Nothing more than a quaint conversation piece. A party favor. You tell me what is the lie."

"It's not true," I tell him. "There's no way."

"How did you even get in here?" He starts to pace, like *he* is the caged thing. "I keep the door bolted. I have the only key."

"The door opened on its own."

"You lie."

"*I* don't have any reason to lie!"

"I do. You know that now, don't you?"

I can't just stand in this room and argue with him like this. I can't keep feeding the monster inside, the one who seems so desperate to break free. So, I do the only thing I can and, pushing off from the desk, I head for the door.

My hope is that he'll let me pass.

Instead, he shifts to block me. When I try to go around him the other way, he thwarts me again.

"Elias, let me go," I command.

"That, I cannot do."

His words terrify me, to the point that I'm ready to start screaming. Will anyone hear me all the way up here? Would anyone come for me if they did?

Giovanni would. And suddenly, it's *his* name I want to shout.

Instead, I reach for the doorknob, but Elias catches me by the upper arms, holding me steady the way he had after the fire, except now his fingers grip me too tightly. I'm ready to start throwing punches again, but when he speaks, his voice, bereft of all its previous strength . . . breaks.

"I will never see her again, Jane."

It's the unfathomable sorrow in the way he says my name that strips me of my fight.

"If you or the others cannot free me," he says, "I will never set eyes on her for the rest of eternity. Can you fathom forever? I have lived long enough that I should be dust and yet . . . *I* cannot."

Could he really be as old as that photo? These journals?

The only other option is that he's not well.

The likeliest answer, however, is that he happens to be both.

"You said she was dead," I whisper through trembling lips.

"A long time dead," he says, "as I soon shall be if fate cannot intervene on my behalf. And if you or someone else cannot, she will not be where I will go."

The shadow of what he's implying looms over my mind, and it makes me pull free of him, and backtrack so that I can see his face.

"What happened?" I ask.

He doesn't answer.

When the silence gets to be too much, I have no choice but to press for more answers.

"You're trying to tell me you're over a hundred years old?"

As he already observed, he doesn't *need* to tell me. Not when the journals, the photo, this explosive reaction to my discovery, do all the talking.

"I asked for a hundred and eighteen years," he replies bitterly. "Wanted to make up for time misspent, you see. Time I thought I was owed. Thought myself quite the haggler. But my tenure, my sentence, will soon expire. At long last, I will turn nineteen."

His tone suggests he's joking, yet that single eye brims with so much sadness that it's beyond plain he's not.

"And that's why your arsonist friend is hanging out," I guess.

"None of you would have come if I'd told you I'd signed a

deal with a devil and that, in a matter of days, I would be paying my dues on that contract and leaving this world for another. A realm that breathes fire down my neck every minute of every hour and, as the days leaf by, inches closer to claiming what is left of my soul."

Pretty sure that was an elaborate way of saying *hell*.

"Are . . . are you dead?"

"I cannot die."

"You're immortal?"

"Until the seventeenth. Midnight of the sixteenth, to be precise."

Of this month I'm assuming, since July 16 is the date he'd specified in the letter.

Because way to plan ahead.

Quiet resettles between us as I try to wrap my head around all of this.

"Who else knows?" I ask.

"Grayson," he whispers. "And now you."

Mr. Poole knows about this? About Elias being . . . whatever he is?

I frown, my mind racing back to my conversation with the housekeeper, and his odd way of phrasing things, the way he danced around the issue of Elias's behavior—and Elias in general.

All that verbal sidestepping made a little more sense now . . .

"I *will* beg you if I must not to quit Fairfax," he says. "You must understand, I had all but given up when Grayson conceived the idea to enlist the help of sensitives. Even then, I expected no miracle. I expected next to nothing. At least . . . not until a strange girl saw through my lies."

His anger has transformed, impossibly, into feverish hope.

Maybe this whole scenario is what Helen wanted. For me to find out about Thea, and for Elias to catch me in the midst of that discovery.

Leave it to Helen to orchestrate a head-on collision like this.

Band-Aids are getting ripped off left and right. Mine. His.

And our wounds—not to mention our coping mechanisms? Well, they look awfully similar.

"Thea is a void in my existence, a tender injury that never heals," he says, almost as if he's having mirroring thoughts about our parallels. "I wager you understand. And for that reason, I know you'll forgive my misconduct. I have faith in that. How can I not when you have tasted as well as I the bitter dregs of bereavement?"

Suppressing a shudder, I wrap my arms around myself, chilled by this room, his words, my understanding of them, and, yes, *him*.

"You're cold," he says, and stepping past me, he leaves the door unguarded to retrieve that robe. I'm not sure why I stay put, waiting for him to get back.

I *should* bolt. Run out of this attic—this house—screaming. But . . . I don't.

For the second time in as many days, Elias loops the robe around my shoulders. Beneath the faded smokiness, the mellower tones of his scent creep over me and, somehow, calm me.

"Go," he says, opening the door and stepping to one side of it as his free hand covers his mouth, like he's shocked by his own utterance. "I've said my piece and I'll not try to stop you again. I'll hold no one against their will. I understand prison too well."

I shift, more discomfited by this show of vulnerability than his anger. Not to mention that stare. The bone-deep tiredness infused in that once again tear-glossed eye . . .

There's a beat of hesitation on my part. And then, gripping the robe more tightly around me, I cross to the door with fast steps.

The moment I'm beyond the threshold, though, the same moment I know he's serious about setting me free, is the moment I vacillate.

"Say I *can* do something about this," I mutter, some of my tension, my trepidation, slipping away now. "Say Ingrid, Giovanni, or I *do* manage to get rid of this thing. Send it back to where it belongs. What happens then—to you?"

He blinks once, slow and plaintive.

"I turn nineteen," he says, "and, mortal once more, I am repaired to the hands of time."

"Your soul is freed," I say. "And when you die, you'll get to see Thea. Is that it?"

"It is a pale hope," he says, "shadowed by the doubt of a misanthrope."

"I thought you said you don't believe in Providence."

"I didn't," he says. "But then *you* arrived. And, what is more . . . you stayed."

Now it's my turn to study the floor.

"How do I know you're telling the truth this time?" I ask.

"What reason have I left to lie?"

For that, I don't have an answer. I do, however, have more questions. So many. But there *is* one that burns brighter than all the rest, and with more intensity.

"What did you agree to, Elias?" I ask. "What exactly was

the deal you made with this thing? It gets your soul . . . in return for what?"

"It's late."

"And, according to you, getting later by the day."

The hour. The minute.

"Tomorrow," he says, "if you are still here tomorrow, if by some miracle I, and the nature of my turmoil, have not frightened you away, I shall show you the answer to that question."

Other than this promise of more information, and the money he's yet to dole out, he has no leverage left to keep me here. And this is his way of admitting it.

Still, I linger, my stare straying to the stairwell that will take me out of his black hole pull and back into the manor. I've been granted access once more to the world at large, and to my life, which I have no reason to risk for this person.

Or . . . do I?

"Elias."

"Jane."

I turn my head his way at the utterance of my name, and once again mustering the reserves of my bravery, I convince myself to look him in that eye.

"The girl who woke you up," I say, "and led you to the fire. It wasn't Ingrid, was it?"

"No," he says. "It wasn't."

I let the silence rest for a moment. And then, even though I have all the information I need regarding who truly *had* roused him, I ask anyway. Just to be sure.

"The girl who did. What color was her hair?"

He takes a deep breath. Then he gestures to the air, like he can't believe his own words.

"Red," he says. "Her hair was red."

We share a pointed stare, and neither of us seem to be able to look away.

Is it because we can't? Or is it because we're each trying to read the other like runes, attempting to decipher what force has brought us from so far away into such close proximity?

Physically, mentally, spiritually . . .

We're locked this way for the eternity of another moment.

And then I make myself go.

I don't let myself glance back as I leave his rooms.

I'm too anxious to get that eye out of my sight and the echo of all those written words—so tender, and heartrending—out of my head.

Because the last thing I need now is to be haunted by him, too.

17

WTF HELEN.

Send.

Two years.

Send.

Two years and nothing.

Send.

Two years and not so much as a wink in the form of a song on the radio.

Send.

And now u show up. And not just to me.

Send.

U said things are thin here. And getting thinner. U led me to that room then bailed.

Send.

U wanted me to find out. Must've wanted him to find me finding out.

Send.

Why??? Because u want me to save him?

Send.

Can't think of any other reason.

Send.

And that makes me even more scared than before.

Send.

Because all this tells me that

Send.

U think I can.

Send.

"Goodness!" Ingrid's voice floats to me from the doorway leading into the massive, bi-level library. Starting, I look up. "Who on earth are you over there rage-texting?"

I click my phone off and move my feet from the settee I'd found my way to after leaving Elias's room last night. Morning had come shortly after, but the nearness of daybreak hadn't been why I'd avoided returning to my room.

After learning all that I had about Elias—and what his predicament implied about this world and the next—would I ever sleep again?

In short, there'd been too much to digest. Too much to sort through and try to solve for. Too much for my overloaded mind to rip apart and to worry to shreds.

Also, there'd been a storm moving in. One that now prevents the stained glass windows of the library from brightening past a dull glow. I could do without being alone in the Moroccan Room during a thunder and lightning fest. Not that being on my own in this huge dark-academia-style library proved to be any cozier. And now I'm *not* alone anymore. But Ingrid sure isn't my first pick for pre-dawn company.

"I'm not rage-texting," I tell her.

"You were glaring like you wanted the thing to combust. Oooh, tell me. Is it a romantic partner?"

I shake my head, and Ingrid frowns as if disappointed before entering with her steaming mug, trailing the scent of coffee. In her other hand, she carries her cards. Because of course she does.

Abort, my brain chants. But can I really afford to be rude—to be rude *back*—to someone who is supposed to be on my side when I have a demon trying to eighty-six me?

"Mr. Poole asked me to track you down," says Ingrid. "He wants to have a chat later with me, you, and Giovanni."

Mr. Poole. Where has he *been* anyway? I hadn't seen him since yesterday.

Unless the dream cameo counts.

"He wants to see us now?" I ask.

"Well, he's making breakfast right at the moment." She gestures over her shoulder in the direction she'd come. "There's time, though, if you want me to read your cards. We could get some insight, perhaps, into the situation with whoever you were just, ah, emphatically hammering away at."

"Sorry," I say, "I'm not much on fortune-telling."

"The cards don't tell the future so much as they decipher energies, offer advice, and present potential solutions," Ingrid says in a practiced infomercial voice, like this is the spiel she gives all the chumps who sign up for her act. "Fate is always at work. That, I know."

I level her with a mordant glare even as Elias's comment about fate intervening swirls through my mind. Or maybe it's *because* of his comment that I'm giving her the stink eye.

Right now, though, fate can kiss my chapped ass.

"But the future itself isn't written for us," she adds. "What fun would *that* be?"

"All the same," I say, "I'm good."

I don't have time for this. I also have bigger things to worry about than Ingrid-filtered bullshit. Like pyromaniac demons, telepathic come-on-strong Italians, shifty housekeepers, and Byronic, lovelorn lords of the manor.

"Oh, come *on*," says Ingrid as she wanders over, a sly smile trying to undo the tight purse of her lips. "It's just for fun."

"For you."

Doesn't she remember the whole "bitter with baggage" tirade she dumped on me before calling me an arachnid?

Guess not, because Ingrid takes the seat next to mine, her perfume invoking visions of expensive department stores and girls with dogs in purses.

Snap, goes a card, followed by another, and then another.

"The High Priestess," she says, pointing to the first card. "Intuitive knowing, secrets revealed, gut feelings, unignorable hunches, and something pulling at you like the moon does the tide."

So, this is happening.

I should steal her coffee. Officially, I need it more.

"The veil behind her asks you to look closer still," says Ingrid, "to peek beyond, for there are secrets yet to be uncovered—the buried-deep-inside kind. And the pomegranates on the tapestry, they are reminiscent of Persephone, who became bound to Lord Hades the moment she tasted the forbidden fruit of the underworld, his kingdom. They indicate something holds you to this situation. You are compelled."

"Do we have to do this?" I ask.

"I'm not wrong, am I?"

I force my face to remain impassive. The description fits, sure. But then, it would for just about any schmuck. That's how these cards work.

"Next to her is the Six of Cups," Ingrid prattles on. "So, the return of some fond friend from the past. Perhaps an ex?"

I force my eyes to the ceiling, refusing to look at the cards or feed Ingrid any indicators one way or another. She's fishing and I'm not giving her squat. Still, Ingrid continues her interpretation.

"The Six of Cups can indicate a past love of some kind, be it a romantic interest or a close friend. Or even both, since there are two figures on the card—children, who represent a bygone era."

"Wish this reading was in a bygone era."

"Temperance," she intones, ignoring me as she points to the next card. "The need to handle your current situation with great care. Also, perhaps the influence of a benevolent force."

Now I have to look. Granted, her descriptions are still overly general, applicable to anyone's situation and not just mine, but . . . there's enough truth ringing in her words that the temptation to survey the images presented is too great. And it's the angel on the Temperance card that steals and holds my attention.

Robed in white, the winged figure stands over a placid pool, pouring water between two golden goblets while, in the distance, the sun rises above jagged hilltops. Or . . . is it a sunset?

But then The Devil card makes a reappearance.

"So, you found it," I say.

"I beg your pardon?"

"That one was still in the study." I point to the card.

Ingrid tilts her head at me.

Oh. Great. It wasn't.

More hallucinations. Huzzah.

"There are seventy-eight cards," says Ingrid. "I have them all, if that's what you mean."

"Just . . . never mind." I wave for her to give me the low-down on this card already. Because, like Elias, I guess I'm now prepared to take help from anywhere I can get it. Not that this *is* helping. Yet . . .

"The Devil is all about control," says Ingrid. "A toxic situation. Being bound or beholden to something. But you'll notice, too, that the chains restraining The Devil's prisoners are loose. There *is* a way out for them. Usually, this card asks you to find your personal power and, with it, free yourself."

Well, that's about as useful as a concrete parachute.

Snap.

"The Hanged Man represents a sacrifice being made in the hopes of achieving enlightenment," she says, "or some higher goal. Something yearned for by the soul rather than the mind or body. Also, there are four Major Arcana cards here. So, it's a big message for sure. Something about the existence of two worlds within you, or even without. Because even the Temperance angel has one foot on the earth and the other in that pool, which represents the waters of the collective unconscious. This is truly bizarre, but I'm almost getting the sense that you've stumbled into a sort of . . . mmm, how do I phrase this?"

"Thinness?" I offer.

Startled, Ingrid's bright blues flash up to me. She blinks wide several times and then glances between me and her spread.

Instead of answering, she pulls another card.

"Three of Swords. Whatever this is, it's been born from major heartache. Let's clarify that."

Ugh. Can we not?

Snap. Snap. Snap.

"Justice followed by the Seven of Swords. Some sort of deal gone awry. Perhaps a contract?"

"We're in a deal right now," I remind her. Because there's no way I'm buying Ingrid is anything but a sham. A fake. "You're just spinning what you know about me into mystical-sounding words."

"We only signed a waiver," she argues. "That's not an official contract."

No. "Contract" is the word *Elias* used.

I push up from the couch, officially done.

"Wait," says Ingrid, "where are you going? I haven't finished yet. Don't you want to know which card is in the final outcome position?"

"*No.*"

"It's Judgement," she calls to me anyway, "the return of something from the long past. The resurgence of an old problem or wound. Spirits of the dead rejuvenated."

I swing around to glower at her from the door. "A spirit is why we're here, isn't it?"

"A *demon* is why we're here," she says. "But *you're* the one assuming these cards are referring to this job. Not me."

"You're not a psychic, you're a cold reader," I accuse.

And a good one. But I'm not about to give her that much credit.

"Please don't be angry." She stands. "Giovanni told me about the fire. And what you said to Elias. About this thing targeting you. I wasn't going to stay. But when Giovanni did, and then you did . . . Well, I think I can help, too. The cards don't just run on nothing. My intention—*our* intention—can be a driving force behind them. Tarot can provide insight. *I* can . . ."

She trails off and I have to tilt my head at her.

"What are you talking about? You stayed because of the bet you made with Giovanni."

Her blinking turns rapid-fire, magazine-cover-worthy lashes batting. "I'm sorry, what?"

I huff, hands going to my hips. "There wasn't any bet, was there?"

What the hell, Giovanni? *Now* who's the shade parade?

I shake my head when she doesn't answer. Because this is just what I need. *Another* liar in the mix.

"Jane," says Ingrid, "I don't know what Giovanni told you, but he's not been forthright with me, either. Frankly, I'm rather worried about him. Not only were his cards a hot mess, but I overheard him on the phone yesterday telling someone he, quote, 'just needs more time.'"

"So, take that up with him."

"I would," she presses. "But you see, *you're* the one he likes." She holds up her deck. "I know . . . I asked."

Scowling, I try to suss out her meaning. She's saying she asked her cards about me and Giovanni. But what exactly is she insinuating by saying I'm the one he "likes"?

"Look, this isn't going well," she says, perhaps picking up on the fact that I'm still considering murder, arms dropping to her sides. "But I *am* sorry for the things I said in the study. I didn't know you were there, but that *doesn't* excuse it. I'm trying to make it up to you. I'm *trying* to help."

"Your cards can't help me," I say. "And sorry, but I'm not exactly sure how they help in this situation, either."

"*Careful*, Jane," calls Ingrid as I exit into the hall. "There *is* a message here for you. A big one. Don't ignore it or write it off. It's obvious—to everyone now, I think—that you're here for a reason. Perhaps we all are."

I storm down the hall and into the kitchen. But even though breakfast clutters the island counter, several platters still steaming, Mr. Poole is nowhere to be found. My stomach lurches with anxiety, and I can't force myself to make a plate.

When I just stand there staring at the spread, I realize I'm waiting for Ingrid. Who doesn't come chasing after me. Which I guess had been my hope.

I take a deep breath and let it out.

Because as far as having enemies goes . . . isn't a demon enough?

My team spirit apparently needs a little dusting off. And, possibly, some CPR.

I grit my teeth and steel myself with artificial niceness.

Genuineness, I can work on later.

I swing back in the direction of the library, bracing myself to choke down Ingrid's weird version of an apology—or at least withstand it—for *Elias's* sake.

But I arrive in the doorway to find her already gone.

18

Alone in my room once more, I pace in front of the portrait of Helen, fingers turning over the bit of charcoal I used to give her eyes more definition.

Outside, the storm blusters and growls, drenching the manor.

While the ambiance of Fairfax Hall needs no more glooming up, the white noise hush of the rain *does* help me think. About Ingrid and her predictions. And whether or not she might really be psychic . . .

Still pacing, I check my phone for the time.

Quarter till noon. Fifteen minutes until my meeting with Giovanni. Though I'm not sure where to find him since we hadn't specified a spot. Maybe, though, I'd better go ahead and try hunting him down. We can go get Ingrid together and—

Bang, bang!

I whirl to face my door, dropping the charcoal bit.

Giovanni. Could it be he's come searching for *me*?

I could sure use a little help. Or a lot. Someone to talk to at the very least. Maybe not about *everything*. But—

"Jane."

The voice behind that door is not Giovanni's. And still, it's one that slams my sternum like a battering ram.

"Jane. Are you there?"

I'm stalled for another heart-stopping moment, and then I force myself to move, to go to the door, which I open only partway.

Elias is there. As in *right* there, leaning into the frame, his forearm braced on the jamb above his head, his drawn face hovering over mine.

Upon seeing me, that eye shuts for a long moment. Then it reopens.

"I *knew* you would not abandon me," he says, and now that eye skewers me. Or maybe it's his words that do that. Because the *way* he says them, his throat tight, his voice hoarse and dry, suggests he really *hadn't* expected me to still be here.

"The moment you arrived," he says, pressing in and then past me—just waltzing right into my room because come on down. "The very second you set foot on these grounds, some . . . *shift* occurred here at Fairfax."

Elias starts pacing in the middle of the floor.

"Then that first night," he continues, "when I pulled you from those flames, did not some part of me—some buried germ of my soul—recognize even *then* that you were not of this earth?" That eye flicks to me. "Not entirely."

I grit my teeth and hold my breath, willing him to stay distracted enough not to notice the bras I'd hung off the fireplace mantel to dry after handwashing them to get the smoke out.

None of them are frilly or anything like that. They're all no-nonsense bargain-bin steals, and one even has a whipstitched strap. But then, maybe that's even *more* embarrassing.

Elias zeroes in on the portrait of Helen instead and, seizing it, draws it close to survey the added suggestion of features.

"And yesterday," he says, "even despite this drawing and the impossibility it hinted at—that you might be . . . an *answer*—I could not stoke my hope into full flame."

I fold my arms, forgoing commentary. Probably better to just wait out this tirade—or whatever it is.

"Before meeting you and, admittedly, even after," he goes on, carrying the sketchpad with him now as he stalks back and forth all Sherlock Holmes–style, "hope had been no more than a single dying ember. But then you discovered my secret. What's more, you believed me. And now, because of your trespass, that hope burns bright. Because of *you*, Jane, it lives."

Guess I can't be *too* miffed about him barging into my room since *I* had outright rooted around in his.

"This . . ." He gestures to the ether with my sketchpad. "The thing I'm feeling. It's almost more than hope. Or perhaps time has made the essence of the emotion foreign enough to me that I've yet to fully identify it. Whatever it is, I've become submerged in it. This heart. It beats anew. It lives. *I* live."

So, *this* is a different side of him.

Kind of makes me want to hose him down or sit him in time-out. Because this? I don't do . . . *this*.

"Elias, what's wrong?" I ask, because something has to be. Or maybe I just need there to be.

The only alternative is that he's being genuine. Why is that harder to accept than that he just requires something from me?

Maybe it's not. Maybe it's just . . . scarier.

Elias goes to prop the portrait of Helen up on the mantel, where he finally takes note of the bras.

I cringe inwardly.

Boundaries—or the lack thereof—are getting to be a thing with us.

"I need you to come with me," he says after a beat. "Now. Before the day escapes."

With that, he does an about-face, brushes past me, and marches back out the door, adding a hasty "Meet me downstairs" over his shoulder.

I frown after him, staying put.

But then I glance back to Helen.

Oh, for the love of . . . Did I *really* draw her with that one look she always gave me?

"*I'm going,*" I bark at her. Annoyed anew, I shove my phone into my back jeans pocket, clench my jaw, and head out, yanking my door shut behind me.

When I arrive in the foyer, however, Elias is nowhere to be found, though the front door hangs wide open. Outside, buckets of rain slap the pavement and gush from the portico in white waterfalls.

There's still no sign of him until I step into the doorway to spy both his black-clad figure and a sleek, steel-gray, rain-beaded sports car whose purr is almost silent under the roar of the storm.

Elias opens the passenger-side door without glancing back at me.

Confused, I venture out a few steps, protected as he is from the downpour by the portico. Then I stop again when the driver's-side door opens and Mr. Poole emerges, an umbrella tucked under one arm. Frowning, the housekeeper glances between me and Elias.

"Thank you, Grayson," says Elias. Because Mr. Poole must have been the one to bring the car around.

"I wasn't aware Miss Reye would be joining you on your ill-advised excursion," Mr. Poole says, and though the housekeeper aims his words at Elias, he fixes his gaze on me.

Instead of the gray nurse scrubs he'd worn in my dream-slash-not-a-dream, Mr. Poole sports a vest, slacks, and a tie—all of the same hue. Those horn-rimmed glasses are identical as well.

I narrow my eyes on the housekeeper.

"No doubt Jane will do as she pleases." Elias rounds to the driver's side. Then he slides behind the wheel, shutting the door after him with a *clap*. A burst of thunder echoes the noise. Lightning flashes a warning—and I can't fight the impression is somehow meant for me.

Mr. Poole then raises a questioning, and perhaps cautioning, pair of brows at me.

I have my misgivings, too. But Elias likely won't wait long for me to make up my mind.

Offering Mr. Poole a tight smile, just like the one the dream-nurse version of him had given *me*, I climb into the passenger seat. At once, I'm hit with the aromas of pine, peppermint, and lemon cleaner. Smooth, black, and streamlined, the spotless interior gives off spaceship vibes, its buttons, knobs, and meters backlit by an ominous neon red.

"Be careful with Jane, sir," says Mr. Poole, who now peers in through my open door. "She's come a long way, been through much, and is rather irreplaceable. She's likely not as *durable* as you are when it comes to withstanding . . . ah, *stunts*, either."

"That'll be all, Grayson," says Elias, but without looking at the housekeeper.

Left with nothing else to say, and probably no way to dissuade me from my choice without bringing trouble on himself, Mr. Poole shuts my door and backs away.

Now it's just me and Elias.

But there's a problem. One that, thanks to Elias's dramatic entrance, attitudinal one-eighty, and all that "not of this earth" blather, I'd *totally* forgotten about until just now.

"Where are we going?" I ask. "I'm—Giovanni's waiting for me."

"Then he waits in vain." Elias strips off his eyepatch to loop it around the stick shift. He keeps his head turned away, but his damaged eye also remains shielded by his hair until he slides on a pair of mirrored sunglasses.

"This is a literal downpour," I say, glancing between him and the windshield. "Is this thing four-wheel drive?"

"Seat belt, Jane." Shifting the car into gear, he hits the gas.

I yelp as we launch out onto the drenched pavement, the car growling with the gunning of its engines. Hands shaking, certain I've made a terrible mistake, maybe my last, I grapple for my seat belt, yanking it down and over my lap.

Elias speeds us around the bend, not even flinching when we hydroplane.

"*Elias!*" I shriek.

"Relax, Jane," he tells me, which of course makes me do the opposite. But at least I've got my seat belt clipped now.

"Where are you taking me?" I demand, my voice tight as we

rocket down the winding drive, the windshield wipers slapping the rain aside only long enough to allow peeks through the torrent. "Can you just . . . pull over for a second?"

And let me out?

"Give it a rest, Jane," he says as we shoot through an enormous puddle, causing twin tsunamis to gush up on either side of us with a tearing roar. "I'm not going to let you drive the Jag, so stop asking."

I grip the sides of the seat, bear down, and shift my gaze forward so that I can see—or at least partially see—my impending doom when it comes. At this point, what else is there to do?

We rip onto the main street, which thankfully remains void of other vehicles. This only encourages Elias's need for speed, and he feeds this beast of a car more gas.

I shut my eyes.

If only I had a happy place to go to.

The car vibrates around me, humming as it catapults us forward. When we turn again, it's with enough force to have me leaning his way—almost into him.

"You're missing it, Jane," he swivels his head to say. And I know because his breath washes warm over my ear. That does things to me. Things I don't like liking. So, when the centrifugal force eases, granting us both back our personal spaces, I talk.

"You mean I'm missing your driving recklessly on the wrong side of the road and not watching where the hell we're going?" I ask, because I might as well get in a joke before we die.

Before *I* do.

"I can see *exactly* where the hell we're going, thank you

very much," he says, "and this far into the countryside, there really is only one side *to* the road."

"Comforting."

Opening my eyes confirms his statement. The street before us is as narrow as it is winding. Every so often, squat stone fences pop up on either side of the road to girdle us in on the straighter portions. We're going fast enough, though, that these structures are gone as soon as they crop up.

We *are* going to hit one. Then we're going to roll until we slam into a tree, or else hurtle into the moors. Maybe, though, we'll hit 1.21 gigawatts first and fly off some cliff in the eighties.

At least this would be a better way to go than burning alive.

Maybe.

"Where are all the stop signs?" I ask when we just keep *going*, never once slowing.

"We don't really . . . have those," Elias replies in a musing way, like he's only just become aware of this himself.

At least the deluge has started to lessen some. Still, the rain ripples down the windshield in a blurring sheet. While Elias maintains his speed, I'm able to relax a little, because I guess I'm acclimating to hyperspace. We haven't hydroplaned again and he continues to manage the relentless climbs, curves, and dips with flawless dexterity.

"Doubtless it's obvious how you've been at the forefront of my thoughts all morning," Elias says. "Since we parted."

I glance his way, and then forward again, blinking a few times.

Normally, people try *not* to think about me.

"I might have gone in search of you sooner," he says, "but after last night, I could not summon the bravery to leave my room, let alone knock on your door. I don't fear much these days. But I became petrified I'd find you had fled. I don't know what I would have done if I'd discovered you'd left truly and for good."

"Just be glad Mr. Poole is a good cook," I mutter.

"Last night," he says, "Jane, you broke through more than my locks."

"I told you, I didn't break in."

"You broke through. To me."

To that, I don't say anything. I'm too busy waiting for my karma from punching Giovanni to kick in and a Mack truck to round the bend and smoosh us flat.

Fingers crossed because things are getting *suuuuper* uncomfortable.

Lightning pulses and a peal of thunder, like the sky above us is cracking open, rattles the car. The Jaguar rumbles on in defiance.

"I've never told anyone about Thea, Jane," he says. "Not a soul."

"You said Mr. Poole—"

"I think he suspects there was someone," he says, "but he only knows what I am. Not who I was . . . before."

I still don't know exactly what's going on with Elias. Am I about to find out?

"You'll notice Grayson never asks me questions," he says. "He never pries."

Not like good ole Jane.

"This is why, in the four years he's been in my employ, I've never dismissed him. He doesn't ask me anything. He just . . . endures."

Well. On the bright side, maybe we *are* making progress here, so long as Elias is admitting he has to be endured.

"I haven't a friend in the world, Jane," he says. "I can't let anyone that close."

My stomach twists as the road ahead of us does. While Elias manages these sudden turns with ease, *I* begin to struggle. Because I don't like the mirror his confession holds up to me.

But then, I'm *nothing* like Elias. I'm not.

Right . . . ?

"I have one foot very literally in hell."

Elias's words draw me out of myself, and my focus back to him.

"If you walk too close to me," he says, "that hell is bound to find you, too. I learned that the hard way."

My breathing gets more difficult, but not because I'm scared of Elias's driving anymore. These roads, he's taking them like he's traveled them a million times. And since he is, in actuality, like Giovanni first claimed, roughly "a billion years old," who's to say he hasn't?

No, it's his *words* that wind me up now. Mostly, I'm dreading what he's *about* to say. *That's* the crash I'm bracing for now. The wreck I can't avoid.

"My steps down this path cost me Thea," he says, his voice fading to the same hushed decibel as the rain. "They cost me *everything*. And so, how could I reach a hand out and risk pulling anyone else into the fire with me?"

My chest is too tight, a barrel of sorrow straining at the seams.

He needs to stop talking, pull over, and let me out of the car.

"I thought if I brought in strangers, I could remain distant. Detached. But then, Jane, you stayed."

"So did Ingrid and Giovanni," I argue.

"Yet they did not meet the man you did last night. No, Jane, you stayed in the face of the worst, in the face of *my* worst."

Since I haven't yet told him about my visits to the hell world, he doesn't know the half of it.

"I told you," I murmur, "I don't have a place lined up to go yet."

"You could have easily departed," he counters. "You could have taken the money and gone anywhere you liked. And aside from that, wouldn't anywhere be better than hell?"

The car gets silent after that. And that silence, it works hard to choke me.

I clamp my mouth shut and shift my focus forward again. The road streams at me just as fast as the rain. Faster than ever. And my eyes blur like the glass.

"The answer, in case you were curious," he says, "is *yes*. Anywhere *is* better than hell. And yet . . . there you sit."

I have to cover my mouth now. And the action reminds me of his from last night.

He'd been feeling *this*—this gutted devastation—then. And now it's my turn.

"Make no mistake," he says, "I *know* I have Helen to thank."

I squeeze my eyes shut, like that can keep my insides from imploding.

God. *Helen*. If only she were here for me to berate for her part in this.

"Perhaps," he says, his voice nearly losing its strength, "perhaps she is where Thea has gone."

The tears I've tried to hold back start falling. And I despise him. At least . . . I try to.

Liking him—identifying with him—is *so* much harder.

"All these years," he continues, "these decades—for over a century, I've waited for her. She never came. Never so much as a sign nor whisper. In my mind, she was either no more, or she loathed me. And, for a time, I convinced myself I hated her, too. Which now strikes me as being as natural a response as loving her. For what is hate if not love in hell?"

And just like that, I'm destroyed. I can't stop the tears, either. So, I don't even bother. Who are they for, though?

Me? Him?

A little of both maybe. And that's not a good sign. Not at all.

Because I can't afford to care about him. I *can't*.

"As I said before, there's something more at play here," he says, his words harkening back to Ingrid's prediction from earlier, too. "You see, no matter how long I waited, how much I prayed—and yes, I prayed—no word arrived in any capacity. Time fed on me and doubt stained the soul I'd already sold. Thea never came. She *never* came. But . . . Jane did."

"*Yes.*" Sniffing, I use the collar of my T-shirt to dab at my eyes because that's all I have. "Jane came. She had *no* fun. Accommodations not as advertised. Whatever you do, don't sleep in the Red Room and *don't* get into pretentious cars with art-swiping, secret-keeping speed demons. One star. Would not *fucking* recommend!"

Elias laughs, and that is almost as unexpected, almost as arresting, as his smile, which all but turns him into someone else. And that smile sends an unnamable zing through me. One composed of a mixture of shock and, more distantly . . . what? I can't say. Whatever it is, the sensation is an echo of that slam that occurred inside me in the kitchen when, fuming, he'd stormed in through that open door, a barely contained walking disaster.

"It's not funny," I grumble, even though I can't help a snort of my own.

"If *you* have not wept in two years," he argues, "*I* have not laughed in twelve times as many—and so it *is* funny."

"Oh, just look at us," I murmur. "Two train wrecks breaking each other's twisted records."

"And, with luck, so much else."

The weight behind this remark, its insinuation—its hope—kills my half-born smile. Because even if Elias thinks I'm equal to his problem, even if *Helen* does, I can't summon the same faith in myself.

Oblivious, or perhaps just impervious, to this change in me, Elias keeps *his* smile as he shifts the car, and we pick up speed.

"Look there, Jane," he says, nodding to the windshield.

His words snap my mind back to the here and now and, reflexively, I obey.

Ahead, the road straightens and, in the distance, the clouds dissipate. Though he and I are still in the rain, under the shadow of the storm, the sun has burst through to bathe the horizon in gold. Its rays paint the surrounding meadows in eye-searing tones of neon green and hazard yellow. They also cast a sheen on the slick blacktop, turning the ribbon of road to silver.

"Let's see if we can make it, shall we?" he asks as he smashes his foot into the gas pedal.

This sends me slamming backward in my seat. Again, I grip

its leather sides, nails digging in as I hold my breath. I don't close my eyes this time, though.

Because, for a moment, it's almost like I'm back in those last days with Helen.

Next to a friend—or, in this instance, someone like a friend (I am still trying not to go there)—who was rushing headlong toward something I had a limited capacity to understand.

Except, this time, maybe, if I'm lucky—if Elias is—there *is* something I can do . . . to stop it.

19

Ironically, the last thing I want to do when Elias finally kills the engine is get out of the car.

So, I don't. Because I *don't* like where we are.

That doesn't stop Elias from shutting the door behind him and walking on without me—not even offering so much as a questioning backward glance.

Always, he's like a damn bullet out of a gun.

I take several deep breaths as he strides through the garden of ancient, tilted, and moss-covered headstones.

He's not going to do what I think.

But then he opens the giant iron door, stained green by acid rain, that leads into a small hut-sized mausoleum.

After that, he passes into the gothic stone structure that, above its entrance, bears the name THORNFIELD.

So, yeah, he does *exactly* what I think.

Note to self: no more effing field trips with Elias.

Hissing a curse, I wrestle free of my seat belt and climb out of the car.

I'm past the same stone angels, obelisks, and markers and through the low stone gate partitioning off the mausoleum's plot in seconds flat. Because being in the car by myself in this massive and ancient cemetery is worse than loitering outside the open door of a family tomb.

Marginally. But still.

The aroma of honeysuckle tempts me to just hang out in the mausoleum's tiny front yard and bird-watch until he comes back out. But then there's the faintest waft of lilac, and I spy him within the darkness, a hand rested atop a marble sarcophagus.

My shoulders slump. And I make myself approach the pair of stone angels that stand sentinel on either side of the door, their wings tucked at their backs, eyes downcast, cheeks stained from the rain, as though with tears.

"I feel ya," I mutter, giving one an arm pat on my way in.

Once I'm past the threshold, the warmth of the burgeoning afternoon is snuffed in favor of cool, stagnant, and stale air. Though there are no windows, the domed skylight casts Elias's dark form and a portion of the two matching sarcophagi he stands between in an absurd spotlight of sunshine.

The pungent odor of moldering flowers replaces the breath of lilac.

The source, a dried bouquet laid atop the lid of the sarcophagus Elias leans on, holds his attention until he sweeps the stems of the spent flowers into a squeezing grip.

"*Hey*." I hurry to his side when droplets of blood blot the stone lid.

He lets me take the flowers, lilies, roses, sweet pea, and snapdragons (incidentally some of my most favorite to draw), and I set them aside before seizing his hand. He lets me do that, too. But the wounds where the thorns of the petrified roses bit him close on their own, sealing over with unmarred skin.

I retract my own hands too quickly.

"I still feel the pain," he says as he curls his hand into a fist, like he wants to reassure me. "Sometimes, that's the only way I can convince myself I *am* still alive."

Elias bangs his fist onto the unyielding stone. Then he spreads his palm flat against its surface and goes still. For a long time, he stays that way, shielded gaze trained on the lid, almost as if he's waiting to feel movement from within. Or like he's checking for a heartbeat.

During this pause, I can't help sparing a glance toward the long stone bench built into the wall across from where we stand, on the other side of the sarcophagus. There's a pillow at one end. A thin blanket trails off the other.

The pillow is the mate to the one on the beaten couch from Elias's room, so these are not the effects of a vagrant.

"I had to purchase vaults for the both of us," he says at last, gesturing to the matching sarcophagus behind him. "To keep up appearances. At the time, it was the thing to do."

His voice echoes in the tight chamber.

And then it's quiet again. Too quiet.

"I think . . . people still do that," I offer.

Because I'm awesome when it comes to comforting phrases.

Is now a good time to ask him to like, share, and follow for more quotable expressions of empathy and compassion?

"Ironic," he says, "that the thing I bartered for was the thing that undid me. Us."

Last night, Elias had vowed to tell me what the deal he'd made had been. Now I'm not sure I need—or want—to know anymore. All that should matter is that I have a job to do. An assignment given by Helen. The more I find out about Elias, though, the more time I spend in his vicinity, the more *he* starts to matter.

"Don't say it was money," I murmur. Because that's why *I'm* here. Or . . . it was.

"It was means," he says, "which is a bit more than just money, isn't it?"

"You tell me." My tone is dry. Because . . . I wouldn't know.

"I was not destitute when I met Thea," he says. "I was gainfully employed. I had good prospects for a modest future, and aspirations for success. The youngest but tallest footman in her father's service, I even made enough money to accumulate a small savings."

Oh wow. He'd worked for Thea's old man. Back in the *day*.

"Pretty sure, in that situation, having a thing for the daughter of your boss was a big no-no."

"Which was why I dared never meet her gaze," replies Elias. "The butler, never mind her father, would have ground me up and fed me to the hunting dogs for a lesser offense."

"Are you trying to say *she* made the first move?"

Go ahead, Thea.

"The planets and the stars," he hisses as he wanders the length of the sarcophagus, trailing that hand across the lid, "celestial beings beyond the stratosphere—the angels and the *gods* made the first move, throwing us together with all their benevolence. All their cruelty."

I slow blink and give all that a moment to breathe. Because why use specifics when you're fluent in Tortured Poet?

"Sooo . . . I don't get it," I say. "You spill a plate of lobster pâté on her or something?"

"Hardly. Her horse almost trampled me on the road that ran through the forests bordering her father's estate. The beast fell with her aboard and she sustained an ankle sprain."

"Let me guess," I say, "you got fired."

"On the contrary," he says, "since she'd been in the act of attempting to run away and her injury prevented the fulfillment of that aim, I was ultimately credited for intervening and praised for escorting her back to the manor."

"Why was she trying to run away?"

"She was being courted by a wealthy man she detested. Someone who her aging father had all but promised her hand to."

"That'll do it," I mutter.

"She detested me after that, too. And, from that point forward, endeavored to have me sacked for the crime of spoiling her flight. Which, by the way, hadn't been well-thought-out at all. I told her as much when, after giving her chaperone the slip, she cornered me with the purpose of making the level of her abhorrence for me known."

"Oh yeah?" A knowing smile tugs at one corner of my mouth. "How'd *that* work out?"

"She cursed me for sentencing her to matrimony with a cold and miserly widower nearly forty years her senior. She accused me as well of stealing from her the prize of true love's kiss, unaware that, while I had never met her gaze, I *had* stolen glances."

"So, you *did* have a thing for her."

"A bit without knowing," he says. "Our stations forbade even the shadow of the thought. But we were alone when she waylaid me. And she was so incensed. And because she'd placed me in a predicament that again jeopardized my situation—not to mention her reputation—I, too, became furious. That was, until I realized she was not truly angry with me. Not . . . in the way I had been led to believe."

The story is getting good. And I'm more than here for what happens next, because can't I already guess?

"It occurred to me she hadn't truly been trying to incite my dismissal," he says. "Not so much as she'd simply been striving to win my attention. And so, in a moment of utter madness, I bestowed on her the kiss she'd charged me with robbing her of. But . . . that act. It made our deficits to each other anything but even."

Okay, so that is officially swoon-worthy. And Elias—he words everything just so.

"There was something cataclysmic about that first kiss," he says, "as though within it a universe had been born. A paradise just outside of reach of us both."

I allow myself an internal sigh. The tale is as beautiful as it is devastating. Beautiful because it really *had* been true love's kiss that brought Elias and Thea together. Devastating because it hadn't ended there. Otherwise, Elias might be sealed in the vault at our backs, the twin to Thea's. He's standing next to me, though, divided from his love by time, space, and a misbegotten bargain.

"Too soon after," he continues, "through covert dalliances and midnight assignations, our fates became irrevocably sealed. We were one and the both of us simultaneously repaired and ruined by the other's love. Yet the threat of our trysts being discovered, never mind her suitor's impending proposal, loomed ever nearer, all of it a question of *when* and not *if*.

Since I could not bear to relinquish Thea to another's arms, nor continue to behave in a way that disrespected her and her family, I swore to her I *would* find a way. And I quit the family's service and her father's house. Weeks later, I returned to find her engaged. But, a gentleman in my own right by then since I had struck my deal, I sought an audience with her father, and I presented to him proof of my newfound wealth, property, and estate—Fairfax Hall."

"Holy crap," I say. "Did he crap? I bet he totally crapped."

"I was too rich for him to be angry, if that's what you mean," says Elias through a subtle laugh. "Indeed, my wealth dwarfed his. When he asked me how I acquired my affluence, I claimed inheritance from a distant relation. When he inquired about my eye, I told him I'd suffered an attack. In short, I lied. So, when he asked why I wished to marry Thea . . . I felt I owed him the truth on that account at least."

"Oh wow," I say. "And he didn't have you drawn and quartered?"

"He commanded me to silence and summoned his daughter to the room," Elias says. "And the shock on her face at seeing me again conveyed to him all he needed to know about us. When he told Thea of my newfound fortune and that I had returned to seek her hand, she begged for his blessing. I was lucky that he loved Thea enough to grant it. And so, I won the one thing I had wanted more than my own soul. A life with Thea who, in marrying me, took on my contract in the same capacity a wife takes on the commitments of any normal husband."

"Wait," I say, startled, "back up. What do you mean? Are you saying she became like you?"

"Not entirely," he says. "Or else she would still be here.

In addition to bottomless wealth, I asked for a hundred and eighteen years with Thea. I was offered instead a hundred and eighteen years of uninterruptable life to do with as I pleased. Because, rightly so, I could not touch Thea directly with my bargain. It would always be her will to remain with me or to go and, of course, I would have it no other way. I was signing away *my* soul after all and not hers. And so, while she could share the benefits of suspended youth via our union in the way couples share in the gains of an investment, invulnerability was mine alone."

"What happened to her?" I ask.

"Only after we were wed did Thea have the chance to notice the change in me. Part of my soul had gone missing, after all. The nature of my contract dictated a down payment, you see."

A down payment? I glance his way, frowning, but he's still focused on the tomb.

"Looking back," he says, "I am only surprised Thea did not mark the change in me sooner. And . . . I sometimes wonder if he took the part of me she loved."

"You're not saying she fell out of love with you." My heart squeezes with the prospect. Because, somewhere along the way, without my even knowing it, I've become . . . invested.

In Elias *and* his love story.

"She just . . . found me harder to love," Elias says. "Especially when we argued after she insisted that I grant her answers. Having done the unspeakable to win her, I felt entitled to my secrets. But Thea was Thea. And . . . she would have them, bar none. Thea found me out. Later, she pried from me a confession. Terrified of me, of what I had done, and of what I had become, she fled my presence and avoided me for days. Just when I was certain she wished to be finished with me, she returned to my side and vowed to sever the tie I had made—to free me."

"Wow."

Thea sounds kind of . . . boss.

"I took comfort in her promise," Elias says, "and what felt like a renewed bond. Our connection, impossibly, had grown stronger. But . . . I should have known better."

Elias's tone drops ominously with his last statement, and leaving the sarcophagus, he goes to the stone bench. Taking a seat, he props his elbows on his knees. When he speaks again, he addresses the floor.

"By dedicating herself to my absolution, Thea became a threat to my soul's shareholder. And the world chewing away at me opened to swallow her, too. As you already know, the demon could not attack until provoked. But Thea . . . she went a step too far. We were married for less than a year before he killed her."

My mouth falls open. For several long beats, stunned silence is my only reply.

Because I don't know what to say.

All this time, almost the entire span of his deal, the deal he made to be with her, Thea had been dead. Leaving Elias alone.

It's been two years for me without the one person in my life I considered family. Those two years have felt like a lifetime. Elias, though . . .

"I'm . . . really sorry," I say at last. What else is there *to* say?

"Sorry," he echoes. "That is the word for what I, in every respect, have since become."

More silence. It blares like a siren. And . . . I let it. Because I already know how empty words, especially those from someone outside the loss of a person, really are. No matter who speaks them, or how sincerely.

So, I lend Elias my presence. It's all I can do. But our thoughts turn dark together.

Because, though the end of Thea's role in Elias's story doesn't come as a surprise, the abruptness—not to mention the grim irony—of it does.

And there's still the mystery of how Elias entered into the agreement in the first place.

"Elias," I say at last, "how . . . how did you even get tied up with this thing?"

"Melekd'mot is what he is," says Elias. "He must do what he must do. And that is to contract with and collect, or perhaps *reap* is a better word . . . souls."

"He found you."

"I went looking," Elias admits. "But one need only come near a demon to gain its attention. Even if you don't go seeking one, as I did, their lot have ways of asking for entry into one's awareness."

My mind goes to the plane ride. And all those instances that built up to that moment when the demon finally manifested in front of me.

"I'm sure it happens differently for everyone who falls prey to such beings," Elias says. "Each instance, I've become certain, is its own perfect storm. Though desperation—or perhaps just pain—I feel, is a key ingredient in any case."

I walk over to take the seat next to him on the marble of the bench, which is freezing despite the warming chamber. And when Elias doesn't say anything else, when his prolonged silence signals the end of his recounting, I lean back on the bench and, folding my arms, bite my bottom lip.

"Jane," Elias says. "You're so silent. Tell me what you're thinking."

My thoughts surround the demon and the things he said, and how he'd threatened me. But . . . I can't tell Elias that.

"I'm thinking this is a pickle," I murmur instead.

Slowly, Elias turns his head my way, brow pinched, eyes still hidden behind mirrored lenses that reflect my uncertainty back at me.

"Forgive me," he says, "but I was under the impression a pickle equated to a punctured tire. Or finding the linen closet void of fresh towels. I think this is a bit more than that."

Understatement of the last century.

Obviously, though, Elias carries the trauma, not to mention the blame, of Thea's demise with him even now. And if he was telling the truth that I'm the only one who knows about her, then that must say something about how he views me.

But . . . before Helen died, she had always been the one to give *me* hope.

She didn't tell me about her diagnosis until she couldn't hide it anymore, either.

I never understood why. Never until now.

Point-blank, Elias is a walking Jenga tower with half the blocks already missing.

I'm not Thea. Elias doesn't see me that way. But he harbors enough remorse, enough regret over his part in her death that, if he caught wind of my hell trips, he'd likely clam up again and retract the hand he's extended to us all from within his own flaming cage. This flaming bed he's made.

And . . . I *do* want to take that hand, even though I still can't yet say why.

Or maybe I'm just not ready to.

"Okay," I allow. "So, at this stage, I'm willing to admit we may be dealing with more of a . . . a . . ."

"Disaster," finishes Elias.

"Yeah, okay," I mumble, "one of those."

Quiet. The passing of seconds. And then, gradually, minutes.

"I cannot be saved," he says, agitated. "Is *that* the reasoning behind your unbearable silence? Perhaps you now think I *should* not be. Say so, Jane, if that is what you are thinking. No matter how bleak your answer, it's sure to be more tolerable than the unending purgatory of your wordlessness."

"*Chill*, Elias," I tell him. "I already told you I was going to help. And of course I think you're . . . You're good, okay? We're good. I just . . . don't know what the punch line to this joke of a psychic artist, a psychometrist, and a tarot card reader walk into a possessed manor is."

He frowns. And scowls. And, mimicking my pose, folds his arms and leans back.

A few more seconds pass before I sit forward to place my hands on my knees, my stare rerouting to the cold marble sarcophagus.

"What I'm saying," I clarify, "is that I don't know how to fight this thing yet, or get him off your back. But like you said, there *is* something more going on here. Helen's involvement proves that. Bottom line, if Thea never gave up—and apparently she didn't—then how can we?"

"You don't think me a monster?"

I give him a blank stare.

"I killed the woman I love," he says.

"You made her a promise," I say. "And maybe you kept it in a screwed-up way. But, at the end of the day, we're all screw-ups. She knew that. I know that. And you didn't kill her. Your demon did. And *he's* the problem. Not you."

Elias lets that sink in. Then, without warning, he stands. Just when I'm sure he's going to pull another him and diva out the door, he steps in front of me to offer his palm.

At first, I'm reluctant. And then I fit my hand in his.

Even after I let him help me to my feet, he doesn't release me, and I'm glad he can't read minds like Giovanni. Some of my thoughts about him . . . I'm not supposed to have.

He squeezes my hand in his. I'm about to tug free. Because his gratitude is overwhelming. Like too much sun after living a life underground.

But then he tugs me against him, enfolding me in a crushing embrace.

My heart riffs Metallica. His thunders against my cheek, like the storm we escaped has found refuge within him.

I squeeze my eyes shut, fighting the instinct to push him away, yell at him, cuss him out. But I can count on one hand the times I've been held like this. By someone who truly gave a damn. And I let myself stay. Breathe him in.

Citrus. Smoke. Sandalwood and sorrow.

"I *know* the worst is yet to come," he tells me, lips and breath brushing my hair, that low voice rumbling through me, tuning me to his frequency even while his warmth syncs my soul with the remnants of his. "For me *and* for you. But no matter the outcome, Jane, know that, at the very least, just by coming, just by staying, just by trying . . . you have restored my faith. In everything. And darkness, can it truly consume what another has already bathed in light?"

He doesn't wait for an answer. Instead, he parts from me, presses a hand to my cheek just like he did that day in the hall, and then . . . he steps around me, his scent a following ghost.

Blinking back more tears, I spin to peer after him. But he's out of the tomb before I'm aware of my next thought.

Still awash in his words, his hope, I lose the battle not to cry again.

And I hate the tears more than ever because this reaction proves I'm already in too deep. Still, I smash the tracks away from my heated face with the heels of my palms while, internally, I command myself to *get a grip*. Because I can't face him again until I can be the Jane I was before he Elias-ed all over me and defused the electric fencing on my barbed-wire world.

Breathe. I need to breathe.

I take a shaky breath as I glance to Thea's tomb.

DOROTHEA ELAINE THORNFIELD reads the engraving on the lid, right above the dates that betray how Elias and Thea shared only ten months together before being separated by death if not eternity.

She must still love him. As much as he does her. Otherwise . . . would *I* be here?

I don't know what's going on, where *she* is, or how I fit into all of this. Only that I do . . .

"I mean, I see the attraction," I say, sniffing as I speak to the vault—address the dead chick inside. "I get it. But, dang, girl. Talk about high-maintenance."

There's no answer. Of course there isn't.

"He was lucky to have you," I say. "Kind of a dumpster fire by himself, isn't he?"

Quiet. So much quiet.

"Listen," I whisper, "I'll do what I can."

Elias honks the horn. Veering on the open doorway of the mausoleum, I flick him off.

Just like last time, though, he can't see it.

I sigh, and drop my hand. Because I guess he's not bossing me around.

He's just in a hurry. Because (no pressure) his soul, not to mention his eternal love life, is on the line or whatever.

I reenter the sunlit cemetery, glaring at the once more rumbling car as I approach.

Because I guess I give a damn now. About that.

About him . . .

20

Elias and I don't talk on the return trip to Fairfax.

Instead, he spends the time deep in thought, and so do I. And there's more mental room to do that this round since he doesn't barrel down the roads like Evel Knievel after nine shots of espresso. He still drives fast, but he must have other things on his mind now than speed.

Thea, of course.

She waltzes through my head, too, the image of her bringing more uninvited feels—these of the snarly, tangly, complicated sort.

I want to like her. I *do* like her. But . . . I also don't.

I don't dare explore why, even though, two guesses . . . So, I just pretend to check my phone for messages before doom-scrolling through social media instead.

Too bad no one's problems are as bad as mine in their posts because—sorry, not sorry—that usually *does* give me a little boost.

Of course, I could pay it forward and return the favor. And how would *that* post go?

Life update: Demons are for real. My dead best friend @HelenBurns is being sketch AF. There's this ripped Italian dude poking at the carcass of my dating life, and just today, my defunct give-a-crap-o-meter got flipped to red by some Hamlet-talking widower who, in addition to being kind of damned, is super unavailable because he's in love with an Edwardian skeleton. 😀

When we arrive at Fairfax again, Elias parks under the portico, just past the front door, the nose of the Jaguar aimed toward the garage. The center bay door of which hangs open.

Within, all the cars seem to have mysteriously . . . popped their hoods.

Elias has spotted these anomalies even before me.

And then, Giovanni—clad in a thin blue hoodie, white tank top, work jeans, and boots—wanders into view.

"*Again?*" Elias growls between his teeth. "That jolter-head. I'll kill him."

And then he's out of the car and stalking toward the garage. Because, apparently, a hundred-odd years and some big fat lessons about impulsivity don't equate to maturity.

Also, why did it sound like he kind of meant what he said?

"*Elias.*" I have to fiddle with the buttons on my door since, whether through force of habit or on purpose, he's locked me in.

By the time I've freed myself from the vehicle, Giovanni has exited the garage and is walking toward Elias with arms spread, as if he'd *like* to be punched in the face again.

I hustle, doing my best to get between the *Titanic* and the iceberg before history repeats itself. And I make it—*barely*.

"Hey, it's Jalias!" calls Giovanni the moment I put my back to him to face Elias. "You two go out for a bite? Did you bring me a hamburger? Your boy Giles is a good cook and all, but sometimes my made-in-America stomach needs beef that's more Whopper than Wellington."

"What do you think you're doing?" snarls Elias.

Giovanni feigns surprise, the toothpick clenched between his teeth dancing.

"Me?" He points a grease-stained hand at himself. "Oh, I've just been making out with Tilly. And Gertrude. Suzy Q, and Eleanor, too. Consolation prize since you apparently get Jane."

"Hey!" I wheel on him.

Those greasy hands go up. "Joke! It was a joke."

Giovanni is genuinely surprised by my reaction. And maybe I am, too.

I glance back to Elias just as his shielded glower transforms to a frown. Apparently, I've prompted some confusion in him, too.

"Where'd you two go anyway?" Giovanni asks.

Can't tell him Elias took me to meet his dead wife, so . . . I don't say anything.

"Just for a ride," says Elias.

"Long ride." Giovanni.

"I told you to stay out of the garage." Elias.

"Yeeeeah, you're right. I'm sorry," says Giovanni. "But since my noon meeting got canceled, Poole gave me the keys when I told him I knew how to repair vintage vehicles. Guess I should have cleared it with *you* first. Welp." Giovanni rubs his stained right hand against his jeans before extending his palm to Elias. "Apology's out of the way now so how 'bout we just put 'er there?"

Elias makes no move to accept Giovanni's handshake. And of course, he won't. Not knowing what Giovanni is. Which he must.

I cut in again, because this bomb apparently still has a few wires left to defuse.

"Listen, Giovanni, I'm really sorry I left you hanging."

"It's cool," he says, but the words are icy as he lowers his snubbed hand. "I get stood up never all the time."

"Don't be cross with Jane," says Elias. "She told me she was to meet with you. She didn't forget. I . . . had to borrow her."

"But just for a ride," Giovanni adds.

Elias takes several backward steps. "Lock the garage when you're finished playing mechanic," he mutters before turning away.

"Yeah, you suck, too!" Giovanni calls, grinning after him. "By the way, I cleaned the carburetor and adjusted the idle on Lucy. That should keep her from stalling on you again. Or, you know, bailing out when you expect her to be there . . ."

His words get progressively quieter as he reroutes them down to me. Guilt, in response, sinks fangs into my empty stomach.

"I *said* I was sorry," I tell him.

"I'm not mad," he grumbles. "Mostly, I've just been . . . worried."

Worried?

"Why would you be worried?"

"Because! For one, you're being stalked by a demon. Two—" He aims a hand after Elias, who vanishes into the manor. "You went for a drive in a hurricane with Kylo Ren!"

I blink and frown. Giovanni must have seen me get in the car. Or did Mr. Poole tell him where I went? Either way, my confusion remains. Because I still don't know why *specifically* he's been worried about me. It's not like we know each other that well. I'm not a stranger but I'm not a worry-level ally either . . . am I?

"I really didn't mean to stand you up," I say at last, because I'm entering hangry territory and that's all I've got for him.

"It wasn't a date," he says. "So how could you stand me up? Or wait, *was* it a date? You know, I think you and I are overdue for a talk about respect and boundaries. Also, we need to schedule a sit-down before you meet my mom. She can be . . . *extra*."

My expression goes deadpan. Though, this time, I'm grateful for the wisecrack. This day has been intense enough.

"Listen, I've *got* to eat something," I say. "Can I come find you later?"

"You're saying Vlad the Impossible didn't take you to lunch? What a tight-ass."

I glare at him.

"Why don't you stick around?" He gestures over his shoulder. "There's some sandwiches in the garage. Some Cornish pasty things and deep-fried egg-ball doodads. Bruce Pain's Poole Boy made them. Gave me the keys to aaaaaaall the shinies when I told him I knew how to fix carburetors and install serpentines."

I register the "sandwiches" part, but not the rest. Because, as the afternoon sun beams down on us, taking the temperature closer to seventy, Giovanni strips off his hoodie.

And it's like watching Apollo disrobe.

Oh. My. God. His *arms*. Also, *chest*.

Pectorals strain against the tank top that is pretty much see-through.

It doesn't help that a light sheen of sweat glosses him. Or that he smells like teakwood, gasoline, and *boy*. Or that he's *totally* doing this on purpose.

The once-over I give him is utterly involuntary and I should be ashamed of myself.

Fully loaded guns? Check. Six-pack? Check. All he's missing is an anchor tattoo with a MOM banner.

"Jane?"

I blink and *fo-cus*.

"Sure," I say. "I like . . . eat."

Sandwiches, Jane.

You.

Like.

Sandwiches.

"Jane like eat," says Giovanni before I can save face. "Giovanni like eat. Jane and Giovanni meant to be."

He flashes one of his killer smiles.

I scoff, trying not to choke on my embarrassment.

"Just. C'mon," I say, and trudge past him into the garage. Because it's about time I told *someone* about the hell world.

21

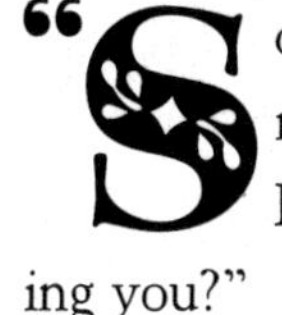

"So, let me get this straight," says Giovanni. "The reason you had that necklace last night was because Bob has been incrementally virtual-reality abducting you?"

"*Don't* tell Elias."

"I heard you the first nine times," Giovanni mutters as he folds shut the hood to the black Rolls-Royce Phantom III that I'm sitting in. A convertible with the top down, it's parked next to a similar-looking 1930s Cadillac, which is parked next to a fire-engine-red vintage Porsche.

Giovanni scowls as he glances between the three cars, like now *he's* the one only half paying attention. Though it's the hot rods that are distracting *him*. I on the other hand remain distracted by his hot bod. Hard not to be when he still hasn't thrown his hoodie back on.

"You know, none of these are replicas?" he says. "Not even the fugly bugly parked way in the back. And that thing's got to be from the Stone Age."

I've got Giovanni's picnic basket in the seat next to me. I'm full, but I nervous-eat a few more chips, doing my best not to drop crumbs.

"Ingrid saw Bob," I say. "You as well. I just don't get why *I'm* the only one dimension-surfing . . . If that's really what's going on."

"Well, that first day, you *did* seem to blip off the radar for a second."

I told Giovanni about dipping in and out of the two versions of Fairfax whenever I run into Bob. I need help figuring out why I'm the odd man out in terms of what everyone has been experiencing.

"It's like I get sucked into some kind of . . . void," I murmur. "It's here but it's also *not* here."

Giovanni must be finished with his tinkering, because he rounds the car. After opening the driver's-side door, he moves the basket to the back seat and takes its place next to me.

"Don't you think it's weird that this demon thing and his world are tangible now, but, according to you—and to a lesser degree, *me*—weren't before? I'm starting to think Cleverus Snape might have some insight on that. Insight he's not sharing. For whatever reason. Which is why I wonder why you don't want him to know about your transdimensional dips."

While I'd wanted Giovanni to know about the hell world, I hadn't banked on him asking probing (if pertinent) questions about Elias.

Time to deflect.

"Giovanni, why did you lie about having a bet with Ingrid?"

"Because, at the time, I had good reason to hide why I

really stuck around this mausoleum. Maybe now, though, if you give *me* a little something to go on, I can enlighten you in return."

"I just told you I've literally been glitching through hell. You know more than anyone."

"I mean about Thornflake."

I don't have chips that I can toss into my mouth so that I won't have to talk, so I avert my gaze to the miniature glove box in front of me. Inside, I find a fancy case with pens.

For some reason, that irritates me, so I snap the case closed and shove it back in the glove box.

"Jane."

My eyes fly to him. Because he doesn't use my actual name much.

"What's going on with this guy?" he asks. "For real. He must have told you something during this cryptic ride through the countryside. It's obvious he's hiding shit. Both him *and* Poole Boy, who, just so you know, goes home every night before dark."

I frown at this last tidbit, though I suppose it makes sense that Mr. Poole would have his own house—his own life. Then again, that would also mean that the dream-nurse version of him couldn't *really* have been him. Not that I'd truly been convinced it was.

"You know neither one of them would shake my hand?" Giovanni asks.

"Giovanni, *I* don't want to shake your hand. No offense."

"Fine," he says. "Nobody likes their dirty laundry aired. But this Thornfield dude, he doesn't just have skeletons in the closet. Homeboy *is* the skeleton."

I grit my teeth. Because I *can't* tell him about Elias. Not when he'd confided in me. Put all his faith in me. Held me to him like that . . .

So, again, I divert.

"Come clean," I say, "why didn't you tell Elias about your dream of Bob during the meeting?"

Giovanni's expression darkens, and I get a glimmer of the more serious and skittish side of him I'd glimpsed last night. "Until I got to Fairfax—saw your drawing—I really thought the dream *had* been unrelated."

"Now you know it wasn't," I say. "So why do you think you and I had run-ins with this thing before we got here? Elias told me that shouldn't have happened. Not until we showed up at Fairfax."

"Well, your case, I'm still not sure about," he admits, and, again, his reply startles me.

I blink at him, and wait. When he doesn't continue, I prompt him. "You're saying you know why *you* saw him?"

"I didn't just see him, Jane," says Giovanni. "I talked to him."

"Wait," I whisper, "*what*? Why didn't you say so?"

"*Because*. I was . . . still in the process of putting two and two together. But then, after the meeting, I figured it out."

"Figured out what?"

"In the dream," says Giovanni, "when Bob showed up as just that pair of eyes, I got this weird sense that . . . whatever was lurking in the darkness, it . . . wanted to talk to me. So, I talked to it. Asked it what it wanted. It . . . *he* said he could help. You know. Help *me*. See, I've had this little problem goin' on back at home and—"

"Problem?" I get a flash of Ingrid's card reading for Giovanni. What had she said? Something about mental anguish—a stressful situation. She'd hit some points with me, too, much as I hate to admit it. Could it be she'd called some truths about Giovanni as well?

"Yeah, it's all good," he assures me. "That fire's out. Ish."

I scowl, unconvinced.

"But long story short," Giovanni continues, "I told Bob, before I knew he was Bob, to go kick rocks and that . . . his offer wasn't one that interested me."

"Oh my God." A hand goes to my mouth. "He tried to get you to . . ."

"See," he says when I trail off, shaking a finger at the steering wheel. "I *knew* you knew something."

Apparently, though, Giovanni had known first.

"When your drawing matched what I saw," he continues, "and when Ingrid said she'd seen Bob, too, and then Thornfrump started talking about there being a demon, I—"

"Put two and two together," I murmur, borrowing his earlier phrasing.

Giovanni, in response, waves a hand like I've hit the nail on the head.

"Then," he goes on to say, "after overhearing Dread Pirate Roberts's response to your ripping him a new one over dismissing us, I knew for sure that this guy was having trouble with this thing because . . . unlike me, he *had* struck a deal."

My mouth falls open.

"But," I say, "then why would you—?"

"Stay?" Giovanni rests a hand on the steering wheel and tilts his head, staring at the sea of cars through the windshield.

"I don't like Thornfield," he admits after a long pause. "No secret he can't stand me, either. But . . . let's just say I know what it's like to have someone breathing down your neck for something."

I fight the urge to interrogate him on that point as Ingrid's words from earlier about Giovanni's phone call replay in my head.

"Basically," Giovanni says before I can speak up, "I'm not taking Thornfield's money without first getting a read on this whole thing. See if something *can* be done or, conversely, if he's just SOL. To do that, I've got to know what you know. And now, since we're playing Truth or Truth, it's your turn, Bird. Where the hell did Dracula take you today?"

I shift, my discomfort growing. God, this is stressful. Trying to help Elias without triggering him into retracting. Trying to convey what I need to Giovanni without revealing too much and betraying Elias's hard-won trust.

"Bird."

"*What?*"

"You might as well tell me. Half the jig is already up. Because you *do* realize I didn't really come in here to work on the cars . . . don't you?"

I swallow hard, narrowing my eyes on him.

He gestures over his shoulder.

"That buggy in the back? Old as it is, did you know it's only had one owner? Matter of fact, *most* of these cars have only had one owner."

"How could you know . . ." I trail off, but don't finish my question.

Giovanni still answers by raising his brows at me.

I blink several times, my heart speeding up.

"Usually," he says, "when it comes to people's stuff, particularly if it's old, the energies get muddy because they've been handled so much and by so many people. No mud on that necklace last night, though, and not much on any of these steering wheels, either."

"Collisions with cars," Ingrid had told Giovanni yesterday. Another prediction she'd nailed. In a way.

He points to the Cadillac. "In case you were wondering, Sir E-Disharmony bought *that* thing right before the Second World War. That pretty Fairlane over there?" He points to the vintage blue-and-white fifties-style Ford. "Had her custom made in the States and imported. The buggy thing I mentioned? Squidward bought that heap brand-new in 1904. But the *lady* was the one who usually drove. By the way, *her* signature is faded as hell and isn't on any of the other cars. His, though? I'm pretty sure he sleeps in that one sometimes." Again, he points. "Also, he babies the *shit* out of these things. Some kind of . . . misplaced sense of responsibility I can't put my finger on. So no wonder he blew a gasket over me being in here. Twice."

Oh jeez.

"Another thing," he adds, "some of the energy in here is a little, uh, jacked. Kind of frayed at the edges and toothy. Almost like there's something missing or unhinged, you know? One of the reasons I got so . . . worried when he made off with you like that."

I'm frozen, caught smack-dab in the scope of Giovanni's gotcha rifle.

"Lastly," he adds, "can I just say that you can tell a lot about someone by how they keep their car? Sorry, *cars*. No special powers needed. And these?" He swirls his finger to indicate our surroundings. "Serial-killer clean. All of 'em."

"He's not a serial killer," I snap.

"Okay." Giovanni nods. "Glad we've established *one* thing he's not. And now, since mass murderer is off the list, my next guess is either day-walking vampire or alien cyborg."

Finally, he shuts up. The silence doesn't help me think any better or faster, though.

"Bird, I know you know," Giovanni says.

"*How?*" Crap. If he can read my thoughts *without* touching me, that's something I need to be made aware of. Stat.

"I don't." He sighs. "But I do now. Because that was a bluff to get *just* that reaction, which is proof that Edward Sullen isn't human."

"He *is* human." I think.

"Jane. Spill."

I grab the door handle, ready to bail. I stop short, though. Because who am I kidding? Giovanni isn't someone I'm going to be able to hide from well. What's more, I need him. *Elias* needs him.

Elias didn't exactly tell me not to blab but . . . doesn't that go without saying? Why else keep Mr. Poole at arm's length? Or lock that attic door . . .

Then again, am I really betraying Elias if Giovanni already knows the truth? Most of it . . .

"Bird," Giovanni says, his tone softer now, "throw me a bone, here. Even *he* knows I'm not his enemy."

Ugh. Rock and a hard place. My favorite stomping grounds, apparently.

I sigh. The release of air brings more relief, though, than it does stress.

Because how can I keep secrets if they aren't keepable in the first place?

22

I make the mistake of letting Giovanni go ahead of me into the manor.

As he walks beneath the shade of the portico, Fairfax Hall degrades, the veneer of reality disintegrating in favor of blackened bricks, crumbling half-fallen walls, and flying embers.

"*No, no, no,*" I murmur as the sky flushes bloody. Then, when the ground splinters with a webwork of glowing fissures, I start running. "Giovanni!"

He turns, but only just as the open doorway floods with a blackness that swallows him whole.

Or maybe *I'm* the one who's been devoured.

Even after my immersion into the demon's realm, I don't stop.

My plan is to charge through that blackness, into the manor, hoping I can still escape—outrun—this latest ambush. But then those eyes burst into being within that rectangle of nothing, bringing my feet—my heart—to a halt.

"You should have left when you had the chance," intones that sonorous voice—the demon's.

He emerges, melting through the shadows that peel back to unveil cracked skin, gleaming horns, snow-white hair, and that dark sneer.

"You see," he says, those unblinking eyes chiseling into mine even as I back away, "it's personal now."

"Because I took off with your necklace?" I snip. "Way to be freaking petty. I gave it back."

And I'm not surprised to find him wearing it again.

"Because you *persist*," he corrects in a hiss, continuing his approach. "You return even when you *know* it is too late. Because you think you can win. But even if I *could* allow that, I wouldn't. Because if you did, that would mean . . . it wasn't worth it. And Jane, I *need* what I did . . . to have been worth it."

At that, I spread my arms, flabbergasted.

"What you did to Thea?"

He touches the necklace—his necklace—with one claw.

"Deals beget dealers," he says. "I told you once you and I are the same. But you don't listen. You leave me no choice but to prove it."

I hesitate, my muscles coiled—my body urging me to run even while my mind pushes me to stay rooted, to press for answers. There's nowhere to run here, though, and he *is* giving me answers. Obtuse, vague, and wrapped in riddles, but still leading.

But why all this breadcrumbing?

Perhaps words, at this juncture, are his only weapons.

Maybe questions are mine.

"Giovanni said you got revenge," I mutter. "He said that's why you are what you are. Which means . . . you weren't always this way. You're not saying you made a deal, too. Like Elias?"

"Not at *all* like him," the demon replies through a dark smile—one that suggests he's not sorry in the least. For anything.

For another instant, I'm stumped. Then I piece his words together with Giovanni's about his read on the necklace. How Giovanni had said this thing had become what he is *because* he'd gotten the revenge he'd desired.

Ingrid, too, had unwittingly unearthed some intel on the nature of our enemy through her cards. Before *we* had labeled this creature a demon, her reading had identified him has a "lost soul."

Ingrid had doubted that message. But she shouldn't have.

Because hadn't the demon even described himself as "a soul without a soul"?

"Deals begat dealers," I mutter, actually taking a step toward him as I repeat his latest clue. "You're trying to tell me you were human once. That's what you meant when you said you were like me."

"Not entirely," he allows—an agreement and a disagreement rolled into one cryptic response.

Still, despite his obtuseness, it's like he wants me to figure it out. Like he wants me to figure *him* out.

And then, in a moment of understanding, I do. One piece of the mystery that is him, at least.

"You were human," I say, "and you made a deal for your soul. In exchange for revenge. And now . . ."

And now that he's become *this*, he needs that deal to have been "worth it."

Which means something about my being here—*our* being here—threatens the centuries-old delusion he's been holding on to that it was.

"Seriously? I rail at him. "Is *that* what this is about? You're stalking me because you cashed in *your* soul for vengeance? Because you're looking for some kind of sick validation?"

New fear courses through my veins. Not of my opponent, but of what this revelation about his fate suggests regarding Elias's.

My outrage, though, sears through the panic.

"You're right," I say, lifting my chin in defiance of him and the arid wind that stirs my hair and his into our faces. "You're *nothing* like him. Elias made a mistake. He didn't want revenge or to hurt anyone. He bartered for *love*."

"There is no such thing!" roars the demon, teeth bared, nostrils flaring, eyes going wide—and feral.

A crack of garbled thunder answers from above. The wind dies and the flying embers freeze.

Everything stays suspended that way—a clear indication my words have brought me to the edge of something not good. *His* edge.

I hesitate, holding on to words I should not say.

But . . . *he* is the one making this personal.

"The girl who the necklace belonged to—what was her name anyway?" I ask him in a whisper. "Or, since you don't believe in love . . . do you even remember?"

Though there's no change in his expression, that luminous serpentine gaze burns a tint brighter.

An eon of nothing passes in which I wait for him to reduce me to ash.

"It's your move," he says at last.

And then his form collapses into a tatty blood-splatter-shaped shadow, which then races for me, skimming over the craggy and fuming terrain until it shoots beneath me.

I skitter back, out of its reach as it zooms on, sweeping away with it the stalled embers and the sky, the rubble, and the crimson-lit ruin.

In the moments before the hell world is vanquished in favor of the summer afternoon, I'm met with the skyline of a crumbling Roman city, its pillars teetering, its towering edifices gutted and half-collapsed—the scene screened behind a haze of red-tinted smoke.

"Ancient," Giovanni had said of the demon. This soul . . . without a soul.

The mirage dissipates in a heat-haze shimmer, which leaves me staring down that winding drive leading away from Fairfax Hall.

"Jane?"

Whirling, the warmer and now floral-scented breeze sending my hair again into a flurry, I find two figures standing at bay.

Ingrid, the one to call out to me, is closest, the wind stirring her pink curls, her wide eyes brimming with worry—and a good dose of terror, too.

"I know you and I just talked about this," says a pale Giovanni, "but . . . you full-on just disappeared."

"Right before . . . *re*appearing," adds a queasy Ingrid.

"Bird." Giovanni takes several steps toward me, hands lifting, as if his plan is to take me by the shoulders. Or something . . . He forces his arms back to his sides and reaches for words instead. "Are you okay?"

There's a beat as I consider the three of us.

A trio of green-ass, psyched-out psychics.

If we don't get our heads out of our butts and start acting like a team—tonight—Elias is done for. And maybe us, too.

"If we're going to do this," I tell them, even while my voice shakes, "if we want to kick this creep's ass and not die in the process . . . then we need to get our shit together. *Now.*"

23

We meet that evening in the dining room. Dinner is laid out, but none of us are hungry.

I've no idea where Elias has gone, but I'm glad he's out of the equation. For the moment.

His absence allows me to take his seat at the head of the table, and talk candidly.

"It's not a secret that none of us know what we're doing," I say. "But here's the lowdown. If we don't vanquish Bob, Elias dies at midnight on his birthday. Technically speaking, the instant the date switches to the seventeenth and he turns nineteen."

"*What?*" says Ingrid, eyes flashing with alarm.

"Also," I say, "you both already know how this demon operates. Elias broke it down for us day one. Basically, we take a swing at Bob, that clears him to take one at us. That pretty much translates to us getting *one* go at this thing." I hold up a finger to emphasize the number. "Because if we screw up and miss, call it a hunch, but I don't think Bob's going to return that particular favor."

"Well, this has all escalated rather quickly," quips Ingrid.

"If you're out," I tell her, "now is the time to leave. *If* this thing will let you."

"I told you I wasn't," she says, affronted.

"So far, we haven't exactly been organized," I say. "Or functional. Part of that's my fault. Part of it's because we haven't had much truth to go off of, either. But now we need a plan."

"Which is going to be hard," offers Giovanni, speaking up at last, "given that we don't know Bob's weaknesses—or if he even has any."

"Maybe he doesn't," I allow, "but obviously his hold over Elias's soul isn't as ironclad as he'd like any of us to believe. Otherwise, why bother with us?"

"Why would he bother with *you*?" Giovanni corrects, his voice quiet, his gaze penetrating.

I plow on, because I don't have an answer. Yet.

"This thing wins, it gets Elias's soul and Elias dies and goes to hell."

And maybe, possibly, becomes something else. Something like Bob.

"The cards *said* he lied," muses Ingrid. "About the property being haunted . . ."

Giovanni and I both regard her. To this, she only shrugs. "I asked them after Giovanni called him out. But . . . this attachment. With Bob. How did this happen?"

"He had a bad day," I say. A bad century, technically, but Ingrid doesn't need to know that. "And he's going to have a worse one if we don't put our heads down and ask questions later. Bottom line, if you're Team Elias, then all you need to know right now is that he made a colossal screwup. I think it's a safe bet to say everyone in here has, at some point, made a bad deal."

"His was just a little more . . . binding," adds Giovanni.

"What we *need* to be talking about," I say, "especially since we have a deadline of four days, is phase one of our plan."

"Which is?" Giovanni asks.

"We use our brains and our extrasensory crap to figure out what makes this demon tick. We look for the chink in his armor."

"How exactly do you propose we do that?" asks Ingrid.

"You tell me," I challenge. "What about these cards of yours is so special? No offense, but what about *you* is so special?"

"Is that a rhetorical question?" Ingrid asks.

"I want a damn answer, Ingrid," I snarl. "What can you do besides sit there and pontificate about Cups and Swords or whatever?"

"The cards provide insight," Ingrid says. "And in answer to your second question, they allow me . . . to see."

"Then get looking," I tell her. "If they don't make sense, look again. I keep glitching into this thing's matrix and that doesn't make sense, but what if it does? Ask them that. Ask them why this thing is singling me out. Ask them why Bob pretends like he knows me. Ask them if he's got any allergies. I don't know. Just do what you do. Giovanni, how open are you to trying to give Bob a handshake?"

"Grab your ChapStick," he says, "because you can kiss my ass."

"Glad you're on board."

"You realize that necklace was like touching a live wire, don't you?" he argues, more frightened than angry. "The more undiluted the energy infused in something—or someone—the more I absorb. Takes a while to shake that shit off, too. And you realize part of the reason I didn't get your name right was because you really *did* have armor on. Even if I could get close enough to touch Bob, he's not going to let me see crap."

"Fine," I say, "then I guess we'll just have to rely on what Ingrid's cards can tell us."

Giovanni folds his arms. He scowls and glares. But I don't care.

If he's sticking around, that means he's also sticking his neck out. He needs to bring his A game. He might not want to touch a demon, and I get that, but we've officially entered go-big-or-go-home territory and, as far as moves and countermoves go, we only have so many.

"What about *you*?" asks Ingrid.

"I'm going to draw him," I say.

"Um," Giovanni interjects, raising a finger, "even though I missed it, I don't think we need a rerun of the Fire Bird episode of the Jane Is a Target show."

"Elias," I clarify. "I'm going to draw Elias."

"Forgive me," says Ingrid, "but, so long as we're being blunt with one another, what do you suppose *that* will do?"

"Like you said," I reply, "we already know it's Elias's soul Bob's attached to. Not Fairfax. And . . . and I think *that's* why things are getting thin here." I borrow Helen's words. They're the only ones I have to describe what's been happening. To me. "When I vanished, I went into Bob's world, which seems to be parallel to this one. I keep phasing in and out of it at random, whenever Bob shows up. Something tells me this is the world Elias is headed for. It's coming to get him. But normally, when I draw spirits, that can strengthen them."

"Yes, you mentioned that," murmurs Ingrid.

"In the past," I continue, "my drawings have helped spirits to come forward into the physical world. So, maybe, if I draw Elias, that will—"

"Help to anchor him," offers Giovanni, like he doesn't think it's a half-bad idea.

"It's what I can do," I say. "Until we get a better idea of how to launch our attack, and make the best of our one shot, all we *can* do is what we know."

"Hear, hear," comes a voice from the doorway.

Mr. Poole stands beneath the archway, a musing smile on his face, like he thinks we're quaint. Like he's walked in on a tabletop role-playing game rather than a war room meeting.

"Glad to see you lot enjoyed the Yorkshire pudding." He sighs, deflating at the untouched dishes.

An uncomfortable silence pulses while Mr. Poole approaches the table where he deposits a plate of chocolate chip cookies. Has he been in the kitchen baking this whole time?

Baking and listening in?

There'd been no rattle of pans, no whir of a mixer, no buzz of a timer.

Until now, there'd been no aroma, either. Now, though, the swirled perfume of chocolate, butter, and vanilla saturates the air. Along with that ever-present aroma of coffee that seems to follow Poole no matter the time of day. Like sunny mornings are just where he happens to live.

"I hope I'm not intruding," says Mr. Poole. "But my earlier summons failed to herd you and, well, now that I've discovered you all together, I'd love a word."

Giovanni raises his hand. "Are we in trouble? Um. More trouble?"

"I wish only to ask a favor," says Mr. Poole as he drifts to the other end of the table, the one opposite mine. There, he rests his fingers on the surface all CEO-style. "Regarding Mr. Thornfield. Man of the never-ending hour." The housekeeper laughs at that—harder than he should, but also a little nervously. Like he's shared an anxiety-inducing inside joke—but only with himself. Quickly, he sobers. "As you may or may not know, Mr. Thornfield's nineteenth birthday coincides with the conclusion of this venture. Rather, it is the day after."

"Jane might have mentioned something about it," mutters Giovanni, his tone remaining dark while Mr. Poole continues on in cheer. Or . . . is it affected cheer?

"Splendid," says the housekeeper. "Though it should be noted that Mr. Thornfield is not fond of his birthday. In fact, he abhors the date."

"What *does* he like?" grumbles Giovanni. "I mean, aside from pretty go-vroom-vrooms?"

"Typically," says Mr. Poole, ignoring Giovanni, "Mr. Thornfield prefers to disregard the day entirely. He takes no calls and receives no visitors."

"He gets visitors?" Giovanni.

"He gives me the day off," continues Mr. Poole, "even when I vow to observe the date just as I would any other."

My heart sinks. Because I know why Elias hates his birthday. It's no secret either why the approaching one is part of the reason he despises all the others.

"So, naturally," says Mr. Poole with a frown, "since this year is different and there are guests in the house, I've decided to arrange, well, something of . . . a birthday party."

Giovanni raises his hand. "Can I opt out?"

"No," says Mr. Poole.

"I have a note."

"Pardon me for saying so, Giovanni," interjects Ingrid, "but it's quite a paradox that you're so keen on helping someone you claim to hate."

"See," explains Giovanni, "that's just it. I don't like him enough to hate him."

His comment draws my attention because it harkens to something Elias had said in the car. About hate. And love. How they, in a way, coexist—act as two sides to the same coin.

"So, this is going well," mumbles Mr. Poole.

"Fine, fine, fine," says Giovanni. "I'm game for taking a break from cracking demon skulls to stage a *literal* pity party. But you said he's not a fan. Are you sure it's not going to piss him off? And get *you* fired?"

"Mr. Thornfield is and has been a student of isolation for so long," says Mr. Poole, "and the presence of peers, meaning yourselves, presents a unique situation that I am reticent to squander."

"Translation," says Giovanni. "You plan to use us as rent-a-friends."

Mr. Poole's shoulders sag. "It's quite bleak sounding when you put it that way."

"When do we discuss rates?" asks Giovanni. "My Bogus Buddy package is ninety-five an hour, but it's extra if I have to smile. This, of course, will be tacked on to my demon-fumigation fee. Which, by the way, is still outstanding."

Ingrid cuts in to chide Giovanni again. And then the three of them banter on about the party.

I chew on my thumbnail, tuning them out. Because suddenly, I'm less concerned with Mr. Poole's hijacking of my meeting than I am with the fact that the housekeeper doesn't seem to know what I do about Elias's impending birthday. That it's truly his one-hundred-and-eighteenth nineteenth birthday. The end of his hundred-and-thirty-sixth year on this planet.

Mr. Poole doesn't seem to know, either, what the three of us do now. That Elias will cease to have any more birthdays after this one. At least, not if we fail. Not if *I* do.

But what then *does* Mr. Poole know about all this? About Elias.

Maybe this is just *his* way of helping. Trying to, since he doesn't have any powers. Since, in many ways, being a more official employee of Elias's, his hands are tied.

"Jane," says Mr. Poole, "you're awfully quiet over there."

"You said yourself we're scheduled to leave the day before his birthday," I say. "My flight is that night."

"Mine too," says Giovanni.

"I'm to catch a bus." Ingrid.

"Yes," says the housekeeper. "I thought it would make the most sense to ambush him that same afternoon. Before we all part ways."

Meaning, the day we either win . . . or lose.

"Just putting this out there," says Giovanni, "but 'ambush' and 'Elias' seem like a bad combo. That's like saying, 'Hey, see that cranky, feral cat over there? Let's throw him in the pool.'"

"Well, it's not a *surprise* if we tell him," argues Ingrid. "And he likely won't come if he smells it brewing."

I frown. Because, can it be everyone is actually sort of . . . on board with this idea?

Should I be, too?

On some level, this party feels like a distraction. But maybe it *could* be . . . a finish line.

For all of us.

"Allow me to be clear," says Mr. Poole. "It is *not* my suggestion that we lob confetti at him or bellow 'surprise' in his face. I merely want him to grasp that, contrary to what I know he has come to believe . . . he is *not* alone."

Everyone gets quiet with this declaration. Even Giovanni, who, knowing him, must have at least a hundred wisecracks sparking off in his head. That he doesn't give voice to a single one speaks volumes.

"Of course," adds Mr. Poole, "you've all already proved as much with your continued presence. Your dedication to help him in spite of the perils, not to mention his at times challenging disposition, speaks to your character. Your spirits. Perhaps, though, the marking of a milestone is the much-needed icing on a rather dry cake?"

"I'm not singing," says Giovanni.

"Yes," says Mr. Poole, exasperated, "you can accept my gratitude for that right now."

I clear my throat. "Can't we all just . . . be in the kitchen at the same time when he comes in or something?"

"You mean . . . just don't tell him we are having a party while we are in the midst of having one?" asks Ingrid.

"You know," says Giovanni, "that could work."

"That's a marvelous idea," says Mr. Poole, almost like that had been his thought the entire time, but he'd been waiting for one of us to say it out loud. "We'll mark the occasion with action rather than words. A clever tactic."

"There can be food," says Ingrid. "And a cake."

"I've aspirations to make a red velvet," offers Mr. Poole. "And perhaps a charcuterie board."

"There going to be any other menu options?" asks Giovanni. "I'm on a strict no-upholstery *or* shark-cooties diet."

"So, it'll be a birthday party," observes Ingrid, "but a . . . clandestine one. It's brilliant."

"He's going to hate us," warns Giovanni.

"Well"—Mr. Poole sighs—"according to your logic at least, he'll first have to like us enough to do so."

"He won't have any room to be mad," I say, "if . . . the job is done by then."

The room gets quiet, everyone's gaze rerouting to me.

Maybe I shouldn't have said this bit out loud. It's a desperate bid on my part to gain some control over the situation as well as this pair of psychics who, like me, don't have a clue regarding how or where to start playing offense.

"It *would* make quite a birthday gift," allows Ingrid after several more beats. "To have his dilemma resolved . . ."

His soul free. His life back.

Some friends to share it with.

"Which means," Giovanni says, his gaze flitting between me, Ingrid, and back to me again, "you, me, and Jane had better get to work."

His meaning is clear.

As is his reason for leaving Mr. Poole out of this statement.

Because the housekeeper is the only one who doesn't know Elias's *actual* birthday . . . might not happen.

24

I am so in over my head.

Send.

All I have to go on is the hope you've given me. All of us, IG.

Send.

You always told me the truth, tho. Even when it was hard to hear. So, you must think he's got a chance.

Send.

Helen, something's happening to me.

Send.

I don't want to like this change. Tbh, it's scarier than Bob.

Send.

I don't want to like these people. Still don't want to like HIM. Even though I do. Maybe too much.

Send.

Prolly just cuz he's into someone else.

Send.

Prob just cuz he needs me.

Send.

Or bc he makes me feel less alone.

Send.

Or it's just the boujee way he talks.

Send.

Srsly, I could listen to him read obituaries and find it hot.

Send.

STFU. I know Giovanni is hot, too. Don't effing remind me.

Send.

I KNOW WE'RE BEING BAD. IDC. 🧝
I GET TO BE BAD. I'M UNDER A LOT OF STRESS FROM GETTING DEMONIC DEATH THREATS.

Send.

Omg. Ur right. What's wrong with me? I'm supposed to be figuring out how to save the guy. Not fantasizing over how good of a kisser he's got to be.

Send.

Still, tho, that's got to be some fine vintage first and second base. 👍

Send.

LOL, YES, I SAID THAT. Ok, ok. 🙃
I'll be good.

Send.

Cuz I want him to live.

Send.

I want him to stay. Around, IG. Me, I mean.

Send.

And just between u and me, cuz ur my ride
or die, I'm going to go ahead and admit right
here that I also kind of want him to

I have to stop typing. Because the doorway leading into the enormous rose-covered stone gazebo I found my way to—the one that stands at the heart of the estate's overgrown gardens—fills with an angular and all-too-familiar shadow.

Light from the waning moon—and the lit-up rear of Fairfax Hall—transforms him into a silhouette. But his is a shape I would know anywhere.

"Elias," I say, and stuff my phone into my knapsack. The movement is borderline frantic. Maybe, though, he won't notice.

"Jane," he says, "what are you doing out here? It's past midnight."

"Oh," I say, and stall, confused. "You mean you didn't come out here looking for me?"

My initial thought was that he'd come by my room, found me missing, gotten worried, and gone on a search. Otherwise . . .

"What are *you* doing out here?" I ask.

"I spend more summer nights in the gardens than I ought,"

he replies, striding into the cool and shadow-draped space. "Thea loved them so. Especially the roses. The seat you occupy now—it was one of her favorite places."

"Here," I say, rising, "I can go."

"Then I shall be alone again," he says, "and these days, I'm half-sick of my own company. Why not stay and tell me to whom you've been writing. Unless, of course, your wish is to retire."

"I'm not sleepy," I lie, and slowly sink back onto the stone bench. "And I wasn't writing to anybody. Well," I amend, "just . . . Helen. In Messenger. She still has an account."

"I see." He moves to take the seat next to mine, that head-spinning scent of his mixing with the headier fragrance of the roses. And that aroma, so distinctly him—I don't want to imagine a world without it. It's also one I'm trying to tell myself doesn't belong on my skin.

"You must have been talking to her about me," Elias says.

Awesome. So, he *did* see me crash-stash my phone.

"Don't flatter yourself, Thornfield," I drone, playing it off.

It doesn't work.

"Your response makes it clearer than ever there's an opinion of me you wish to conceal."

"This from the guy who locks his journal room."

"Mm," he says, "you make your point."

Quiet. And I shift. There's something about being in the dark with someone that's both comforting and unnerving. On one hand, you can't see their expression and they can't see yours. On the other, since there's nothing to focus on but Elias's voice, and his presence, it's like I'm here with him a bit more . . . authentically. Intimately.

Kind of like . . . talking to someone's ghost. Their soul.

"I confess your name has flowed from *my* pen once or twice since our meeting," he says.

"Oh yeah?"

Great. He waxed poetic to his dead wife about me. Talk about a fat friendzone cue.

"You think we would have gotten along?" I ask him. "Me and your old lady?"

He laughs, a softer sound than before, when we'd been together in the car.

"I suppose you mean Thea. You remind me of her," he admits. "She was such a force to be reckoned with. A rare creature whose will could not be withstood. Or, rather, resisted . . ."

My hands, poised on my knees, contract into fists. This answer. It rankles me.

I don't want to be like her.

This fool. I want him to see *me*.

Maybe, though, he can't. And maybe I shouldn't hope he still will.

Time for a conversational segue.

"Hey, listen," I say. "While we're on the subject, I need to ask about her. If you know what she did. To attack Bob, I mean."

"I never knew," he replies, his tone quieter than before, as if I've brought up a taboo subject. Or maybe just brought him slamming back into his own darkness. That place of blame he'd been fermenting in for longer than any still-edible cheese known to man. "But I do know why you ask."

"Just good to note what didn't work the last time." I sigh.

"Thea was so independent," he says. "And fiercely protective. She took the whole undertaking on by herself. Keeping her secrets in turn. Her fear, I think, was that if she shared her plot with anyone, least of all me, our foe would gain the advantage of foresight."

"She overcorrected," I mutter. "Tried to."

"She must have attempted to destroy him," Elias says. "Whatever her tactic, its failure still granted him the leave he needed to retaliate. And she perished. So, I hope you understand there is no winning a battle of might."

Well, there goes the drop-an-anvil-on-his-head idea.

"Grayson," says Elias, "presented me with the idea of inviting sensitives like yourselves because he thought you might be able to *detach* the entity from me. Untether my tie to him, and his to me. And even if that cost me the portion of my soul he holds, the effort might still be worth it."

"Yeah," I murmur. "Me and the others. We're sorting through some . . . approaches."

"What are you planning, Jane?" he asks. "What, if anything, new have you uncovered?"

I open my mouth, about to tell him of the hell world. I clamp my jaw shut, though, some faraway fragment of my being again warning me against going there. At least . . . just yet.

Skittish as he is, Elias is likely better off not knowing what I've learned about Bob. Or what that could—will—mean for *him* if the others and I can't pull off this rescue mission.

But *can't* is not an option anyway. I won't let it be. So . . .

"I'm glad you asked for a strategy update," I say instead. "Because the answer is . . . I need you to sit for a portrait. Tomorrow."

"Pardon?"

"I need to draw you. Sooner the better."

He's quiet. For a long time.

"What?" I ask. But he doesn't answer. "It's not a root canal, Elias. You just sit there."

"Why do you want to draw my portrait?" And now he's the one trying to stuff shit away so I don't see it—verbally at least. "I'm not one of your spirits."

Except . . . isn't he?

"You said this demon's got part of your soul," I say.

"Yes."

"Well," I continue, "if I draw you, then what if that helps keep the part of you that's still here . . . here? Could buy us more time."

"Ah," he says. But like he thinks it's a shit idea.

"What do you mean, 'ah'?" I ask him.

"I mean, of course," he replies quickly. "Tomorrow, we'll make plans."

I scowl, turning my head his way, and now I'm desperate to read his features. So desperate that I dig my phone back out and activate the flashlight, which I then shine straight into his face.

That eye squints and blinks, but he doesn't try to hide.

"You don't want me to draw your picture," I accuse.

Elias doesn't answer, but his hand finds mine—the one holding the phone—and he gently takes the device from me. He can't get in to see my messages to Helen because I've got the screen locked behind a passcode. But information isn't what he's after. Instead, he turns the phone's flashlight on me, becoming a shadow once more while it's my turn under the interrogation lamp.

"If you are so set on wasting your paper and charcoal on me," he says, "I shall sit for your portrait, Miss Reye. My fear is only that you will do me too much justice."

I take the phone back and aim it at him again. "Smooth talking doesn't get you out of the hot seat, Shakespeare. What's the *real* reason you don't want me to draw you?"

He blinks in the glare of the light, and I forbid myself from staring at his lips, which tilt up in a rueful smile.

"There *is* one other worry," he admits. "My spirit is in the clutches of something that seeks to transmute me. Though I'm not partial to the idea of your tampering with that connection, primarily because you've already endured one harrowing attack born from a similar action . . . I *shall* acquiesce."

His hand creeps up my wrist this time, like he's afraid I'll snatch the phone away from him if he doesn't come in soft. His strategy works. I let him claim the device again, because this lingering, drawn-out touch, one that sends a ripple of electricity through my entire body, isn't one I want to fight.

Instead, it's one I want more of. *Lots* more.

"For I must do what Thea did not by accepting aid," he continues, like he's trying to convince himself more than me. "Besides that, as already stated, yours is a pull I would not deign to try and resist anyway."

His words lull me like a spell. Which must have been his plan. Because instead of turning the light on me again, he rises with the stolen phone and walks to stand beneath the center of the gazebo's dome ceiling, his profile cast in the screen's harsh white glow.

I grip the edge of the stone bench, but then, when he thumbs up on the screen and begins to type in a code, I launch myself at him.

Elias has to catch me because my momentum is so much that I almost fall. The only thing I care about, though, is getting my phone away from him. He lets me have it, but he has to steady me and set me to my feet.

"What have you written of me that would be so devastating if I knew?" he asks.

"How do you know my code?" I demand.

"I don't," he whispers, and his words serve as a battering ram to the gut.

A bluff? Really? And just like with Giovanni in the garage, I fell for it. Only Elias set a much more nefarious trap. Because the truth he'd been after . . . was mine.

Also, why isn't he letting me go?

I force myself to look up at him.

"You must have said something truly horrible about me," he murmurs, and I swear he leans down.

"Just that you're the only one I know with problems more jacked than mine."

"Mm," he says, as if in agreement. "And hourly, they only grow more complex."

"Sucks to be you."

"You have no idea."

I don't know how to respond to that. Words have dried up. Because he's holding me against him. With those last words, he'd also leaned down by another small degree, enough so that the swoop of hair covering his hidden eye falls to tickle my cheek.

For one heart-stopping moment, I'm sure it'll happen.

That he has read my mind or, worse, Helen somehow ratted me out to him on what I want—even though I never got to finish telling her.

But then, without warning, he releases me and steps back.

"I *must* go," he says. And then . . . he does.

Leaving me standing there, staring after him as he stalks off through the darkness.

Again though, why does it feel like his words weren't really meant for me?

That, instead, he'd once more spoken them aloud . . . for himself.

25

Elias doesn't show up the next day. Or the day after that.

And every time I or anyone else goes looking for him, he's gone from the manor—off in one of his bazillion cars. Either that or he's hiding.

Twice now, I've gone to cop-knock on his door like he did me, but if he was in there, he never answered. And the door stayed locked because, yes, I tried it.

And *of course*, he doesn't have a phone.

He's avoiding me. A *duh* that hurts like hell. And confuses the crap out of me.

Because we had a plan.

And it's not like we *did* kiss. He doesn't know what I said about him in Messenger, either.

But whatever. Screw him. I'll save his life without him.

Which is why I've called another meeting.

Because we're running out of time. And Ingrid's cards aren't ponying up. Giovanni hasn't been able to grab anything new off any artifact in the manor, either.

And now my stress level has elevated high enough that I actually wish Bob *would* make another appearance. He doesn't have to yet, though. Which tells me he's gotten something he wanted.

Namely? Me in limbo.

The whole thing on the plane, the fire—the Pop Goes the Bob event with the necklace. Those had been scare tactics. Probably to send us scattering. To send *me*, as Giovanni had said, flying.

He must know we're in it to win it. And now he's just sitting back with his Flamin' Hot hell Doritos and watching us scramble while the game clock ticks toward zero.

Not on my watch.

Which is why I've got my sketchbook. Because it's the only weapon I have.

"I get the logic, Bird," says Giovanni, who leans against the huge mahogany table in the library, arms crossed, brow pinched. "But I still don't dig this idea."

"Elias has apparently tapped out on his own rescue mission," I say as I head over to flop my sketchbook down next to him, "so, it's not like we have a lot of options here. *Or* time."

"Why don't *I* try talking to him?" he asks. "Tonight."

"Sure," I say, spreading my hands. "Have at it. You can totally take a turn at playing whack-a-mole. But in the meantime, until you can pin Elias down, we need to do something that's going to actually get us somewhere."

"What happened anyway?" Giovanni asks, picking up a

paperweight—a glass ball with a petrified rose inside. "Between you two?"

"Nothing."

"Something must have," says Ingrid, who sits at a large desk, snapping down those annoying-ass cards. "He is obviously avoiding you."

"Thanks for the astute observation, Ingrid," I say. "But it shouldn't take fortune-telling cards to arrive there since *everyone* avoids me."

"That might have been true once," murmurs Ingrid as, infuriatingly, she pops down yet another card with a *snap*.

"You were supposed to draw him," says Giovanni. "I'm guessing that didn't happen."

"Kind of need him to sit still for that," I say.

"You can't just draw him from memory?" asks Ingrid.

"Can you read cards for no one?" I counter.

"I can read for someone who isn't present, if that's what you mean."

"It's different for me." I run a hand through my hair. "I mean, I can do a loose sketch. *Maybe*. But it won't be the same. I need to get him *right*. Because I'm not just drawing his face."

"Now that, I understand," says Ingrid.

"Except now you want to loose-sketch Bob instead," says Giovanni. "Because you're panicking, and summoning a demon is apparently the answer."

"You got a better idea?"

"I don't get it. You and Thornfrap have a fight?" asks Giovanni, a note of hope edging his tone.

"Mm," answers Ingrid. "More like they had a close call. A near miss, if you will."

I swing around to glare at her. She's not paying any attention to me. Instead, she's shuffling and squinting at her spread. Which I have to hold myself back from marching over to arm-sweep off the table. Because okay, maybe she *is* psychic.

"Close call?" Giovanni repeats, but the question is meant for me.

"How the hell do you *do* that?" I mutter at Ingrid, avoiding Giovanni's question. Right along with that probing stare.

"The cards speak in symbology," Ingrid answers, apparently not picking up on the fact that, this time, my question *had* been rhetorical. "Strung together, they tell a story using the imagery of archetypes. In a nutshell, they help me to tap into the collective unconscious, of which we are all a part. And here we have The Lovers paired with the Seven of Wands, which suggests some heartfelt exchange was . . . blocked. Or perhaps . . . cut short?"

She peeks up at me for confirmation. I feint at her, fist raised.

We're ten yards apart, and the threat isn't real. But she needs to shut up.

"Thought he was seeing someone," Giovanni mutters to the paperweight, but only loud enough for me to hear.

"He is," I say, then veer on Ingrid again. "Hey, I have an idea. Why don't you try asking where he's been?"

"I have," Ingrid bites back. "All I get is that Elias is avoiding you because there's some big secret that yet remains. At least, that's what The High Priestess paired with The Magician in reverse suggests."

"I don't suppose you've gotten anything *useful* out of that parlor trick yet," I say. "You know. Regarding Bob?"

"In this country," she chides, "tea, no matter in what form

it comes, brewed, steeped, or in this instance, spilled, is *always* useful."

I'm about to ask Giovanni to hold my proverbial American beer while I find a new place for Ingrid to store her cards when Ingrid looks up.

"And you'll recall I've *told* you what I've gathered on Bob," she says. "The Eight of Wands crossed by The Hanged Man. He has a plan of attack, but he is *waiting*. I keep asking and the cards keep saying the same thing. Because the energy—his—is just not changing."

"Still no clue as to why he's badgering Jane?" asks Giovanni. "Or was until now."

"I keep getting the Strength card in reverse," says Ingrid. "Which suggests a battle of wills. He wants to break her. Because, in his mind, it's—"

"Personal," I say, interrupting her, and attracting both their gazes.

"See," say Giovanni, "this is why I'm not a fan of trying to dial this thing's number via your sketchpad. Your sketching a demon is a bad idea. Was the first time. Is this time."

"Bob's waiting for us to make our move," I say, "for me to make mine. If he doesn't get that, then he's just as happy waiting for the sand to run out of the hourglass. He's got the luxury of time, but guess what? *We* don't."

"Bird," Giovanni says, "calm down. We *all* want to save him."

"Don't tell me to calm down." I round the desk, my charcoal bit already in hand.

"All I'm trying to say is that this feels a little knee-jerk and I think we'd better try tracking Gomez Addams down one more time before you go for another Bob portrait."

"Elias has days, Giovanni," I remind him. "*Days*. And he isn't cooperating."

"And you think this demon will?"

I shut my mouth and glare at my sketchpad, at the blank page I'd flipped to on the way down from my room. I lift the charcoal bit, ready to go.

My plan is to do a take-two on Bob's portrait. See if I can find him, smoke him out of hiding.

Har, har.

From there, I want to spring for another chat. And while I'm distracting the demon, Giovanni's going to go in for some touch-based intel. At least, he'd agreed to try.

"I *don't* like it, Bird," says Giovanni. "And not just because I don't want to give Bob a high five."

"This isn't go time," I reason. "We're not taking our shot yet. We're just going to try to get something more to go on. And what's Bob going to do if I draw him? Draw *me*?"

Giovanni doesn't answer. Those soulful eyes linger on me. But then they go back to studying the paperweight.

"I'm afraid I have to agree with Jane," says Ingrid, though she still doesn't look up from her cards. "We need more information. *I* do, at least. I can't interpret these messages. They just say the reason the demon is after Jane specifically is because he wants something from her. But with The Moon and the Judgement card both here in reverse . . . I just don't *know*. Maybe if we knew what, specifically, he wanted, we'd have our answer regarding his weakness."

"Thornfield is still hiding shit," says Giovanni. "*That's* the hang-up. And, Jane. He's hiding it from you."

I narrow my glare on him. "Elias *did* tell me the truth."

Giovanni shrugs and sets the paperweight aside. "Maybe some of it."

"You talk like *you* know something." I fold my arms.

"Because maybe I think I might," he replies, folding his arms as well. "I was hoping he'd have summoned the guts to tell you himself by now, though."

"What is it?" asks Ingrid. "Did you pick up on something else through some other object?"

"No," Giovanni says. "I just—"

He stops, gaze lifting to something above us—something on the library's upper gallery level. Something that makes him snap his mouth shut, jaw going tight.

I spin and follow his gaze. Ingrid, gasping, launches to her feet.

I don't say or do anything. I just stare. Because I guess I'm a bit more desensitized to his appearance, his presence. The demon's . . .

He strolls along the second-floor gallery, pallid hand trailing the banister, claws scraping the varnished wood. He has his hood up again, but his nose pokes out, betraying the hint of his splintered profile.

As Ingrid joins us, Giovanni takes a step forward, extending an arm to goalie both me and Ingrid off from whatever's about to go down.

"No need to summon me with a drawing if you wish to speak," says the demon, his voice soft as crackling fire, while the lights around us gutter and then die.

Sun pours in through the room's stained glass windows, but in the next instant, that grows dim, too. As if another storm has swept in, darkness creeps over the three of us.

Then, in a snap, it devours us whole.

Ingrid grips my arm with both hands, nails digging in.

Either she has faith in my ass-kicking abilities, or she's desperate for comfort.

In the blackness, the demon has become just that pair of eyes. Two glowing orbs that, in the next instant, wink out of existence. Right before reappearing on the ground floor, in the center of the room, mere yards from our huddle.

Ingrid shrieks and Giovanni presses us back, barring us from this thing, which, in the nothing, crackles into view, the firelight glow between the fissures in his form providing the luminescence by which to see him and now, part of our surroundings.

"You think I don't hear every word of your scheming?" he asks. "You think I don't know everything about your ploy? Each of you . . ."

"Leave," orders Giovanni.

"But you *wanted* to find me," he says, that low voice menacing in its calmness. "Jane did."

"She changed her mind," whimpers Ingrid. "*We* changed our minds!"

"I know your plans," says the demon, once again addressing Giovanni. "And since I am here, don't you care to know mine?"

The demon lifts an arm, opening a clawed palm toward us—toward him.

Giovanni shakes his head. "Nah, man."

"*Luchessssi*," says the demon. "Running hasn't worked for you yet, has it? Take the truth you seek."

Before I can stop Giovanni, tell him that Ingrid's right, he bursts forward from us.

Instead of taking the demon's outstretched hand, though, Giovanni halts in front of the entity.

"Why Jane?" he asks. "*That's* what I want to know."

"Not 'why Jane,'" corrects the demon, extending his hand farther, claws beckoning. "*Will* Jane? That, at least, is what *I* want to know."

"I'm not touchin' you, man," says Giovanni. "So, you might as well get lost."

"Lost," repeats the demon. "Isn't that what *you* are? The three of you?"

He starts to back away, the lit cracks between his skin dying to blackness, erasing him by one more degree with each retreating step. He's about to go—to leave as commanded.

Because, possibly, like he'd said, the next move is still mine. Or maybe he's just trying to goad us into attacking. Into giving him some kind of ammunition, the way Thea had. Or maybe his hope is to lure us—one or all—into a trap.

Giovanni had been right. I should have let this sleeping dog lie. Looked for another approach.

Maybe, though, since he's leaving, I get to learn my lesson *and* stay alive.

The demon fades, flaring out like one of those embers.

Relief pours through me.

But then Giovanni surges forward and grabs the demon's hand, which, in turn, snaps closed around his like a trap. The demon blazes into full light, his fire glow encompassing Giovanni.

"Giovanni!" I screech, lunging toward him.

Ingrid hauls me back while the demon, rotating Giovanni, yanks his captive against him, clawed hand now clasping Giovanni by the throat.

"Let him go!" I command.

The demon's blazing gaze finds mine. And he holds my stare even as he whispers something to Giovanni, who struggles against the creature's hold. Then he releases Giovanni, who, eyes rolling into the back of his head, collapses in time with the demon.

Except, while the demon vanishes into the floor, his sudden absence bringing a return of the lights, Giovanni lands hard, skull bouncing against the carpet.

I fly to him, dropping to my knees at his side.

My hands are on him, patting his face, checking his pulse.

His heart is beating. But . . .

"Go get help!" I shriek at Ingrid. "He's not breathing."

26

At my command, Ingrid ran past me. And that's all I know about where she's gone.

My focus belongs to Giovanni, who is out cold, and still not inhaling.

"Giovanni!" I shout, and shake him.

I don't know what to do. I certainly don't know CPR, or if that's even what I *should* be doing. There's no medical protocol for demonic attacks.

I take his face in my hands and tilt his head back to help clear his airway.

Then I shriek when his eyes pop wide and he arches with a sudden, noisy intake of air.

"*Giovanni.*" I latch on to his shoulders as he sits up.

"Jane," he rasps as my hands go to cup his face, "you scoundrel. I thought I told you never to touch me."

I'm too shocked to stop him when he grasps me by the nape of the neck—and pulls me to him. Crashes my mouth against his.

His lips burn against mine as though it was a lake of fire he'd just come up for air from, instead of the carpet.

I have sense enough only to submit as he lures me into a kiss, one fueled by this impulse, which his urgency suggests, up until this instant, he'd been trying too hard to suppress.

My body is a traitor. Because I *want* to resist. Not because I'm not every bit here for this intoxicating thrill ride of holy hot. But because of what he must be picking up off me.

In short? Everything.

How I feel about him. How I feel about Elias.

All the things that are wrong with me.

All the reasons why he should run the other way.

All my bitter. All my baggage.

All my confusion.

But there's no resisting the lips that chase mine with no reprieve. Like he'll never be able to get enough, even if he never let me go.

Why does he have to taste like apples and pine and summer? The scents of aftershave, mint, and more distantly, motor oil cloak me in a promise of familiarity. Home. And, somehow, safety.

But those things. They're foreign enough to my understanding that I have to pause.

That comes one second after his tongue sweeps mine, a final tease of just what I'm missing before he pauses, too.

Then, the next moment, he breaks the kiss.

"I couldn't help it," he whispers, his breath playing on my lips, eyes lingering there, like all he wants is to dive back in. "I didn't want a near miss. Not with you, Bird. Hate me if you want. It . . . was worth it."

"Right," drones a voice from the entryway, and I jerk my head in that direction.

Accompanied by Ingrid, Mr. Poole stands there with arms crossed, a kitchen towel slung over one shoulder.

"Seems this . . . *emergency* has expired," says the housekeeper. "So, I'll be off. *Do* alert me again, though, when there's another life-threateningly awkward moment I can be a part of. Truly, I get paid enough for it."

Stripping the towel from his shoulder, he stalks off again.

Giovanni sits up with a grunt, offering Ingrid a sheepish smile. She, in turn, shifts her weight to one foot, puts her hands on her hips, and glares.

"Next time Giovanni is unresponsive," she says, her stare shooting to me, "*I* want to stay with him. Perhaps, if you like, we could even begin taking turns."

"Giovanni," I say, "I'm . . . so sorry."

And I am. That stolen kiss aside, he could have died. And if he had, that would have been because of me. Because of my desperateness.

Hadn't Elias said, in his own way, that demons could smell desperation? And pain.

I'd let myself get desperate. Again, I'd tried to go it alone. Do things *my* way.

Isn't that what had killed Thea?

"Bird," Giovanni says, tucking a stray strand of hair behind my ear. Which I let him do. "Your idea worked. I got a read."

"On a weakness?" I ask, blinking.

"Not exactly," he admits. "But . . . it's something."

♥ ♥ ♥

Hey.

Send.

Giovanni said Bob HAS to collect a soul, or the demon CAN'T go back to where he came from. Not without some serious repercussions.

Send.

He said Bob's like us. He HAS to do his job, or else.

Send.

Asked him what the "or else" was but he didn't know. Like he'd said before, Bob could control what information he got.

Send.

Asked Giovanni what the demon whispered to him. Demon said he had two options. Tell me the truth about Bob being bound to his task of delivering a soul, or lie and say nothing can be done.

Send.

Said the demon told him, "one will save him, and one will save her."

Send.

G said he wanted to lie to me. Because he knew the demon wanted the opposite.

Send.

When I asked Giovanni why he didn't lie, he said it wouldn't have done any good.

Send.

Asked why he thought that, and he said he'd tell me after I did the drawing of Elias.

Send.

Said the drawing of Elias was the most important part of the plan and that I needed to do it ASAP.

Send.

Asked him why and he said that it wasn't his business to tell??

Send.

Also reminded me that the energy he picked up off that one car Elias sleeps in was recent. Really recent.

Send.

So, I'm going out there tonight. Late. When E won't be expecting a visit.

Send.

And, Helen, I think I already know why I have to draw him.

27

Upbeat music drifts from a lavish, modern blood-red convertible, providing a ludicrous soundtrack to the moment as it echoes through the garage, the side door to which I'd found unlocked.

And it's the drumbeat, lyrics, and the pair of crossed boots hanging out the passenger side of the back seat that tell me where to find Elias.

I round to the side opposite the boots and, gripping the door, peek over the edge, into his upside-down face.

Eye shut, he's sprawled across the rear seats, an arm draped over his stomach. The other is lolled off onto the baseboard.

He's not asleep, though. The pointer finger of the hand on his stomach keeps time with the drums, guitars, and eighties-style synthesizer.

"Is this the Cure?" I ask, and that one eye pops wide.

"Jane." He's surprised to see me.

"Elias."

There's that smile. This time, though, it only touches one side of that mouth that, because I seem to be a glutton for punishment, I haven't been able to stop thinking about.

Not even after that incinerating kiss with Giovanni. Which should, in theory, have ruined me for all other kisses.

Lifting a hand, the one draped over his stomach, Elias messes with my already fried mind by unhooking a portion of my hair held back by my shoulder.

Dark straight strands tumble free, and he traces fingertips down their length before allowing his arm to collapse again.

"'Just Like Heaven,'" he says as the song ends. "From their album . . . Well, best not get me started."

He sits up and, after tugging on the handle of the door nearest me to pop it open, he scoots over.

"Don't You (Forget About Me)" by Simple Minds, another familiar eighties tune, begins to drift out of the radio, but as I take the invitation to climb in, Elias leans forward to switch us to silence.

That trend continues even with us seated together. I hold my sketchpad in my lap, and Elias, flicking a glance between it and me, frowns.

Without a word, I flip open the sketchpad to a clean page.

"I had hoped to avoid you another day," he admits.

"It's almost two in the morning on the day before your birthday," I tell him.

My way of reminding him he's officially out of days with which to avoid me or, spoiler alert, anything else.

Least of all Bob.

"Must you do this?" he asks as I get started.

"Look at me," I tell him, because a profile isn't what I'm after.

Elias's movements drip reluctance as he angles toward me. Leaning back, he lounges in the seat, one arm draped along the backrest. As instructed, he faces me straight on, that eye boring into me like it had that day in the kitchen.

I trade my attention between it and my paper—him and the whiteness that loses its purity as I set down parameters in the form of lines and the barest impressions of shadows. Those shadows get deeper as I go, the process of drawing him mimicking the process of getting to know him.

His stare accuses me while I work. Maybe it resents me.

Since this whole scenario is do-or-die, I give zero.

In minutes, Elias's face surfaces like a mirage, the shadows illuminating the light, which is portrayed by the paper itself. Here and there, I use my thumb and fingers to smudge the harsher lines into submission.

His lips are the most entrancing and easiest part to draw. Because they fascinate me so much. I give his cheeks their underlying darkness, and then I outline his eyes, which I have to focus intensely on to get just right. I try hard, too, to capture that . . . something. That essence, that *glimmer* deep within his uncovered eye. Really, *that's* the thing I'm after. It's so far away, though, and there's not anything about it that can be defined in terms of darkness or light. The spark I'm seeking to capture is just . . . there.

I satisfy myself with doing as much as I can with it.

Then? Then I shift my attention . . . giving definition to his *other* eye.

I don't have to glance back up to Elias to get this part of

him down. After all, I'm not using my physical sight to "see" his other eye. I can't since he's wearing the patch. Instead, it's my other "sight" that I lean on in my search for the true state of his spirit. The same extra sense that allowed me to see and sketch Bob on the plane.

The only reason I find anything there to draw is because it—that eye—belongs to the other world. The one that's come looking for him.

Now that this moment has come, I'm not sure why I never "looked" until now.

Really, I should have suspected long before.

Giovanni had figured it out, hadn't he?

Always putting two and two together—that's Giovanni. Because he'd found out first that Bob . . . hadn't always been Bob.

When I'm done, I glance up from my sketchpad. Elias stares at me for a long moment. Though I expect him to ask to see the drawing, he doesn't. Instead, he lifts a hand to the patch, which he strips free.

The hidden eye, a match to Bob's glowing gaze, isn't a surprise. I'd already captured the truth of what lies behind that patch on my paper. Which Elias must have realized, or else he wouldn't have abandoned his charade.

Even though that piercing, luminous orange eye, slit through with its black pupil, is *his* this time—Elias's—its strangeness (*and* familiarity) still manages to strike me with terror.

I keep that emotion hidden behind a mask of impassiveness. As much as I can.

Because this. My discovery. For whatever reason, it must be what he's been trying to avoid.

"I don't understand," I tell him. "After the bed fire, the journals—*Bob*—did you really think that was going to scare me off?"

He blinks slowly, that amber glow dying and then reappearing.

"I just knew . . . the drawing wouldn't do any good," he says. "That and . . . I *didn't* want you to see."

"Because you thought I would give up on you?"

"Because I have once again become torn, in more ways than one. And the fissure that now divides me, her name is Jane."

I blink at him, gazing into that eye. His "damaged" one.

Except that isn't the right word for it. "Compromised," maybe. Or even "captured."

Elias isn't damaged. At least . . . no more than I am.

"Your eye doesn't bother me," I tell him. Which isn't totally true. But it will be soon. In another minute maybe. When I can get over the aftershock.

"I am part demon," he says. "And *that* should disturb you."

So. *That's* what he'd meant the other night when he'd said the demon sought to "transmute" him. Elias is on the same path that Bob had turned down. Long ago . . .

"Are you really part demon, though?" I ask. "You don't act like it. And no offense, Elias, but you'd make a crap demon. You'd never talk anyone into selling their soul. You use too many deluxe words and you're too . . . likable."

"Yet neither my vernacular nor my supposed affability, I think, would afford me the leisure of disobeying my future generals."

I roll my eyes. "And I rest my case."

"Jane, I never expect to be whole again," he says. "I only

wanted to salvage what I could. But win or lose, live or die—I am still rent one way or another."

"I'm going to fix it," I tell him. "We are. Tomorrow. I mean, I guess, today."

Because we have to.

"May I?" Elias asks, and he holds a hand out for the sketchpad.

I fork it over and, after flipping the sketchpad around, Elias draws it into his lap. As he examines his likeness, my hand automatically curls around my pencil.

Why is his scrutiny more nerve-wracking than his secrets? Even this latest one . . .

"Hmph," he says, "Am I truly *this* ghastly-looking?"

"*I* think you're beautiful."

The words fly out on their own. They're a knee-jerk response that I have no control over. I can't possibly shove them back in my big fat mouth, either. And since I have no way to cover for the lapse, no way to *re*cover, I snatch the sketchpad away. I don't dare look him in the eye again, though. Instead, I peer down into the portrait that's nearly finished, allowing my hair to tumble around my burning features.

While I busy myself with touching up the details and darkening the spots that don't need darkening, I wait for the moment to pass.

When it refuses to do so, I make myself talk. Because I *do* have something else I want to address with him.

"Speaking of tomorrow," I say, "I want to talk to you about . . . what happens. After."

"After," he repeats in that infuriating deadpan way that asks for more without giving a thing.

"When this is over and you're free," I say. "Look, I've been thinking—"

"Free," he repeats.

"Y-yeah," I say. Because . . . isn't that why I'm here?

Please don't say he's already given up on himself. On me. I've gotten so used to being his hope. And, I guess . . . his friend.

I take a deep breath and, after folding up the sketchpad, I stuff it into my knapsack and drop both into the front seat.

"I want to stay for a little while," I blurt out.

"Stay?" He repeats. "Here at Fairfax?"

The question is a cold demand. Like he already suspects the answer. Also like that answer isn't one he's going to welcome.

Well. I've already said too much as it is, so . . . too effing bad. For both of us.

"Because it . . ." My words are scarcely audible, getting smaller with every syllable. "It's . . . where *you* are."

"*God*," he snaps. Like he's annoyed. Or angry. Or both.

This reaction. It's enough to gut me.

My face becomes a furnace. I twist away so he won't see and I grab the door handle, ready to flee his presence. Because I only meant to tell him I care. That I give a shit.

I only meant to do what Mr. Poole had wanted to do with the absurd party. But I've said too much. Or maybe he just saw it in my eyes. The *real* truth.

He must think I'm pathetic.

"Jane, don't go." He catches me by the crook of my elbow.

Skin-to-skin contact is more than I can bear, and I rip free of his hold.

I hate him. So much. I tell myself this at least, because it's the only balm I have as I try to make my escape.

He won't let me fly.

Clack.

Though he doesn't try to grab me again, he's hit the internal locks on the doors like he did the other day.

This doesn't really trap me. But, at the same time . . . it does.

Like when he stole my drawings from my room.

Like that action, this one counts as enough—*just* enough—to hold me in his thrall.

I veer on him.

"Luchesi warned me of this," he says. "I did not believe him. Tell me it's not true, Jane."

So, Giovanni had found Elias before I had. Apparently, through that stolen kiss, he'd gotten a read on me, too. But then. Of course he did.

And Elias.

Could his skull be any thicker?

I can't answer him with words. And I don't have anything left to lose.

So, scooting down the seat to eliminate the distance between us that, until this moment, might as well have been an ocean . . . I kiss him.

28

Elias grabs me, those big sinewy hands seizing me by the upper arms.

Clearly, I've crossed a forbidden boundary.

Any second, he'll throw me off. Away. From him. From Fairfax. From . . . *this*.

I'm completely out of line. Out of touch with reality.

Especially since he's all but already rejected me.

But I couldn't help myself. Not after the other night in the gazebo. Our "near miss."

Giovanni had taken a risk and had gotten *his* answer. I have to get mine, too.

No matter the cost.

Elias's grip on me tightens, *almost* becoming painful.

He's willing himself to act, to push me back. He's willing himself to tell me I'm appalling. To rail at me and to restate what I already know better than I want to.

That he loves a dead girl.

At least, that's what I'm sure the battle raging in him must be until . . . until the moment the rigidness in him breaks. And he begins to kiss me back.

And the instant his lips part, become pliant and inviting even as they go chasing after mine, a rush overtakes me.

The intensity, it's too much. Enough to elicit from me a whimper as I breathe him in, inhaling deep, like I can take the remnants of his soul into my lungs and hold them captive—safe—within me.

One of Elias's hands releases me. His fingers, warm, find their way past my hair as they wrap around the base of my neck.

This hand is tender, gentle, coaxing.

His other keeps its viselike grip on my arm, a representative of the side of him that's trying to convince himself to let me go—to stop this.

We don't stop. *I* can't.

He's like an oasis in the desert of this world—of my whole damn life.

I've never kissed anyone like this, either. Like I need them more than air.

Elias keeps up with my insistence. Even more detrimental to my senses, my already obliterated mind—he answers it.

We're in a moment out of time—neither of us where or when we're supposed to be, but this connection, it's too magnetic, too charged, to break free from. Not that I want to.

If Elias wants to, he doesn't show it. Not more than in the deep furrow in his brow.

That shadow of hesitancy in him, of confliction, is enough, though, to make me force myself to break away.

I stay close, because he's still holding me that way. Elias grits his teeth, both eyes searching my face, darting everywhere and still refusing to meet mine.

"*Jane.*" His voice is edged with rawness—frayed with the turmoil of someone caught in the throes of some wrenching dilemma.

His fingers curl against the nape of my neck, thumb smoothing flesh as he closes that fist, tries to disconnect. The "shouldn't" side of him is winning out, all while the "should" side delivers to my senses a death blow, the merest taste of what caresses I'm sure those hands are capable of.

I want them all over me. I want to kiss him again. But . . . I can't.

He brings our foreheads together. "Jane, I—"

"I know," I tell him in a whisper. Because the pressure of having to tell me what I already know—it's got to be immense. As if he needed any more.

"You *don't* know," he says, wincing.

My hands go to cup his face.

"Thea," I say. "I . . . I *know* you love Thea."

And I'm not her. I'm Jane.

I'm not trying to replace anyone—least of all her.

But Elias has a life to live when this is all over. After I save him.

I have a life to live, too. What's more, he makes me *want* to live it.

And if we make it out of this mess, if we survive, he couldn't just go back to being that lost lonely person. No more than *I* could go back to being just Jane. Not when he has made me into something else—*someone* else. Someone I'd sworn to myself I'd never be again. Someone who gives a damn.

Who loves someone.

"I know I shouldn't have," I whisper, drawing back from him. "It wasn't fair of m—"

"*Fair?*" The word is a bitter growl, and he catches me, pulling me to him again. "*Nothing* about this is fair," he says, his voice catching in a way that shatters my heart.

And then his lips crash into mine.

With this second barrier obliterated, I can't possibly hold myself back. His permission granted, bestowed, I give myself leave to drink him in—as much as he'll let me.

My hands are in his hair. His drop to my waist.

And then everything becomes simultaneously not enough and too much as he draws me onto his lap, my legs straddling his.

His scent is everywhere—in my bloodstream, mixed up with the tatters of my own shredded soul.

My veins are alive in a way that makes me question if I ever truly was before this. Before him.

Elias. I'm kissing Elias.

And it was *my* name on his lips just now and it's *my* heart in his hands.

And those hands, they travel up my sides, sneaking past the barrier of my T-shirt, tracking heat that further unwinds me.

Once more, we've gone from zero to eighty in the span of a heartbeat. And there's no sign of stopping. Especially not when we're fused together this way—and Elias keeps upping the danger, his teeth trapping and releasing my bottom lip, his hands falling to my hips, drawing them snug with his own in a movement quick and forceful enough to make me gasp.

Then his tongue sweeps mine, setting me on fire. I press into him, delivering the same attack.

Elias's low and answering murmur is something I feel more than hear, but it heralds a shift in him and, taking my face in his hands, he kisses me like this is goodbye, like the two of us truly *are* in the midst of burning away to nothing.

Like we're that couple in my drawings.

The ones always together, and ever apart.

And now I'm the one keeping up with him. It's a battle he sweeps out from under me as he grabs me and, swiveling in the same motion, guides me off him—and onto my back.

He's the one hovering over me then, hair hanging down around an expression of consternation and bewilderment. Agony and bliss.

"This can't be so," he says. "This is a dream. And yet . . . I stopped dreaming long ago."

I prop myself up on my elbows, wishing he wouldn't talk, that he wouldn't steal from me like this. Not when all I want is to keep stealing from him. Siphon all that emptiness into my own and, in so doing, convert it into something that might just fill us both back up.

This is complicated, though. *I've* complicated it. And, impossibly, him.

"I'm not asking you to forget her," I whisper. "I just—"

"Jane, *God*—how can this be happening again?" he asks, his eye—*both* eyes—brimming with anguish, his words pleading. Wrenched with something I don't understand. Yet another thing I don't understand.

Again?

I blink up at him. And then I see it.

There, in the depths of that half-glowing stare—the truth flashing at me like a warning sign.

Sitting up, I scoot back from him, and this time Elias makes no move to stop me. And when he doesn't say anything else, when he won't meet my gaze any longer, slowly, bit by terrible bit . . . I start to understand.

The sensation that overwhelms me with my too-gradual realization—dark and horrifying—is familiar. A black tide that whispers of despair.

I've drowned in its waters once already. At the same time, it's like my soul has remained adrift in them every day since. Or maybe forever is just how long the numbing death they bring lasts.

"Elias." I swallow hard.

Still, he won't look at me.

That last word he'd uttered just now, it needles at me, prodding the wound that has never healed because it can't.

What did he mean by "again"?

"*Elias*," I hiss.

I want him to tell me what he's referring to. And yet, I'm too afraid to ask him directly.

Words have suddenly become dangerous.

At the same time, his parting comment from that night in the gazebo returns to take on a catastrophic new meaning.

I must go.

Must.

His portrait. He said he'd *known* it wouldn't do any good.

"Jane," says Elias as he climbs out of the car, shutting the door behind him, the clap quiet yet, in a way, booming. "You can't stay at Fairfax past tomorrow. No matter the outcome."

"Why?" I demand through gritted teeth.

I know why. But I need him to say it. Or else I won't let myself believe.

I never let myself when it was Helen. Not even in those last days. Those final hours.

And after my fleeting moment in heaven with Elias, the only thing that could hurt worse than being hurtled straight to the hell I'm in now would be if he let me hope that I was reading this—him—all wrong.

He's not that callous. At the same time, there's no mercy in his delivery of the truth.

"Because," he replies simply as he walks away, heading for the door without a moment's hesitation, or backward glance. "I won't be here."

29

e's going to die anyway.

Elias is *going* to die.

No matter *what* happens.

No matter what I do. No matter what *any* of us do.

Worst of all, he'd known.

The. Whole. Time.

The two of us—me and him. When we'd been in the attic and I'd asked, he'd *lied* about what would happen to him if we were successful. Just like he had about the demon being attached to the property.

At the time, his reasoning about *that* lie had been because no one would help him if they knew the full truth.

He'd been *right*.

Because the last place anyone would want to be is where I am.

Walking alone down a deserted road in the middle of the English countryside in the dead of night, trying to get away from the place, the situation, the *person* who had just destroyed what was left of me.

I don't know how long I've been walking, but it's been long and far enough that if I look back, I won't see Fairfax jutting over the hillside.

The pain of Elias's impending death, though. It chases after me. Fills me up.

It doesn't help, either, that I still smell like him. That the smoke of his burning soul has infused my clothes, my hair, my heart.

Breathing is painful, but I try anyway. The air won't take, so I let it out in a raw scream that carries through the surrounding woods and down the empty road—inaudible to anyone in this whole world but me.

With every step, I keep waiting to wake up. To jar out of this nightmare that, like Elias had said, *can't* be happening again. I don't care where I wake up, either, or when—or even as who. Just so long as it's not here, not now. And not Jane Reye.

I *don't* wake up, though. I'm still me.

And I don't know how to cope.

So, I keep walking.

There's nowhere to go.

But in my current state, nowhere is where I belong. That's the best place for someone who can't touch something worth holding in this world without it slipping out of her grasp and into some abyss.

My parents. Helen. Elias.

Elias. I can't ever see him again.

I can't be there when . . .

I can't *do* it again.

I can't do this.

My steps start to slow when my mind conjures before me that eye. His soul is buried so deep within that window of pain and loss. It's only a glimmer—like a shard of diamond captured in ice. Barely discernable, easy to miss.

I'd glimpsed it that day in the hall, though, when I'd told him off. Washed by those tears, it had glinted at me from the void, a spark of life and light in a man who had already given up on himself. And I had made the horrible mistake of looking closer—too close—after I'd *sworn* to myself I'd never do that.

I don't have anything on me to throw. Officially, since I'm not going to turn around, since I *can't*, I no longer have anything in my possession but the clothes on my back. So, I have to stop and find something. A rock. I hurl it into the surrounding woods with another roar.

There's no relief. Still, I burn.

So, I continue on my escape route.

The road dips. Minutes later, it rises. It, like the night, like the screaming inside me, just goes on and on.

Even worse, my surroundings, oblivious to my pain, are flush with the echoes of life.

Crickets and night birds. The rushing hush of the wind through the trees.

Sounds that mock me. Taunt me.

They remind me of how I'm stuck here. In this place full of everything and nothing. A place that, for me, keeps doling out too much of the latter.

I hate being here. In a world full of strangers. A world that insists on taking everyone who isn't.

I find another rock. I chuck it into the trees.

There's no way else to expend this . . . rage.

I want to yell again, but I don't because it won't help.

So, I flick off the sky. With both hands.

That *does* help. Impossibly. Miraculously.

But not enough.

So, I keep walking, trying to outpace the decimation that's already laid waste to everything but the last shreds of my sanity.

But then a distant growl—growing nearer—breaks through my awareness.

That . . . of an engine.

I'm following the side of the road, which now bends sharply. If I just keep walking, whoever is approaching from behind will pass me by. They'll ignore me like everyone else does. Like everyone else *should*. Like I want them to.

The car gets nearer, its engine a seamless purr that conjures images of all those cars in Elias's arsenal.

He wouldn't dare, though.

He has to know better.

The car gets nearer, and soon, the light from a pair of high beams appears to throw my shadow long before me. I follow the willowy dark wraith like *it* can lead me somewhere better, and I don't look back—not even when the car begins to slow instead of passing.

Then it pulls up beside me. I clench my hands into fists.

My prayers for it to be a concerned stranger—or even an axe murderer—are ignored.

It's the Lamborghini—Elias's.

I just keep walking.

The vehicle, rumbling low, growling an obnoxious purr that's the very *breath* of money, crawls along beside me.

My fury at last overtakes me and I wheel on the car, kicking its door.

"Get away from me!" I shriek.

Vrrrrrrrrp. The tinted window zips down to unveil a sleek interior illuminated by neon red and blue lights. And a familiar face that is *not* Elias's.

"*Hey*," calls Giovanni, glowering at me from the driver's seat. "Watch the paint!"

I have to blink a few times. To be sure it's really him.

And hold up. Is . . . is that a *black eye*?

His lip is busted, too. Even though the bruise that I left on his cheek is nearly healed, he still looks like he's been in a fight.

His injuries are enough to distract me from all my other questions about how he knew where to find me, and whether or not he's stolen this car.

"Giovanni? Wh-what are you doing here?"

"Could ask you the same thing, Bird," he says, checking his rearview mirrors before peering back to me. "Creepy as all get-out out here. Why don't you hop in and we can go back to the terrifying demon-infested manor instead?"

I'm not about to tell Giovanni what just happened. At least . . . not the part about making out with Elias.

"How did . . . you find me?" I ask him. "And what happened to your face?"

My mind goes all over the place. And really, isn't there only one person who could be responsible for that shiner?

"Poole Boy called me," says Giovanni, pointedly ignoring my

second question. "Said you'd be out on the road. By yourself. And, well . . . here you are."

My sense of mental whiplash only grows. "Mr. Poole? How did he—?"

"Didn't say," he says. "But he told me to tell you the security cameras on and in the garage are motion-sensing and that he's got remote access."

"Oh God." Both hands leap to cover my face.

"Yeaaaaah. He said you'd say that. Do you . . . want to get in and tell me about it?"

"I'm not going back there," I shout.

"That's weird," he mumbles. "Poole said you might say something like that, too. Starting to think that guy's got a little shine himself."

I hesitate, uncertain now what to do with myself. Not that I had much clue before Giovanni showed up.

My options—per usual—are limited.

I can keep walking. Or I can get into the damn Lamborghini.

Except, I can't do either. I can't do anything. Nothing, apparently, but fall apart.

"Heeeey," says Giovanni as my disintegration—overdue—begins. Then he's out of the car and rounding it to get to me. "What is it? What's going on?"

He stops in front of me, just short of me, like he's back to curbing that impulse to touch me.

"Silly question," he says as I hitch. "Looks like you finally caught up to the Count of Monty Python."

I might have laughed at that one. If the part of me capable of laughing had survived this night. Instead, tears streak my face, which crumples.

"Oh, Bird," he says. "I'd offer to whoop his ass, but that's kind of off the table now. Best I can do is a kick-me sign and maybe a mean tweet."

I *can't* tell Giovanni what happened. I can't ever tell anyone.

But Giovanni. He isn't someone who needs words to understand.

And when I rush into him, he opens his arms, and, catching me, folds me into him.

"Ah, Bird," he says, like someone fretting over a fractured vase there's no hope of putting back together.

I shut my eyes.

And officially stop caring about what he'll see.

30

"*Awwr, yeeaahhr*," Giovanni groans around his mouthful of french fries. "Mmmmmm—migod," he adds as he chews.

I sit stiffly in the seat next to him, a grease-stained paper bag open between us.

After driving us into the nearest town, the historic village Elias had mentioned, Giovanni had located an actual twenty-four-hour McDonald's.

He hadn't asked me if I'd wanted anything as he'd rolled into the drive-through. Still, he'd ordered two large Big Mac meals with sodas, a pair of cheeseburgers, an additional large fry, and a fish sandwich.

Now we're parked in front of the golden arches, awash in their dayglow aura.

After he promised me he wouldn't take me back to Fairfax, I'd gotten into the car with him.

Giovanni had driven us here without asking any more questions. Since he isn't prodding me for answers, or revealing what or how much he'd picked up off me during our embrace, I don't press him for answers about his injuries yet, either.

I'm going to have to say something in the next few seconds, though.

Because Giovanni is *literally* moaning into his hamburger, and the sounds he's making are not okay.

"Thas tha hicket," he says, bits of shredded lettuce falling from the burger as he chews.

"Did you know?" I finally work up the nerve to ask, my voice small.

"About the eye? Yeah. 'S why I wanted you to draw him."

He takes another bite, this time chewing in silence.

I hadn't been asking him about the eye. I'd been asking about . . . the other part.

The part that matters.

But the fact that Giovanni assumed I'd meant the eye must mean he *doesn't* know about Elias . . . His impending death.

"I figured out why he really wore that eyepatch after touching Bob's necklace," he says. "That was part of the reason I got . . . so upset right after. Because I suddenly realized what would have happened to *me*. You know. Eventually. If I *had* taken up Bob on his offer. Made me realize, too, what a demon really was. Ours at least. Also, what Thornfield was really facing."

"You should have said something."

"Wouldn't have changed anything." He shrugs. "He'd still be just as damned and we'd still be just as clueless on how to . . . *un-damn* him."

"Then why was it so important for *me* to know? Before, you said the drawing was important."

"I said the drawing was important," he replies, "because I

knew it would force him to fess up to you. About the eye, yeah. But . . . also about however he feels or whatever. For you."

"You knew he cared for me?" I ask.

"You care for him, too," he says. "Actually, Bird, impossible as it sounds, you love that asshole. My condolences, by the way."

"Our kiss," I whisper.

"God, that kiss." He lets his head thud against the headrest. "Never in my life have I ever had a kiss like that. Bird. It was lightning and thunder. It was punk rock music but also Vivaldi."

I'm here enough, in this moment with him—meaning far enough away from my pain over Elias—to blush.

"You know like when you lick a battery?" he asks. "Kind of like that, but . . . on steroids."

He's licked a battery?

"But," he goes on to say, "none of that—the flash and the boom, I mean, the frickin' *voltage* in that kiss . . . was for me. Which is wack, by the way, because Cyrano de Schnoz doesn't have *half* the game I do."

When I don't say anything, Giovanni digs out another hamburger, which he sets on the dashboard in front of me.

"It's okay," he says. "I'll get over it. One day. Maybe. In the meantime, you should eat. You gotta be hungry. We've had nothing but crumpets and iceberg wedges for days now. Eat your Bird food. You know you want to."

Really, I'm not sure I'm going to be able to ingest anything ever again.

So, I just shake my head.

"Okay. This Burger King says have it your way." His hand

goes into the bag again and he retrieves a handful of fries. Half of which he purposefully drops.

"Oooooops," he says before shoving the other half into his face.

My eyes widen on him.

"Wha?" he asks, popping the lid off his soda before picking it up.

"Awrh," he says, "accidentally" sloshing orange Fanta onto the floorboard before bringing the straw to his lips.

"Omigod, what are you doing?" I ask.

"Having the first decent meal of my entire English life," he says. "What's it *look* like I'm doing? Fair warning, I *will* eat yours if you wait much longer."

"He's going to murder you," I say, shifting my gaze forward again.

"Go fish!" Giovanni tosses a handful of fries over his shoulder into the rear of the car. Then he takes another slurp from his soda. "Ah, yeah, that's good. The fizzy burn. The sugar rush. The whispered promise of ulcers in every bubble. Also, you know the real reason Loki buys posh cars without back seats is not because that's how the fancy new ones come, but because he doesn't have any friends. Or . . . he didn't."

That gets my attention.

"Forever riding shotgun with his missing personality," Giovanni mutters as he checks his busted lip in the rearview mirror. "The salt is killin' this thing."

"Giovanni, are you going to tell me what happened to your face? *Please* don't say you got in a fight with Elias."

It's the only answer I can come up with. And if Giovanni looks like this . . .

"A fight?" He squint-winces. "With *that* dweeb-oid?"

I relax a little. But I'm still unsettled.

"Nah," says Giovanni, "it wasn't a fight."

I stiffen again. "Giovanni. What. Happened."

"Lost a bet or two," he says as he reaches across me to unlatch the glove box. He starts rooting through its contents, throwing things into the back area as he comes across them. Another pen case, a billfold of important-looking papers, a tire gauge. He stops when he gets to a pair of sunglasses, which he pauses to inspect. "Dawg, are these Versace?"

He puts them on, his face going suddenly sober as he turns his gaze on me.

"*Hello*," he says in a terrible British accent, "my name is Elias Thorn-in-your-arse, and I'm a very complex and tortured individual with *issues*."

It's the way he says "issues," with too many hissing s's.

A smile, born from some part of me I don't recognize, sneaks onto my face.

"No one likes me because I am insufferable," drones Giovanni, continuing with the terrible impersonation. "Though I *do* have a mean right hook. Probably because I happen to be older than candle wax and scrappy as a mofo."

"Oh my God," I say, looking away. "You two *did* get in a fight."

"Told you it wasn't a fight." Giovanni strips off the glasses and tosses them into the back. "By the way, did you know Thornfungus has a billiards room in the basement?"

I'm not going to let him change the subject.

"When did this happen?" I demand. Though it would've had to have been within the last hour or so. Because when I'd been with Elias, he hadn't had a scratch on him. Of course, then, with the way he healed, he wouldn't. Still. I have to ask. "Is he okay?"

Giovanni gapes at me. Affronted, he points to his eye.

"Are *you* okay?" I amend.

"No!" he says. "I challenged Edgar Allan Troll to a game of eight-ball earlier and got my ass handed to me."

Earlier?

So . . . before I found Elias. Who *said* he'd spoken to Giovanni.

"Winner got a free shot," he adds.

I pinch the bridge of my nose. "You are *not* serious."

"My idea," he says. "He wasn't going to go for it, but then I let it slip accidentally on purpose that I kissed you, and from there, it was game on."

"You goaded him."

"I was setting him up," Giovanni corrects. "Or . . . so I thought. See, I'm a pool hustler. It's what I do. Well. It's *one* of the things I do. Nights and weekends. Figured Professor Moriarty just had the upper hand since we were on his turf, you know? So, I played him again and . . . lost again. He got another free shot. That's how I got this."

He points to his black eye.

"What the hell," I pipe. "What is *wrong* with you two?"

"Gave me a choice the third time," says Giovanni. "Told me I could take my lick, or fess up as to why I wanted the money from the job so bad. Said he smelled desperation all over me. I called him a hypocrite and told him he needed to get over himself and tell you how he felt about you *and* about the eye, because you were falling for him. Also, because, if he wasn't interested, *I* was. Then he cracked his knuckles, and I like my teeth so I told him I haven't been home in three months because I hustled the wrong guys."

My head snaps his way. "You *are* still in trouble. You said that fire was out!"

"Because I figured it would be!" he says. "Mostly out. Whenever we got . . . paid."

"You could have asked for the money, Giovanni. Elias *said* he would pay us."

"I didn't want to look desperate," he snaps. "Desperate is what got Thornfield where *he* is. Besides. His problem was worse than mine. *Is*. Though, I didn't think . . ."

He trails off. Then, after a beat, he dips a hand into the bag again and this time he retrieves the fish sandwich, which he promptly throws into the glove box before shutting the little door.

"Don't like fish," he mutters as he takes yet another handful of fries and tucks them behind the driver's-side sun visor.

"You seriously haven't been home in three months?" I ask him.

"Been crashing with friends out of state," he says. "Hanging out in the DC area mostly. Spent a couple nights in some motels. Worked at a body shop in the city under a fake name trying to rustle up the bread, you know? Drops in the bucket for what these dudes were wanting. And these guys. They're the kind who say they know a guy. Know what I'm saying?"

"You mean they threatened to kill you?"

"They didn't have to! That's what knowing a guy means."

"Why didn't you call the police?"

"Because, Bird." He sighs. "First, I got a record, and second, that's not the kind of thing that's going to endear me to these dudes. Also, just because *I* can leave my house and go on hiatus, that doesn't mean my mom can."

I get quiet, letting everything sink in. And I know how easy it is for someone on the outside of the problem to assume there's an easy fix.

"She must miss you," I say.

"She thinks I'm in school."

Oh jeez. This just keeps getting worse.

"Does she even know you're in England?"

"She thinks I'm at Hogwarts. She was so proud when I got my owl."

I let my head thud against the seat. "At least tell me Elias gave you the money."

"No," he grumbles as he pats the navigation screen, leaving huge grease prints. "Gatsby extorted some particulars out of me and then . . . then he made some calls. Before I knew it, he had my shit paid off. All of it. Because even *this* job wasn't going to cover everything."

I go quiet.

"He helped you," I murmur.

"*No*," says Giovanni. "He just . . . paid me in advance. And tipped me well. That's all."

Heat and agitation enter Giovanni's tone and demeanor now. Elias, it seems, has conjured some conflicting emotions in him, too.

Clearly, though, Giovanni plans to go back.

He's going to return to Fairfax and face Elias's demon. Elias, too.

But . . . he still doesn't know the worst part. He hadn't

picked up on what sent me out onto that road. The truth about Elias's deal, and what happens to him when his contract ends. Regardless.

"Did you tell Elias that you were taking his intervention as payment in advance?" I ask.

"Yeah, I told him that! I'm not owing that punk anything. I hate his guts. I just traded one devil for another. But at least this one's a deal I can handle. Ish."

Silence returns to the car. Giovanni's humor evaporates and now he's the one glaring through the windshield—out at nothing.

"You . . . didn't pick up why I was on the road," I say.

"Hell yeah, I did," he snaps, his words shocking me. "Why do you think I've been trashing his ride? Ugly-ass Masterpiece-Theatre-talkin', James-Bond-villain-lookin', jerk-nut, ass-can, trash-haired, beak-nosed—"

Giovanni doesn't trail off so much as he stops short. I check on him with a side glance. His jaw, clenched, ticks.

Then, squeezing his eyes shut, he drops his forehead to the top of the steering wheel.

And now the silence goes off like a bomb.

Because it occurs to me how, this whole time, everything Giovanni's been saying about how he regards Elias—he's meant the opposite.

On and on the quiet stretches.

And there's something to be said about suddenly having someone in the fallout shelter with me. Some part of having company in my despair . . . Well, it makes the prospect of walking out, into a destroyed existence, if not less painful, then more bearable.

"Bird, you have to know I can't do this by myself," he says at last, his throat tight. By "this," he's talking about the job. "He loves *you*."

I gape at him. Is he saying that because he knows? Could a few punches give him that kind of information? My punch, he'd said, had given him nothing.

"No, I don't know that because he clocked me," Giovanni says. "I know it because I picked it up off of *you*. On the road just now. His energy was still . . . all over you. Should have made me hella jealous. Would have, if it hadn't echoed whatever had infused that damn kiss."

My head starts spinning as I try to keep up. Try to latch on to his words. Believe them . . .

"And another thing," he adds. "It's not over until it's over. I mean, dude's walking around just fine right now. So, what if he's wrong? Or hell, what if he's right? Say he *does* kick it even if we win. At least he's not . . . At least he won't be . . ."

A demon in hell. Those are the words Giovanni can't bring himself to say.

"Look," he starts again, "I'm sorry about Helen. I am."

I snap my head forward once more.

"And I understand it feels like it's happening all over again," he says. "Especially since you've caught some . . . pretty intense feelings for him. And tonsil hockey sessions *always* make things more complicated."

Aaaaaawe-some. So, Giovanni *had* seen that, too.

Augh. Just. Why couldn't *I* be the one on the death spiral?

"But it's *different* this time," he hurries on. "This time? If we walk away, he goes down no matter what. *Literally*. We stay, he's got a chance. *Maybe* even to live. He might be an antique, but he doesn't know everything. Shit, I had to explain Tinder to him."

Are we seriously here right now? In Elias's car, with Giovanni making a case for him?

Maybe Giovanni isn't defending Elias, but he certainly isn't giving me much room to hold on to my conviction to run.

"B. T. Dubs," he adds, "you might want to know that *I've* started to blip into hell world. As of today."

Numbly, I glance his way. "You went there? Saw Bob?"

"Not him yet," says Giovanni. "But the house got all screwy for a good while. Tried to figure out what the difference was. What might have happened to trigger this newest bull. Didn't take long for me to realize . . . it's got to do something with . . . Jane, there was something inside that kiss. Something old and indestructible. Something . . . incredible. Something that belongs to you and to him. And has. Since before you got here. Since before I met you. And . . . I think that's why you saw the hell world first. Because you cared . . . first."

I blink, absorbing all this, my mind whispering impossible explanations. Explanations that tie into why I've fallen so hard and so fast for Elias. Why the demon seems to know me . . .

But my brain can't handle those possibilities. Not yet.

Instead, it focuses on the Giovanni-shaped anomaly in his conclusion.

"Which would mean . . . he really did grow on you," I say.

To that, Giovanni whisks a hand between us, like he's not sure if that's the answer, but it's one he'll take since it's the only one we've got.

The car gets quiet again. Then Giovanni runs that hand through his hair and sighs long and loud.

"Look, *I'm* going back to Fairfax," he says. "I *have* to. I got a friend there who needs a solid. But in the meantime, you tell me, Bird. Where to?"

Friend.

Giovanni and Elias are . . . friends?

And Elias and I. What are we?

What are we really?

If he loves me and I love him, then maybe the answer doesn't matter.

And maybe even death, regardless of which of us it claims—or even when—doesn't, either.

Giovanni is right, too. Hope still *does* exist.

But even though I want to latch onto Giovanni's assurance that Elias might not have all the answers, that he might still have the chance to live, I can't let that particular uncertainty be the reason I walk back into that house.

Instead, I just have to hope that my hope—the one thing the demon had said separated me from him—will be enough to undo the worst.

Thea had never given up hope.

And so, neither will Jane.

31

Still unnerved by the previous day's run-in with Bob and wanting to stick together while we wait for daybreak, Giovanni and I crash in the drawing room. He gives me the sofa and takes the big chair and ottoman near the fireplace. I sleep for almost an hour, comforted by his soft snores. If nothing else . . .

Then, when the morning light starts to sneak in through the curtains, that same aroma of coffee that drew me to the kitchen that first day coaxes me to full consciousness.

Giovanni snores on while I slip out into the hall, following the rich scent to the kitchen.

Mr. Poole isn't the first person I want to see. But then . . . he's not the last.

"Miss Reye," he says as I slink in through the door.

"'Sup," I reply without inflection.

"I must say, I'm glad you're all right." He places a giant steaming mug on the counter before gesturing to it.

I make a beeline for the coffee, arriving just as Mr. Poole sets a carafe of cream next to the mug. When he doesn't ask me if I want sugar, I narrow my eyes on him. Because how does *he* know how I take my coffee?

"Quite an arduous night," says Mr. Poole, returning to the stove where he's assembled breakfast ingredients.

"Mm," I say. An answer that I hope sends the message that my most recent interlude with Elias *isn't* up for discussion. Nor is yesterday's episode with Giovanni.

I didn't come in here to chat about my ill-advised escapades with the resident fire boys of Fairfax anyway.

I *do* want to dish on how much he knows. And find out if that knowledge base holds any insight that has evaded the rest of us.

And Mr. Poole. He does know *something*. Something he isn't saying out loud—for whatever reason.

"I *do* hope you were able to get some rest," Poole prattles on, flipping a frying pan before setting it on a burner. "Of course, you must be hungry. Why don't you have a sit and let me make you a fry-up?"

I don't know what a fry-up is, but I'm game because I'm starving. Even if this *is* a trap.

Instead of going to the kitchen table to sit, though, I stay standing at the counter and sip the coffee. The caffeine will kick in hopefully any second. Jump-start my prefrontal cortex. Override mortification mode and prime my preloaded passive-aggressiveness so I'm better armed for when we start talking about the whole kiss-cam thing.

"This is Mr. Thornfield's favorite meal," Mr. Poole tells me as he cracks a pair of eggs into the pan. "Simple as it is, it's the only thing he seems not to have grown tired of. Aside from black dark-roast coffee, that is," he adds bleakly. "So, I make it quite a lot."

I take a breath and hold it. Because, officially, Elias has entered the conversational building. Is this Mr. Poole's way, however, of trying to gauge how much I know about the specifics of his employer's predicament?

That game, I can play.

"Breakfast is something you can have for a hundred years and it'll still taste good," I say. "The ultimate comfort food, in my opinion."

Mr. Poole remains quiet until there's the softest of sizzles followed by the unmistakable aroma of frying bacon.

"He's lost his taste for so much," says Mr. Poole. "And he never finishes *any* dish I set before him. Truly, I haven't seen him passionate about anything or anyone for a very long time. Not even the cars, really. Those just seem to be . . . a distraction. Something to care about and for. Though they make for cold companions. So, I was surprised at what I saw on the security footage when my alarm went off."

And there it is.

"Kinda surprised myself," I say, snagging a paper napkin from a nearby stack, which I then start to shred. "Not a life choice I would make again. Especially not if I knew there were caaaaaameras."

I sing the last word. Because I can't embarrass myself any more than I already have.

"I'm glad you insisted on returning," he says after another long stretch of silence. "Furthermore, I'm glad I was the one to help you get back here in the first place."

I tilt my head at him. It's true that I *did* come back to Fairfax. But I didn't really insist so much as I just . . . returned. And he'd done the official hiring for the job, I guess, but what does he mean by helping me get *back* here?

Frowning, I let these questions go. Because there are other more important bases to cover.

"Yeah, well"—I sigh—"we'll see if Elias thinks the same thing."

"Jane."

"Poole." I keep my eyes poised on what's left of my napkin.

Is this it? The lecture? Am I going to have to tell Poole, king of good manners, where he can stick his spatula?

"Please don't tell anyone else this yet," he says, "but I want you to know today is also *my* last day in Mr. Thornfield's employ."

I peek up at him. "You're not saying Elias fired you."

"His exact words were *I will no longer be in need of your services.*"

Oh. Ouch.

"It's not because he doesn't want you around," I hurry to tell him. "Or anything you did."

I say this because, apparently, I feel the need to reassure Mr. Poole (who knows Elias better than I do), that he isn't being discarded. It's not like I can tell the housekeeper Elias is letting him go because he's going to die. That'll only complicate things. Which . . . is probably why Elias didn't tell *me.*

Elias hadn't expected either of us to develop feelings for the other. That's why he'd always kept Mr. Poole, and everyone, at a distance. To avoid inflicting pain on himself or anyone else.

His tactics had worked about as well as dull scissors.

Not that I forgive him for lying. I don't.

"I'm well aware my dismissal has little to do with me," says Mr. Poole. "But that . . . well, it almost makes it *more* difficult."

This conversation. It's so strange. I'm not sure what Mr. Poole is trying to get out of it—trying to get out of *me.*

So, I don't say anything. And, until he's done cooking—which doesn't take much longer—he doesn't speak, either.

"Sit," he instructs when I try to take the plate of food from him, and he waves me to the nearby two-seater table—the small one near the windows overlooking the rear porch that Giovanni and I had shared the night I'd "borrowed" Bob's necklace.

Obediently, I go.

When Mr. Poole sets the food in front of me and wanders off again, I'm hopeful I'm being let off the hook for all further discussion. But then he returns with his own mug of coffee and he takes the seat across from mine.

"When he walked away from you last night," says Mr. Poole, "and you reacted as you did, I knew it must have been because he told you the truth. Which he hasn't even told me. Not . . . in so many words."

Slowly, I eat.

Eat because I'm starving. Slowly because I'm confused.

Mr. Poole's wording suggests *he* knows the truth.

"He's been here for so long," says Mr. Poole. "Yet he pines for something else. To be some*where* else. The tragedy, Jane, is that I think now a part of him, a large part, because of you and the others, wishes he *could* stay."

Wow. So. Mr. Poole *does* know.

Of course, Elias dismissing him had to be a huge clue.

Still, this chitchat is hitting home. Nicking all those gory spots that, though they've stopped bleeding, still smart like heck.

"I don't know what you're asking me to do," I whisper. "Aside from whatever I can . . . to try and stop it."

Obviously, Mr. Poole cares about Elias. And *not* just because he's paid to.

"I'm not asking you to do anything," he replies. "I'm *telling* you that . . . even if you don't think so, what you three are doing for him. Well, it *has* made a difference."

I glance up from my plate. Mr. Poole wears an uneasy expression, or maybe he's just tired.

"We really haven't done anything yet," I say.

"Course you have," replies Mr. Poole. "*You* made him smile. And—God forbid—*laugh*. More than once if I'm not mistaken. Not even I've ever managed to do that."

My chewing slows. Because wait. When had I made Elias laugh in front of Mr. Poole?

"Mr. Luchesi and his precarious situation elicited compassion," continues Mr. Poole. "Albeit only after a brief interlude of one-sided and agreed-upon violence but, particulars aside, I still count that whole matter as definite progress."

"Hold up," I say, "were you *there* for that?"

"Goodness, no," he says with that halting and haughty smile-free laugh of his. "I can't be here after dark these days."

Giovanni had mentioned something about Poole clocking out and going home in the evenings.

"Besides," adds the housekeeper, bringing his mug to his lips and pausing before another sip, "the air surrounding him. It's begun to thin too much the *other* way."

I set my fork down, blinking at him. The other . . . way?

"And lastly," he adds, "again just between you and me,

Miss White—Ingrid—played quite the trick on him early this morning. Before my arrival. After she went looking for you and Mr. Luchesi. After she found Mr. Thornfield stewing in the study instead."

My brain becomes one of those corkboards homicide detectives use in the movies to connect the dots in serial-killer cases—all pushpins and crisscrossing string.

Because what is this dude *talking* about?

Mr. Poole said Ingrid found Elias *before* he, Mr. Poole, had gotten here. Which . . . what?

"Okay. Time-out." I make a T with my hands. The words are out of my mouth before I can stop them. "What are you, the Phantom of the Fairfax? Are there like . . . cameras installed everywhere or something?"

Because Elias and I had been driving through the countryside in his car when I'd made him laugh. And we'd been alone.

"I am nothing if not Mr. Thornfield's main confidant," says Mr. Poole before taking a relaxed and non-fussed sip of his coffee. "Which was the whole reason you approached me in the first place."

I purse my lips. Because that isn't an answer. Not one that makes any damn sense.

"You're saying he *told* you about all that? And what do you mean *I* approached *you*? I applied for the job, yeah, but *you* approached *me* about coming here."

"Tomato, tomato," Mr. Poole says with a flip of his hand, altering the pronunciation of the *a* in each utterance of the word.

Another shifty nonanswer.

"Look," he elaborates when I level him with an I'm-not-buying-it squint. "I know these things because I keep tabs on Mr. Thornfield—and have for ages. As I told you before, it's my job to care. Yet my influence, as you know, is limited. Mostly because I'm no longer the only one tasked with keeping up with him. And the other, Bob, you call him, currently holds more sway. This is my way of telling you I'm well aware of the direness underscoring the battle that lies ahead. But I also wish to say that Mr. Thornfield has never been more himself than in the last few days. And, well, I suppose I just wanted to thank you. For doing what *I* could not by reminding him he *is* worth saving."

Augh.

Poole one, Jane zero.

"M-Mr. Poole, I—"

"I *know* it was a difficult choice to return," says Mr. Poole. "This whole arrangement has been exacting to the nth degree. And perhaps the odds are against us no matter our tactics. You and I went into this knowing that. But understanding what I do about you—about you both, really—I also understand, or perhaps appreciate is a better word, that there ultimately *was* no choice. And that, despite my misgivings . . . you were right."

"About *what*?" I have so many questions but that's the one that leaps forward.

"That it *is* better to try and fail, than to stand idly by, accept defeat, and fail by default."

I blink, baffled as he rises with his coffee mug.

"Wh—? *I* never said that."

"You did," he assures me. "Though you cannot recall that particular conversation, you will no doubt remember how I told you this idea to have you to the manor was *partly* my idea. Its initial conception, however, was yours. Yes, Jane, *you* were my co-conspirator. Though your name was not then Jane."

I gape at him outright.

"But please," he adds, "do *not* do anything drastic. Trading one evil for another is not a victory. Neither was that part of *our* deal. And I'm going to have enough explaining to do when this is all over."

He walks away after that—sliding packets of documents I hadn't noticed before off the counter as he takes his coffee with him, leaving me alone with my fry-up and my now-total incomprehension.

Deal? I'd never made any deal with Mr. Poole.

Unless . . . I had.

I study the remnants of eggs, bacon, fried mushrooms, and beans. Then I glance out the window, like the porch might hold the answer to whether or not I really could be what—*who*—I think.

Instead, I spy Ingrid sitting alone on the stone steps leading down into the gardens.

And I'm pretty sure . . . she's crying.

32

"Let me guess," I say as I hover over the step Ingrid's seated on. "He told you the truth. That he was going to die anyway."

Ingrid sniffles, hand clutching a wad of tissues, which she dabs her eyes with. At one of her elbows, a box of fresh tissues sits next to a pile of crumpled ones. At her other, there waits a large thermos.

"I don't look for that kind of thing," she says. "I don't ask the cards about that. It's unethical to read for death. And the Death card, it doesn't mean death anyway. It means transformation."

"You saw it in his cards?" I take a seat next to her.

"He did," she replies. "Elias, I mean. Though, I think that's what Bob *wanted* him to see. Because the reading—it went all wrong."

I put my arm around her. Ingrid, in response, leans into me, her designer perfume kind of . . . not half bad anymore. It's light, airy, and floral, but with a deeper undertone of something sweet.

Like Ingrid herself, I guess.

"What happened?" I ask. "Mr. Poole said you went looking for us. Me and Giovanni."

"I don't know how *he* would have known since, at the time, Elias was the only one in the manor."

"Ya got me there," I mutter, glancing once behind, toward the kitchen, which remains empty of Poole or anyone.

"I couldn't sleep," explains Ingrid. "And with tomorrow being what it is, I doubted I was the only one. I tried texting Giovanni, but he never answered. I finally found Elias in the study. He had your sketches everywhere. And he'd laid the one you did of him out on the desk. Straightaway, I saw the eye you had drawn."

I frowned down at our shoes—Ingrid's pale pink, rhinestone-encrusted flats, my beat-up Converse sneakers.

"He was quite shocked to see me," she said. "He told me you and Giovanni had both gone and that, when he'd found a car missing from the garage, he was certain the three of us had fled together. Elias asked to borrow my phone, and thinking he would try to contact one of you, I gave it to him. Instead, he called a cab. For me. So, since I couldn't make any headway with *him*, I began setting down my cards. Asking *them* where you two had gone."

Oh boy. "What'd they say?"

"They all . . . came up black," mutters Ingrid. "Elias took the omen as proof I needed to go. He said Fairfax had become too dangerous—that the demon's world was drawing nearer to ours. Then he told me to go and gather my things, that I needed to leave straightaway. That I should never have come. Any of us. That he should never have asked us to."

"And yet, there you sit," I mutter, borrowing Elias's words from our helter-skelter car ride.

"I demanded that he tell me the truth," says Ingrid, "or I would ask the cards for that, too. In response, Elias stripped off the patch and *invited* me to read for him. Actually, Jane, he dared me. Thanks to your drawing, the eye was less of a shock than it might have been, though it still frightened me. However, I laid his cards. This time . . . they were Death. All of them." She hitches. "But the Death card is just . . . transformation."

Is she trying to reassure me? Or herself?

"He told me everything, Jane," Ingrid continues. "About Thea, the demon, their deal. What would happen at midnight tonight. I told him I knew he was in love with *you* now. I'd seen it in the cards. Elias did not deny it, but neither would he hear me out when I told him you *would* return. Because you loved him, too."

"What did he say?"

"He only repeated that I needed to go. And that if I refused, *he* would have to depart since the demon—hell itself—would soon be coming for him. So, I did the only thing I could. I allowed him to escort me to the cab and see me in. But just before the driver reached the main road, I ordered him to let me off. From there, I walked back. And I've been out here all morning. Waiting."

"For?"

"You," she murmurs through another sniff. "After the reading I did for you that day in the library, I *knew* you'd be back. And, well, here you are."

"Here we *all* are," I echo. "Giovanni's in the drawing room."

"Jane, where did you go?" she asks.

"To take a walk with me, myself, and . . . I'm pretty sure, Thea."

At that, Ingrid eyes me with incomprehension.

I shake my head, because it's too much to explain. Even to myself still.

"Elias still thinks you're gone," I guess in a monotone.

Ingrid nods.

"He really thinks the three of us bailed on him," I mutter.

"Well," says Ingrid, "he'll soon find out how wrong he is about that. When daybreak came, Mr. Poole appeared suddenly. He'd brought me coffee. And a box of tissues. Honestly, I don't know how he knew I was out here, *or* that I was crying. But he suggested I return to the kitchen . . . at noon."

"The party," I say.

"Poor fellow. I don't think he knows anything about what's really going on."

"Unless . . ." I reply, squinting toward the climbing sun, which reminds me of the card Ingrid had pulled for me with the angel on it, since it had featured a sunrise, too. The Temperance card. "Unless he actually happens to know . . . everything."

♥ ♥ ♥

U watching all this?

Send.

Don't tell me you're only allowed one phone call.

Send.

What's bail btw? I'll pay it. We can put it on Elias's tab.

Send.

U said it yourself. We're running out of time.

Send.

He's running out of time.

Send.

U must have known the truth all along. About me, I mean.

Send.

That's why u showed up instead of her. Thea.

Send.

Must be why you led me to the journals, too.

Send.

Poole Boy give you a hall pass? That why he was in the dream?

Send.

In case it's not obvious, this is me using my Phone-a-Friend option.

Send.

Please, please, please, pick up, Helen.

Send.

Everyone says I love him.

Send.

That doesn't make much sense.

Send.

But neither does the fact that I'm starting to think that maybe

Send.

I always have.

Send.

33

"Yes, Mr. Thornfield," drones Mr. Poole, his voice floating down the hall, growing nearer to the kitchen, where the three of us, Ingrid, Giovanni, and I, loiter around the island counter. "I *shall* be on my way shortly, but there's one final matter that needs your attention."

I hold my breath when Mr. Poole sweeps into the room, making his way to the counter where he deposits a ring of keys—right next to the red velvet cake he'd made.

"This isn't about the paperwork, is it?" asks Elias, and now *his* voice is the one drawing near. Setting my destroyed heart aflame and somehow—simultaneously—resurrecting it. "I thought the last of it was already in—"

Elias's dark form fills the doorway. He halts there, as if an invisible barrier has stopped him from entering, and not his shock.

I tell myself not to look at him, but of course I do.

He scans us all, brow pinched with confusion—and something that might be pain. The bittersweet kind that comes with realizing you were wrong, and that the part of you that died by the hand of your previous convictions, impossibly, breathes yet.

"Not the paperwork, sir," answers Mr. Poole. "I just wanted to be sure you knew where I had placed my keys. And there they are. On the counter."

Elias doesn't respond. And he won't meet anyone's gaze—not even mine.

Stricken, he's silent for ages. Until, finally, he speaks.

"For God's sake," he says, as if trying to muster any emotion other than the one gripping him, "is that a cake?"

"*No*," says the housekeeper. "It is *not* a cake. It is, rather, a confection of absolutely zero significance, concocted by yours truly for the sheer purpose of seeing if I could accomplish the task. Red velvets are *infamously* difficult to execute."

"It's a birthday cake," says Giovanni.

Elias scowls.

"You have evening flights," he reminds me and Giovanni. "I'd thought—*hoped*—you'd gone."

"Yeah, well," says Giovanni as Mr. Poole sets to cutting the cake. "I had to come back because I forgot my toothbrush."

"I left my camera," Ingrid adds. "And my laptop. I can't possibly continue my channel without them."

"I came back because I forgot to tell you I hate you," I say. "But . . . you know what they say about hate."

Elias shuts that eye.

"You four planned this," he accuses, his words going soft, bereft of much voice at all even though they try to be angry.

"Poole's idea," says Giovanni.

Mr. Poole shoots Giovanni a death-ray glare.

"None of you should be here," continues Elias. "It's too late. As it was from the start. This dark pact. It cannot be undone. I . . . cannot be helped."

"You all hear something?" asks Giovanni as Mr. Poole starts doling out slices of cake. "It's like . . . lyrics to bad emo music except there's no whiny-ass guitar."

I pick up one of the plates. After adding a fork, I carry it over to Elias, who, at last, peers down at me.

"You should be here least of all," he says.

"We can argue about that tomorrow." I hold the plate out to him.

For several seconds, he doesn't say anything. He doesn't move, either. But then, when I refuse to back down, he finally accepts the plate. I spin away from him after that and return to the counter to claim my own piece.

I dig in. And as far as potential last meals go, the red velvet makes for an epic one.

"Thih ihs tha besh thing you've mahe, Poole," says Giovanni after breaking the prolonged silence with a smack of his lips. "Do I detect a hint of lemon in the frosting?"

"Well, what do you know?" says Mr. Poole. "Your palate *does* have a pulse."

"Hmph," says Giovanni. "Needs salt."

"Mr. Poole," chirps Ingrid, "this red velvet is *divine*."

"Why, thank you, Miss White," says Mr. Poole. "One wonders if you say that because you know."

I blink at that, my gaze cutting sharply to Mr. Poole, who bounces his brows at me, like he's meant that comment for me more than Ingrid.

"Best cake I've ever had," I admit. And it's not a lie.

"It's got potential," allows Giovanni.

"What do *you* think, Elias?" asks Ingrid.

"Yes," says Mr. Poole, "I *do* hope you'll at least try—"

Mr. Poole snaps his mouth shut when Elias deposits his plate—empty—onto the counter next to Mr. Poole's keys.

For several long moments, the housekeeper stares at the few remaining crumbs. Then, without warning, Mr. Poole moves out from behind the counter.

"If you'll excuse me," he says.

"Wait," calls Ingrid, "where are you going?"

"Jane, I've done all I can," Mr. Poole says, pausing in the doorway before adding over his shoulder in a warning tone, "Remember what I said."

And then he's gone.

I abandon the counter and the kitchen to go after him. Because I'd wanted to talk to him again. One-on-one. Also his leaving like this—never mind his words—it can't be a good sign.

"Mr. Poole," I call as I turn the corner. "Mr. Poole?"

I stop when I reach the foyer and go to the windows to find the Fiesta gone from its normal spot.

There's no sign of it on the drive, though, and there's no way he could have driven off so quickly without a trace. I'd been right on his heels.

His absence is resounding. And I have to sigh.

Because, for better or for worse, it looks like this "party" . . . is officially over.

34

I'm about to turn away from the window, head back in the direction of the kitchen to rejoin what's left of my army, Elias's, when the horizon tints crimson. The sky reddens, too, stationary clouds going the deep pink of raw meat as they drain into whirlpools.

The embers are back, chasing up as the walls paint themselves the hue of charcoal.

Turning around seems like a bad idea.

Instead, I want to believe my safest bet is not to move—to just stand here, shut my eyes, and wait for his influence to drain away.

If only sticking my head in the sand really worked. With this demon or anything else . . .

He's all over the back of my awareness—that molten stare crawling along my shoulders like so many cockroaches.

When I turn, though, I don't find him where I sense him—near the crumbling stairs, which climb up to the still intact second floor.

I drift in that direction anyway, eyes going to the portrait of Thea that hangs just as it does in the real version of Fairfax. Except the frame is fractured, and the canvas torn. And *this* portrait features a dead Thea, her face rotted with empty sockets for eyes, her skull exposed.

Her collarbone juts from the yellowed and stained garments that now hang off her skeletal frame. What flesh remains is papery, ripped, and hanging, the dingy hue of dish-soap water. The roses in her lap have become dust.

Bob's energy shifts and shorts, blipping to the front door, which creaks open to again reveal a portal of blackness. Then those eyes appear.

"Love what you've done with the place," I tell him.

That gets something of a smile out of him as he emerges from the nothing. At the same time, it's the quiet slim sort of smile that suggests he doesn't *actually* think I'm funny.

"We make our own hell," the demon says.

His way of saying he wasn't in charge of interior decorating but, rather, Elias?

In so many ways, that makes sense. But there's something—more than a few things—that still don't.

"You don't actually *want* to do this," I whisper, gaze narrowing on him, "do you?"

He doesn't reply. And those eyes, they just keep boring into me.

"You have to," I stress, approaching him, my words more for my own thought process. "You wanted us to know that. Why? And if you don't really want to take his soul . . . what *do* you want?"

"At this moment?" asks the demon. "To warn you. That if *you* get help . . . *I* get help."

He backs into the darkness, which folds around him, swallowing him whole again.

I almost call after him. But it's the igniting of more sets of eyes within that void that stalls me. At first, only a few pairs—all of them slit-pupiled and molten orange—pop into being. But soon there are ten, twelve, twenty sets.

"Your time wanes," whispers the demon. "*His* does. Don't waste it."

I back away and, turning, head for the study, my mind racing ahead of me.

I hurry though the dilapidated, burned-out, and ruined hall until it gives way to the restored corridors of the true Fairfax, the two versions of the manor blending and mixing, like they're overlapping. Converging.

I find the study whole and unblemished, and going to the desk, I seize my sketchpad.

The sketch of Elias peers back at me. I shake my head at it, and flip to a clean page—one of the few I have left. I locate my knapsack nearby, where Elias had dropped it. Grabbing it, I hook the strap over my head and veer back into the hall, abandoning all the drawings Elias had again exhumed. The same ones from before—all those sketches featuring the mysterious couple. The renderings that had, all this time, these past few years, been me—the most buried parts of *my* soul—whispering the truth to myself.

In the foyer, the skeletal portrait of Thea still hangs above the half-wrecked staircase. The window, too, reflects the hell world. And though the doorway leading outside remains open, it contradicts everything by showing only the clear and sunny afternoon.

"Things are thin here. And getting thinner."

Helen's words from my dream, from her visit, echo in my head as I retrace my route to the kitchen, the path flowing once again from blackened and crumbling to wallpapered and wood paneled.

Evidence that things aren't just thin anymore. More like now they're starting to tear.

I arrive at the doorway to find Giovanni blocking the entry, his back to me. In front of him, Ingrid stands with Elias, grasping one of his arms with both hands. In his fist, Elias clutches Mr. Poole's ring of keys.

"What's happening?" I demand.

"Thornfield has the bright idea of trying to roll out."

"Since you three refuse to leave Fairfax," says Elias, "then I *must* go."

"Dude," says Giovanni. "The villain is never supposed to *reveal* his plans."

"Stand aside," commands Elias.

"Jane," says Ingrid, trying to tug Elias back from Giovanni, "I'm starting to think you and I should just . . . knock them both out and go from there."

All things considered, it's not a bad plan.

"What exactly are you going to do if I *don't* stand aside?" challenges Giovanni.

"Remove you from my path," growls Elias.

"Try me, Thornwimp."

Tilting his head at Giovanni, Elias arches his brows.

A beat. And then—

"You know what?" Giovanni sidesteps from Elias's path before aiming a thumb my way. "On second thought, I'm gonna let my muscle handle this one."

And just like that, Elias and I stand opposite one another. Opponents in a war we've both already lost.

"My God, the hall," Ingrid says in a hushed tone, taking in the change that has occurred behind me. A change that has started to slow creep its way closer to the kitchen. "What's happening?"

So. She sees it now, too. And here we all are with Elias. In hell. His hell.

Does that mean we, the three of us, all now have claims on parts of his soul, too?

Elias steps forward, moving toward me, and Ingrid's shock is enough that she allows him to slip free of her hold. Giovanni, throwing his hands up in surrender, doesn't try to stop him, either.

They don't have to stop him, though. Officially? That's my job.

"You're not going anywhere," I tell him. "And neither are we."

"Jane Reye," says Elias. "Yours is a will I cannot—and never have been able to—resist. And so, I'm left to beg you. Let me go."

"Never."

"It was cruel of you to return."

"Payback," I tell him through clenched teeth, before rushing into him, wrapping my arms around him, even while I still clutch my sketchbook in one hand.

Elias catches me, enfolding me in his arms as well. Again, he crushes me to him, just like he had in Thea's tomb.

"I am a time bomb," he says. "Yet you cling to me."

"You're a pain in the ass," I mutter against him, "and I'm not afraid. Not anymore."

"That's what scares me," he says.

I pull back from him, enough to reach up and unhook the patch, which I lift free. Elias's eyes, his unaffected one and that blazing demon's eye, search my expression.

He lifts a hand to my jaw, thumb brushing my cheek.

"This soul of yours," he says, "I would know it anywhere. And yet, too preoccupied with my impending fate, I failed to recognize you until this day. I would plead for forgiveness, if your presence, your constancy, did not already speak to its bestowment."

"Shut up, Elias," I say.

"Indeed," he replies—and kisses me.

And now, in this moment that, though it's still weighted by so much darkness, is now unfettered by the chains of disbelief, I'm transported. Time melts out of existence and, in my mind, I'm thrown backward through decades—roughly a century and some change—to a moment just like this one.

The twin to this kiss glimmers on the edges of my rationality, still half-lost behind a gossamer curtain of time, space, and eternity.

All the same, like that kiss, this one stands as its own universe. One that belongs to Elias and me alone.

Like Giovanni said. Thunder. Lightning. Punk rock—but also Vivaldi.

"*Of course* Jane gets a taste of both the snacks," scoffs Ingrid. "How *else* would the cosmos have it?"

My laugh breaks the kiss. But the time for jokes—let alone make-out sessions—is growing short. Hadn't Bob himself tried to warn me about that? Along with his sudden right to enlist his own posse?

Heck of a good reason to wrangle mine.

"Everybody," I say. "Asses in the dining room. Now. I'm calling another meeting."

I press a hand flat to Elias's chest before clutching the material of his shirt in my fist.

"That includes you," I say as I shove him backward through the kitchen doorway. "Because I know what we have to do now. And it's going to take all of us."

"Wait," says Giovanni as we pass him, as Elias yields to my shoving, even while his eyes search mine with a mixture of shock and heartbreaking disbelief. "Are you serious? You know how to get rid of Bob?"

"We're not going to get rid of him," I tell Giovanni—everyone—my gaze still locked with Elias's. "We're going to free him."

35

Thea had never known what I now do.

Like Elias had said in the gazebo the night of our "near miss"—she'd gone it all alone with Bob last time. Meaning, she hadn't had any help.

Jane does, though.

"Jane," says Ingrid, "what is that? What on earth are you doing?"

"It's called drawing, Ingrid," I mutter as I outline a face—Bob's.

"Just a side note," says Giovanni as he hovers at the window, peering through the curtains, "in case anyone's interested in a weather report. I'd say it's looking cloudy with a chance of fire and brimstone."

"What in the hell is happening to Fairfax?" asks Ingrid.

"I think you just answered your own question there, Ingrid," replies Giovanni.

"Things are getting thin," I clarify while I hurry along with the drawing. "Hell is barreling down on us. It's coming for Elias. Which is why everything has gotten a little too real."

I let the outline I'm constructing be rough. I don't need Bob to be perfect. I just need to get him down. And I don't have my subject here, but that doesn't stop me from chasing after him with my mind.

I find him on the edge—at that place where *his* hell ends, and Elias's begins.

I don't give definition, or even much thought, to the burned-out Roman city jutting behind him, though. Neither do I focus on his monstrousness. Instead, this time, I channel—try to—the soul. His. The one he'd lost. Sold.

"Bird," says Giovanni. "You want to start expounding on this left-field tree-hugger approach of yours? We're a little lost and I told you I was only telepathic-*ish*."

"Think about it," I say as I continue sketching, that long white hair now showing up black on my paper—the way it had once been, "long ago," as the demon had said. "If we take our shot in the form of an attack, if *any* of us do, we're dead meat. That's what happened to Thea. We can't make the same mistake twice. *I* can't."

"You said we need to free Bob," says Ingrid. "And I suppose, on the surface, that approach makes sense. Logically speaking, that is."

"We free Bob," adds Giovanni, "Elias is free, too. By default."

"Bingo," I say, outlining the eyes and putting into place that narrow nose.

"Pardon me for saying so," says Ingrid, "but there just seems to be one minor problem to this plan."

"Yeah," says Giovanni. "Given what we know about how

Bob operates, the strategy sounds good in theory. But how the heck are we supposed to free a freaking demon? Somebody *already* on the other side of one of these deals."

"Ingrid," I say, fingers smudging lines, blending shadows, "I was actually hoping *you'd* be able to offer some insight there."

"Me?" she pipes, panic raising her voice an octave.

I pause from my drawing to glance up at her. She stares at me with wide and frightened eyes.

"I thought you were supposed to be Ingrid with an Eye or whatever," I say. "So, get out your cards and start seeing. You haven't been wrong yet, have you?"

She frowns and shakes her head. "The cards . . . I told you, they wouldn't work last time. The reading, it was a disaster."

Because Bob had been messing with her—the same way he'd been messing with me on the plane and all of us after our arrival. Well, maybe not the *exact* same way. Still, regarding the reading in question, the one Ingrid had done for Elias, the demon must have been influencing the things she and Elias saw, manipulating how the cards played out and appeared. What had been his goal in that instance? Same goal from the start of all of this. To frighten us. Scare us into cashing out.

Concerning Ingrid's last reading, Bob's plan had both worked *and* backfired.

Worked because the cards had "proved" Elias's case that things were hopeless, leading him to call that cab and send Ingrid packing. Backfired because Ingrid hadn't fallen for the false flag. She was still here.

Like me and Giovanni, she'd come back. She'd walked through the gate of fire.

In other words, she'd passed his test.

We all, each in our own way, had.

He'd tried to get us to tap out. We hadn't. But he'd needed us to commit—to really commit—before he could rally his own ranks.

"He won't interfere with your readings again," I tell her, and return to my drawing, adding definition to Bob's jawline.

"How do you know?" she presses, her voice shaking. Because she's terrified of making things worse. And maybe, possibly, of seeing the truth.

I am, too. Especially if the truth conveys what Elias had, until possibly this moment, come to believe without a doubt. That this whole pursuit is a fool's errand. Or, worse, a suicide mission.

"He's not going to screw with us again until it's time to collect," I say.

"How can you be so sure?"

This question, it comes from Elias, who has been silent until this moment. He drifts to stand behind me, his shadow falling over Bob's countenance, which has evolved from outline status to a full-on sketch. Still, it's lacking details. And now that I have all my guidelines in place, I zero in on the most important of those details. Bob's eyes.

"Because we're not playing by his rules anymore," I say. "We're not taking the bait to launch missiles. So, he can't, either."

At that, everyone goes quiet and I try to ignore the stares that I know must be on me.

Instead, I funnel my attention into Bob's.

More silence passes as I continue working. Then, finally, Ingrid takes the seat across from mine. And I have to smile with a surge of satisfaction and some weird sense of pride when she lays down her first card.

"The Strength card reversed," she intones. "It's come up again."

The demon's pupils are black as before, but now I make them round instead of slit.

"The Tower upright," Ingrid continues after the next snap.

I tilt my head at the drawing as I fill in Bob's irises. They're dark instead of blazing, and infused with rage. But, just as there had been something deeper to the sorrow in Elias's eye, that glittering glint of hope we, as a team, had managed to fan to fuller flame within him, there's something more in Bob's as well. I dive for it. Because that's what I'd done with Elias.

"The Judgement card reappears, too," murmurs Ingrid, "*also* reversed. Jane, this isn't good."

"Fear," I whisper, at last spying the emotion—identifying it. "Oh my God, it's fear."

I slap the sketchbook down and stand. Placing my hands flat on the table, I lean forward and survey the three cards Ingrid has selected.

"Jane, are you listening to me?" Ingrid asks.

"Stop commenting without context," I tell her while Giovanni scoops the drawing of Bob up and holds it at a distance between both hands as he surveys the final product. "Translate already."

"Talk about a glow-up," mutters Giovanni, tilting his head at the portrait one way, and then the other. "Or I guess, technically, a serious crash and burn since this is the *before* picture."

"The Strength card in reverse, in this position, represents *us*," Ingrid explains, pointing at the card. "It indicates a lack of confidence. Also, that our aspirations are . . . well, to be blunt, rather hopeless. The odds are against us. We are outnumbered."

"Yeah, okay," allows Giovanni, still examining the portrait, "I could see this dude having a girlfriend."

Elias holds his hand out for the drawing. Giovanni forks it over without comment.

"The Tower represents the situation," continues Ingrid. "It signifies catastrophe. The tower falls because its foundation is unstable. And the people inside are doomed because there are no doors. They've no choice but to leap to their deaths. Fire consumes all."

"Okay," I say, and take a breath. "We've got one more card to go. That one's got to be good, right? Like you said, it's shown up before."

"The final outcome for all is Judgement," says Ingrid. "And, paired with The Tower, it is the most powerful of omens. But not a good one in this instance, I'm afraid. We are ignoring what is staring us straight in the face. And that, the cards say, is certain defeat."

Though I *want* to glare at Ingrid, I scowl at the images on the cards instead. After all, how can I be mad at her? Like before in the study, after I'd first arrived, she's just playing the role of messenger. And even if I'd wanted to hate her for the things she'd said then, I can't now.

The truth is the truth.

But . . . is this newest (and bleakest) interpretation of hers *really* the truth?

"You said tarot doesn't really tell the future," I remind her, continuing to scan the cards. "You said it's just advice. *You* said it offers solutions."

"Yes," murmurs Ingrid, "I suppose I did say that."

"You also said energies can change," I continue. "So, if tarot is just advice, and energies can change, doesn't that mean that what these three cards are saying is just a warning?"

Ingrid's eyes, uncertain, flick up to me. I offer her a shrug. And then tilt my head at the cards. Because what was all this jargon about "reverse" and "upright" anyway?

I reach across the table and, one at a time, I rotate the cards so that their positions are now inverted.

"There," I say. "That's what I saw from my side of the table. *My* vantage point. The vantage point of believing there *is* a way to win. So, tell me what they say now."

Ingrid blinks and bites her bottom lip. She clutches her deck more tightly in her hand, gaze falling with reluctance to the spread that is the same, and yet . . . isn't.

"Strength upright urges us to summon our inner courage," she says. "To tap into our reserves. It challenges us as well to dig for an answer—a solution—that is *not* obvious. The woman depicted on the card, you see she is trying to close the mouth of a lion. You could even say she is trying to tame . . . a demon. Yet, in the upright position, her strength is expressed through gentleness, rather than force. That is why the lion submits. Because he recognizes her action is one . . . of compassion."

Now we're getting somewhere.

"Next," I say.

"The Tower is now in reverse," replies Ingrid. "The meaning is altered only slightly here. Destruction is still imminent, but the fire has become the cleansing sort. The forces against us are what are unstable. And the tower—well, it falls because *it* is weak, not the people."

"And last but not least," I say, tapping the final card. "Judgement in reverse. Before, in the library, when you read my cards, you said it meant the return of an old wound."

"You *were* paying attention," she says, pressing a manicured hand to her chest, touched.

"What's the final outcome now, Ingrid?" I press.

"The need to undergo a transformation," she says. "And . . . a fear of being judged."

"Bob's afraid," I say. "And I'm pretty sure . . . he has been the whole time. Maybe even more than any of us."

"Eeeh," says Giovanni, with a squint and a head tilt. "That last statement might be pushing things a bit."

"What is it, do you think," says Elias, speaking up at last, "that he fears so intensely?"

"The truth," I say, the words tumbling from my lips. "Because that's the only thing left for him *to* fear."

"The truth?" Ingrid prods.

"That love *is* real," I tell her. "Because he has to change if he buys that—if *we* prove that. He won't have a choice, will he? So, in essence, death—*transformation*—comes for *him*."

"Oh my God," murmurs Ingrid, perusing the cards before her again. "Jane . . . you might just have a talent for tarot yourself."

"So, spell this out for me real quick," says Giovanni. "What exactly does 'death' look like for a demon? And how does it help us free him and, by proxy, Elias? Bird, the sketch is great. Ingrid, you're spot-on—per usual. But none of this gives us much of a clue regarding *how* to put Bob's problem in reverse, never mind our own."

"It's true," I agree, peering at Giovanni. "We *don't* understand much about this demon. What—exactly—is going on with his soul, I mean."

"I thought he didn't have one anymore," argues Giovanni.

"I thought so, too," I say. "But selling your soul, what does that really look like? On that point, what does being a demon really *mean*? Maybe Bob's told us already. Because when you took his hand, didn't he reveal to you how collecting on this deal was *his* job? And that he was just as bound to his side of the contract as Elias was to his? That he had consequences waiting for him, too."

"So, what's that got to do with Bob's soul?" Giovanni asks.

"His weakness," I say. "It's been in plain sight all along. That necklace. My hell world visits. Ingrid's readings. They've already given us all the puzzle pieces. The answer to what makes Bob tick."

"Which is?" Ingrid asks.

"That Bob's not really running on empty," I say. "In other words, there *is* someone inside that stare. Bob's still there. Deep down."

Giovanni's mouth falls open. Because he knows I'm right. And he's about to say something—to ask another question. Maybe, though, his brain delivers the answer for him. Because he clamps his mouth shut again, jaw jutting with thought.

"If only there was someone around who could shed some light on the whole demon soul thing, though," I say, my gaze shifting to the window, to where Elias has drifted during our conversation. "Someone who could tell us what a demon's soul really looks like. If it's really *missing*. And, if it isn't, what, exactly, is wrong with it."

Hands in his pockets, Elias angles toward us. He blinks once, slowly, like he knows what I'm getting at. Also, like he knows it's the right answer. And that the ball is now, officially, in *his* court.

He pivots toward us and strides to Giovanni.

Stopping before him, Elias meets his gaze with both eyes, one human, one demonic.

Then he extends his right hand.

A hand that, without even the slightest hesitation, Giovanni takes.

36

I dig my phone out of my knapsack. There's only one tiny service bar. I guess hell doesn't get great reception.

But then, Helen has never needed cell tower service to receive my messages.

Good news. Sort of. Giovanni says Elias still has all of his soul.

Send.

Just part of it's been messed with. Corrupted, he said. Like a computer hard drive. Files are all still there, but only accessible to something else.

Send.

Handshake messed with Giovanni pretty bad. He asked for some time out.

Send.

Time is the one thing we're short on. But I said okay.

Send.

U prob already know midnight is when Bob comes to collect, cuz that's when he has to.

Send.

This ticking clock. Helen, I think it HAS to run out. Cuz the contract MUST be fulfilled.

Send.

Maybe that's why I came back when I did. Cuz it had to be that way.

Send.

Cuz Bob messed with a shard of Elias's soul as down payment tho, we know something about our demon that we didn't before. And wouldn't have without that puzzle piece.

Send.

Which makes me wonder if Bob has just been crying for help this whole time.

Send.

Would explain why he approached Giovanni about a deal. So someone in our group had a heads up on all Elias wasn't telling us. Also helps explain why Bob has been on my case. Cuz I was the one he COULD reach right from the start. Cuz he did know me.

Send.

The necklace. HE was the one to tear it off—not me. He must have known what I would do with it.

Send.

He has to know our plan too. But he also has to play his part. "Or else," Giovanni had said.

Send.

All we've got is a shot in the dark plan. But then, that's all we've ever had.

Send.

I hope it works.

Send.

For all our sakes. Bob's included, IG.

Send.

I'm so scared of losing Elias like I lost u.

Send.

Yeah, I know ur still there. At least, I do now.

Send.

Okay. I'll stop spiraling. Ur right. He needs me to be strong. WE do. Strength card vibes.

Send.

Yeah, I kno u love me. I love u, too.

Send.

Shut up.

Send.

I'm not crying.

Send.

"Jane," says Elias, interrupting my texting session, "come here."

I let my arms fall to my sides, but I don't move to meet him. I can't. Because everything's gotten to be too much for me, too.

So, standing in Elias's sprawling bedroom, beneath the skylight—which, like most of the windows in Fairfax, has flooded with orange firelight and tattered gory clouds—I wait as he crosses to me from where he'd been rummaging in his wardrobe.

When he arrives, I let him pull me to him, and rest my cheek against his chest while the flying embers outside cast screens of moving shadows along the floor and walls.

"I wish there was something I could say," he murmurs, that low voice rumbling through me. "But my troubles, they have become yours. And I already know how little comfort can be found through the avenue of words."

Sigh. Elias Frickin' Thornfield.

"Did you find it?" I ask, my tears soaking into his shirt.

While Giovanni went down to the billiards room with Ingrid to shoot a few rounds to help clear his head, Elias and I had come up here looking for his wedding ring. The thought being that, if worse came to worst, if we lost, if the plan we'd cobbled together failed and Elias *did* go to the other side with Bob, he'd still have *something* to remind him of what had taken him there. A touchstone.

Giovanni had speculated that Bob's necklace could be the thing that—if we succeeded tonight—saved Bob's soul, since it alone had tethered the demon to his lost humanity. So, the ring was something of a fail-safe, a backup plan. Another Hail Mary in case the one we'd only just concocted ended up going the way of The Tower upright.

"There's time yet to locate the token," Elias assures me.

"Let me help you look," I say with a sniff, slipping past him, wiping my face with the back of one wrist. Along the way, I drop my phone off on the worn couch.

I don't wait for him to grant permission before inviting myself to his wardrobe, which he's already done a good job of ransacking. For real, though, hanging way in the back, is that a leather jacket?

"You really don't remember where you put it?" I ask, opening and rifling through the little drawers, each filled with everything from cuff links to sew-on band patches. *The Clash, Ramones, Misfits . . .*

Could it be Elias seriously went through a goth-slash-punk phase? Or maybe he's just a closet punk. He *does* like the Cure.

And the music paraphernalia . . . It makes me halfway want to reconsider which of us brought the punk rock to our equation, and which the Vivaldi.

Elias drifts to stand in my periphery.

"You're not very organized for a supposedly lovesick old man," I say.

Elias opens his hand to me, making me pause. Because the ring is there, a golden circle in the center of his palm.

"I wasn't ready to put it back on," he admits.

"Because you miss her?"

"How *can* I miss her?" he asks. "And on that point, if you want to get technical about things, am I truly any older than *you* must be?"

I angle toward him, taking the ring between my fingers.

"That whole thing," I say. "You really think . . . it could happen?"

"Is there any other answer?"

I take his left hand in mine, and slide the ring into place. Elias prohibits my escape by threading his fingers through mine.

I squeeze his hand and the metal—still cold—bites into my skin.

I strive to recall its feel, this sensation, but I can't. Like so many interludes that have come before, though, there *is* something familiar about this moment. And that's him. His nearness, his presence, that scent. His . . . himness.

That bone-deep familiarity surrounding the essence of his soul is what now tempts and beckons me. Grants me courage.

Lifting my free hand, I place it on his chest, my palm marking the beats of his heart. They come rapid-fire, like my touch is something that ignites the muscle into frenzy, brings him alive. And that, in turn, is what sets *me* on fire.

Time pulses by, stretching on and on—one second elapsing for every year apart.

We're waiting each other out.

Trying to.

My strength to resist is failing me. Going . . . going . . .

It's one more heartbeat before Elias is the one who caves.

He pulls me into him, his mouth taking mine.

My arms wind around his shoulders, pulling him down to me. There's no slow build this time, either. This time, we pick up right where we left off in his car, right before everything went to hell—literally.

Elias's hands trace down my sides, finding their way to my hips, which he yanks against him. Unlooping my hands from his shoulders, I grab hold of his collar—and tug, taking a retreating step.

Elias follows my lead, bends—as ever—to my will, and starts backing me toward that already tossed-up bed of his. By the time I bump into the mattress, I'm already too drunk on him to do much else than drown in his kiss, so I'm glad when, taking the lead, he hoists me onto the covers.

Then, in a reversal of our first meeting, I draw him onto the bed after me.

He follows without protest. And this latest make-out session, its intensity matches our first, except now *neither* of us are torn. Unlike before, though—unlike *any* time before—neither of us are the same, either.

I lure him after me as I lie back. An arm braces him over me while his other hand again wanders up my side.

My fingers pry at the buttons of his waistcoat and then his shirt. He lets me unfasten everything, kissing me all the while. Then, the very moment he can, he sheds waistcoat and shirt.

I let my hands wander up that chest I'd admired once before and then down his shoulders, relishing the warmth, the contours of muscles—the delicious coiled tenseness in all of him.

"*Jane.*"

His voice is a raw plea as he hooks a hand under one of my knees, drawing it to his waist as he descends on me, simultaneously pulling me into him so that our hips collide.

A whimper that is equal parts surprise and bliss escapes me, but Elias, returning his lips to mine, quickly devours that.

I wrap his shoulders in my arms again, and when he presses into me a second time, I'm all but overcome with the need to climb into him.

Since that's impossible, I grip him by the biceps, and pushing upward, flip him onto his back. Elias concedes, giving the lead to me even while his hands go to brace my thighs so as to keep them fastened around him. As if he's afraid I would leave him here. Anywhere.

As if I could.

The need he exudes to keep us locked together drives me even further toward the edge of abandon.

Sitting upright on him, I grip the hem of my T-shirt and, like the skeleton girl in my drawing, the one with her ribs full of all the same flowers Elias brought Thea—I lift the garment over my head so that now we're both shirtless.

Elias has already seen my bras. Knows I don't have anything lacy or fancy, but when he sits up to press his lips to my sternum, trailing kisses closer and closer to the small swells of my breasts, I'm instilled with the sense that its reveal is still appreciated.

My hands return to his shoulders, bracing there and then clamping down as his caresses intensify.

"*Elias.*"

His name is a sigh as the room continues to dim, taking on a fiery red glow as the burning world without continues its slow creep over us.

This fire, we ignore. Even as Elias and I set our own.

He sweeps me under him again, and I let him.

After that, I'm too entranced, too engaged, too distracted by the heaven we spin in the midst of the chaos to notice any hell.

Or anything at all . . . but him.

37

y phone rings.

Except. My phone never rings.

No one ever calls me.

Not since Helen died.

So, of course, I open my eyes.

A deeper, bloodier scarlet glow bathes the room now, blanketing all in a pall that silently echoes the word "danger."

Thankfully, the hell world hasn't eroded the ceiling yet, or taken the floor out beneath me. All the same, it's beating down on the skylight, turning it into a bellowing mouth of fire and flaming ash.

I gasp, sitting bolt upright. My eyes fly to the pillow next to mine.

Empty.

Elias is gone.

We'd just dozed for a second. *I* had . . .

I curse, wrapping myself in the bedsheet before fumbling toward the couch where I'd left my phone.

"Hello?" I answer.

"Th . . . ell . . . re . . . y-ou . . . ird?" asks Giovanni between pops and bursts of static. "It's 11:10. Wh-t happ-n -o -eeting . . . li-bra-ry . . . quar-t-r -ill?"

"Tell me Elias is with you," I say.

"What?" Giovanni asks. "I . . . ought -e -as -ith you!"

Again, I curse. Then, "I'm coming."

After hanging up, I hurry to retrieve the garments I'd shed. Then, when I'm dressed again, I tear out the door and down those winding stone stairs.

Alone, I run through the infrared hall, taking the reverse path I had the night I'd followed Helen to Elias's room. The one night things here might just have been thin in the *other* direction. Whatever direction Mr. Poole had come from . . .

But then, isn't there only one other?

"Elias!" I shout, my heart clawing its way into my throat with the fear he's abandoned us after all. Gone off to face this demon on his own even after everything.

He wouldn't do that to us, would he? He wouldn't do that to *me*.

I don't find him in any of the open doorways I pass.

When it comes down to it, though, Elias *has* to still be here.

The row of curtained windows that had allowed in the moonlight the last time I'd run past them are now flushed crimson—ten shades brighter than everything else. So, I have to assume Elias is somewhere on the estate.

Because the hell world, by Bob's own admission, follows *him*, Elias.

"Elias?"

I've reached the half-destroyed stairway leading into the foyer, one of the places within Fairfax where the hell world has bled through, and *still*, there's no sign of him.

I mind my steps as I descend, sticking close to the wall, where the footing is more solid.

But I have to stop next to Thea's portrait. Because it has changed yet again.

Dead Thea is gone. But so is the living Thea, and I gape at the image that has transformed from horror-movie prop to museum-gallery piece. And even though the hell world still fumes around me, slowly eats away at the manor one inch at a time, one hour at a time, the girl in the portrait—now rendered completely in charcoal—remains unscathed. Even if the same can't be said for the fractured frame that holds her, or the crack-riddled wall that supports her image.

She sits in that chair, same as before—the chair that matches the one in Elias's journal room. The roses tumble from her lap as before. She wears the hat, too. But her face . . .

Now her face . . . is mine.

I lift fingers to touch the portrait, to see if the charcoal will rub away onto my fingers—fingers that could have drawn this portrait. But didn't.

This time, *Elias* had rendered it. His mind had, at least.

"I'm here, Jane," comes that voice.

I suck in a breath, relief pouring through me as I clear the rest of the charred stairs, hurrying to where Elias stands in the mouth of the front door. Behind him, there's only the quiet, normal night. Still, the windows tell a different story. Reflect a different realm.

Maybe, since there are people present in this ordeal who still have full possession of their souls, the rules insist on the existence of an escape hatch.

"Where did you go?" I demand.

"To post a missive," he says, that gaze finding and holding mine. And the small, almost imperceptible smile he wears—it's enough to make me blush.

"You went to mail something from hell?" I ask, fighting off this newest brand of fluster the sight of him brings.

"The postbox remains accessible," he says—a verbal shrug. Like it's just another storm bearing down on us, and not the freaking apocalypse. "The matter was rather important and I was loath to wake you. I apologize for causing you dismay."

"Dismay," I repeat. "Elias, I swear, if you're not overstating things, you're understating them."

"Good thing I don't need words when it comes to you, Jane."

He targets me with those eyes and then he closes the distance between us.

I tilt my chin up, ready—always—for another taste of him. But our next kiss remains unborn.

"Hey!"

I jump when Giovanni calls to us from the direction of the study, and then he appears in the half-decimated hall, arms spread in a what-gives? manner.

"Can't you two hanky-panky *after* Project Save the Bob? We're kind of on a tight schedule here."

Elias winks at me with his gray eye. A signal that the joke's on Giovanni, but also that the conspiracy of our interlude—our latest one—is still ours.

"Forgive us for the delay," Elias says then, speaking to Giovanni as he takes my hand and leads me down the hall, past the study and Giovanni, who follows on our heels.

"Yeah, no problem," grumbles Giovanni. "Ingrid and I each

only had a *minor* nuclear meltdown wondering where the heck you two had gone."

"We are, all of us, reunited now," says Elias, his voice calm—maybe too calm.

"And not a minute too soon," chimes Ingrid as the three of us enter the library to find her already involved in phase one of our plan.

Giovanni and Ingrid have shifted furniture aside, allowing a clear surface on the polished wood for her to place her cards. She does so in a wide circle, taping every other one down with shipping tape.

"Eight of Swords next to the Eight of Wands," Ingrid chants as she kneels to snap the cards down. "Nine of Swords beside the Nine of Wands. Ten of Swords. Ten of Wands."

After these are in place, she tapes down the Sword cards but leaves the Wand cards loose.

According to Ingrid, the Swords suit represents the mind, intellect, and thoughts. The Wands suit represents the spirit. The soul.

"Double-edged," the Sword cards will, we hope, create a cage composed of our thoughts—our intentions. One that will trap Bob *in* the ring and, consequently, hold him and therefore Elias *out* of the reach of the encroaching hell world.

There's no rule saying Bob has to show up inside that circle or enter it at all. But . . . we do have one guarantee that, at some point after midnight, he'll have to.

Elias gives my hand a final squeeze before he steps beyond the circle of cards to stand at its center.

And, damn. Even acting as bait, he looks good.

"So, Bob enters the circle to get Elias," I say, rounding the circumference, checking to make sure all the cards are present and in order, that the Swords are the taped, immovable ones and the Wand cards, interspersed between, remain loose. "The demon claims Elias's soul by the time the clock runs out. But the Sword cards—totems of our intentions—put him in check. He can't leave."

"That's when the three of us invert the Wand cards," says Ingrid. "Which should, if we're lucky, invert his soul. *Revert* it. Bob's."

"Because, deep down," says Giovanni, "it's still there. Corrupted after he sold it—but there."

"The cards and our intentions, we hope," I add, "will *uncorrupt* his soul. That should break Elias and Bob's connection. Restore the tampered-with portion of Elias's soul and allow him—Elias—to leave the circle."

"Then it's all me." Giovanni sighs.

"You offer Bob a safe place to put *his* soul," I say. "To *download* it."

"He can either agree," says Ingrid, "and leave the circle by way of another Giovanni handshake."

"Or refuse," I say, "and take his own restored soul—since he *has* to deliver one—back to where he came from. Either way, Elias is off the hook."

"If Bob takes us up on our offer," says Giovanni, "then, when Bob's spirit is out of the circle, I release it."

"Bob goes the way of the Judgement card," Ingrid says.

"He's out of our hands," I say.

"And hair," adds Ingrid through a huff.

"No more demons," Giovanni says.

"Equals no more deals," Elias finishes.

It's a snap-trap plan, lashed together with the tools and talents at our disposal. Maybe, possibly, it's desperate enough to work.

For me, losing—losing *again*—isn't an option.

The room grows dim as I retrace Ingrid's circle, triple-checking it as I round Elias once more. He turns to follow me with that probing gaze as, around us, the lamps flicker, several of them dying with quiet pops.

The demon's presence tickles the back of my awareness—along with the frayed and gnarly energies of countless others. Because apparently, an army of three empowered Bob to summon a legion.

But then, what about us gave him a reason for that kind of backup?

"Giovanni, what time is it?" I demand.

"Go time, apparently," he mutters, drawing my gaze—and everyone's—even as charred blackness crawls in from the perimeters of the room to claim the floorboards and stain the eroding walls.

Above us, the ceiling disintegrates, singeing away to reveal the inflamed sky, which churns with its slow-motion hurricane clouds.

The stained glass windows lose their panes, frames becoming decorative skeletons.

The distortion of the hell world continues with its too-rapid conquest, clambering down the walls and bookshelves, decimating them and reducing all to firelit ruins before abandoning us to dry wind, flaring, flying embers, and, spearing the horizon, soundless crimson lightning.

Only the varnished wood floor within Ingrid's circle remains untouched by the corruption. A sign we might have a chance?

"It can't be midnight yet," I argue.

"Looks like Bob's fashionably early," replies Giovanni, his stare fixed on one shadowed corner where a pair of walls still meet. Within that patch of pitch watch those eyes.

As planned, Ingrid and Giovanni move to flank me and, together, we create a barrier between the demon and Elias.

"I know you didn't show up now just so we could shoot the shit for ten minutes," I say to Bob.

He doesn't reply. Those eyes don't move.

"Fine," I say. "Don't talk. But do your job and take the bait now. You know our plan. We know yours. So, like you said before—no sense in wasting time."

Those eyes close, erasing him.

"Of course I must," says the demon, his voice, now emanating from behind, causing me, Giovanni, and Ingrid, to whirl. And now the demon stands in the circle with Elias, whose upper body he's hooked with one pale and cracked arm.

Elias grips the creature's wrist and forearm, but already his skin starts to pale, going white and cracked as well. Pain etches his features—strain, too. Like he's been rendered speechless as well as immobile.

This can't be happening, though. It's not midnight. It's not time.

"Now!" I shout, falling to my knees next to the cards in tandem with Giovanni and Ingrid, all of us frantically flipping the Wand suit.

This plan. It has to work. It *has* to.

When I peer up, I find that Elias's hair has gone white, white as the demon's, who bores those still-blazing eyes into me, hatred beaming from their centers. But also that fear I'd uncovered in my drawing.

What is he afraid of? That we'll win? Or . . . that we won't?

Ingrid finishes flipping the Wand cards, and for one heart-stopping instant, Bob's eyes do wash clean of their molten hue, flashing dark brown. The spell over Elias is broken, and the cracks vining his skin evaporate as he regains his color.

This, our Strength card move, our act of compassion—it's working.

But then, something horrible happens. Something I hadn't accounted for. But something we all should have seen coming—a reversal that proves we're *all* caught in a cosmic catch-22. And always have been. Since the moment we showed up here.

And in my case, my soul's case, since the moment Elias sealed that deal.

Flames burst from the floor to consume the ring of cards, incinerating them in a split second and obliterating our circle. Thrown back by an invisible force that catapults the three of us in separate directions, I go airborne, my shout—along with Ingrid's scream—rising above the roar of the fire, which, an instant later, dies with a *whuff*.

Flurries of embers surge into the air when I collide with the burnt floor, my shoulder jarring hard as I skid to a halt, my skin and clothes stained with the soot of this realm. But I don't have time for pain.

I push through the ache and, rising, spin to find I'm the first one back on my feet. Ingrid is next, because Giovanni got slammed against a fallen table.

Reeling from pain, gripping his side, he remains kneeling.

The demon still has his hold on Elias, whose form has been

reclaimed by the demonic transformation—all except for that one gray eye, which finds me. And pleads.

Not for help. But rather, for release. From me and my efforts. From having to watch me get hurt.

But I already told him I'd never let him go.

Still, I don't know who to run to. Who to rush for first since our plan's gone to shit and I don't have another one.

But there's no time to reach anyone anyway.

The demon isn't done retaliating.

"Ingrid, watch out!" I screech.

She only has enough time to duck and raise her arms before all the ruined furniture in the room—blackened tables, broken chairs, even charred books—rushes, tumbles, rolls, and flips toward her as though drawn by magnetic force.

Instead of being skewered or pummeled, though—crushed—she's gated in by these objects, which clamber and climb up and over one another, defying gravity and physics to form a cage.

And of course, it makes sense. Ingrid had been the one to lay the Sword cards. She'd been the one to try to trap the demon.

Why hadn't I thought far enough ahead to realize what that strategy would do? Why hadn't I foreseen—?

I wheel back toward Elias and the demon, whose eyes have gone serpentine once more. Even though fissures climb Elias's face, webbing their way over once more ashen features, he still has that single gray eye. At least, he does for one more instant before that last shard of him is claimed, too, and that eye becomes a match to his other.

"No!" I shout.

Because this—the early loss of Elias—has to be my fault,

too. We'd tried to revert Bob's soul. Had that given him and his world permission to fully transform Elias's?

That must be it.

Because Elias's time isn't up.

And now, thanks to me, my crap plan, we can't do anything to stop this.

Giovanni, though, must think otherwise.

Because he appears from nowhere to launch himself at the pair.

"Giovanni, don't!"

Giovanni's arms wrap around only air as, a second before he can catch either Elias or Bob, the demon collapses into—and then through—the floor. Like he had the last time he'd been in this library with us.

Except this time, he takes the transformed Elias—demon Elias—*with* him.

I rush to Giovanni, who, with a grunt, pushes himself up from the floor. Before I can help him to rise, though, the vat of shadows still swathing the floorboards beneath him shifts and stirs. Then that darkness grows arms—countless ashen hands shooting through the murk to grab, pull, and pin Giovanni to the floor, where they hold him captive.

"Giovanni!" Helpless, I drop to my knees next to him.

Giovanni reaches for me, but the hands snatch his arm and slam it, too, to the floor, claws digging in.

My friends. They tried to catch the demon. And now, the demon's "friends" . . .

"Let him go!" I scrape at the arms that, though they flake and shed embers at my touch, might as well be made of stone.

"Bird," huffs Giovanni, one side of his face pressed to the

blackness that must not be able to take him as it had Elias. "Back off. Don't give them an invite."

I heed his warning, but only because I still have hope that this isn't going to go down this way.

"What do I do?" I beg. "Giovanni, what do I do?"

The hands that have hold of him—demon hands. Whatever Giovanni is picking up from them, it's got to be killing him right now. Maybe even literally. But maybe he's also trying to tell me we still have a chance. Maybe he's gotten something from these hands that can still help me.

Help Elias . . .

"Bob," grunts Giovanni. "He . . . doesn't want Elias's soul. Elias isn't the one they—hell has been after. That's why they're early. That's why Bob is. He's got Elias, but he can't take him yet. So, Bob's using him to set a trap of his own. Turn *our* trap around on us. But it's done, Jane, do you understand me? Don't fall for it. You have to let him go. You have to let them *both* go."

"*Jane.*"

I push up from the floor, pivoting toward that echoing whisper.

"Jane, *don't* follow that call," urges Ingrid. "The cards. Remember the cards!"

I do remember the cards. What they'd said before I turned them around. What they'd said after.

And me. Aren't I—metaphorically speaking—now the last card we have left?

Looks like we have one turn-around, one reversal still to go.

"*Jane Reye.*"

The hell world, it peels back, rushes toward the open doorway leading out into the rest of Fairfax, the embers draining in a spiral through that entryway even as the manor restores itself around us.

Still, Ingrid's cage stands. Giovanni's wardens, too, keep a firm hold.

With no one to stop me, with no choice left but to play this game, I start toward the restored archway, the one through which hell has already escaped, taking Elias with it.

The one from which my whispered name had emanated.

"Jane, *nooo*!" Giovanni bellows into the floor.

Because he must know my new plan. If you can call it that.

The one where I answer that haunting summons.

The demon's.

38

"Jane, stop. You *can't*!"

Ingrid's pleas echo after me as I plunge into the halls of Fairfax, which, like the library, have now been leached of hell's influence. Bob's signature, though, plagues my awareness yet.

"Jaaaaane!" roars Giovanni, his voice hoarse, raw with anguish, like he already knows he can't reach me anymore.

"*Jane.*"

That whispered voice, the last one, is the only one I heed.

I turn the corner ahead, and then another, actually catching up to the hell world as it makes its final retreat, all the embers, all the blackness, the ruin, and the flurrying cinders funneling into that still-open front door. Which now, in opposition to before, frames that familiar blackness.

The thinness. I've chased the last of it here, to this final portal, within which Bob again stands—a single pair of eyes.

"You knew it wouldn't work," I accuse.

"So did you."

Is that true? Maybe. Mr. Poole had said he'd helped me get here. By me, he must have meant Thea. The soul that she and I share. He'd also said something about the odds still being against us and how it was better to try and fail than to not try at all. Like he'd known better than anyone how much of a long shot my coming here had been.

But this can't be how it ends. This can't be how we—me and Elias—end.

"Where is Elias?" I demand.

"It's midnight," says the demon, his voice drifting nearer, along with those eyes, until he breaches the darkness, that screen of shadow that yields enough to let him surface halfway.

"Midnight," I repeat, my arms locked at my sides, hands clenched into useless fists. "That means time's up. But you're still here."

"My mistake," he says, and begins to slide back, the shadows consuming him again. "I thought we might yet have business."

"Wait!" I call, having to resist the panicked urge to catch him. "Don't go."

The demon hesitates another moment, eyes beaming brighter, burning the way they had that day I'd challenged him outside Fairfax. Except now, rather than fury, it's the fires of new interest and, perhaps, intrigue that fuel their inhuman glow.

"And there she stands," intones the demon, "so grave and quiet at the mouth of hell, eyes clear, resolute, and perhaps, dare I wonder . . . decided?"

"Yeah," I tell him. "You win. And this must be what you wanted. *That's* why you were on the plane. And that's really why you told Giovanni the truth about needing a soul—any soul."

"I have been paid," the demon reminds me. A clue that his time is not mine to waste. Or, possibly, even his.

"Fine," I blurt. "I'll trade. Whatever."

The demon huffs a laugh—an impossibly human response.

Is he laughing at me? I don't care.

"What's so funny?" I ask. "Why laugh when you *knew* I'd do it. That's why we're here, isn't it? *This* bargain. This whole time, it's what you *really* wanted."

"He's right about you," drones the demon, and, in a blip of a movement, he lifts a hand, claws tucking under my chin—raising my face to his with surprising gentleness. "You *are* a rare creature. One we could use. Persistent. Cunning. Broken."

I wince as his influence, his essence, his poison, floods me. Cringing, I keep my hands clenched at my sides, even as my limbs dry and grow brittle. Fissures crawl up my face, wind over my skull and down my spine. In just a few blinks, the darkness behind him gains depth and greater sharpness.

Too many horned silhouettes, blacker than black, shift into being, their forms brought into relief by my transformed and heightened sight. Yet the details of their faces, their figures, remain indiscernible, their realm untraversable, since I've yet to strike this bargain officially and become fully as they are.

The demon blinks at me. He tilts his head as if surveying his handiwork—my new look.

I don't care what I've become, though. I just want to see Elias. I just want to be with him.

No matter what.

"Say it then," says the demon. "Your soul for his. Speak the words and he goes free."

"No," I snip through teeth that have gone sharp and jagged. "I'm not trading my soul for his. I'm trading it . . . for *yours*."

39

The demon retracts his claws from me, snatching his hand away as if my words have scalded him. With the severing of our connection, his influence drains away from my body, and my limbs become flush once more with warmth, and life, the fissures resealing.

I draw breath, too, unaware until the oxygen floods my system that I'd even lost the ability.

Confused, the demon regards me with that fear. The exact fear I glimpsed in that portrait I'd rendered of him, the one that had shown he did, in some capacity, still have a soul, even if it didn't belong to him, and hadn't for centuries.

"You . . . would follow him to hell?" he asks.

"There's no such place," I say. "At least . . . not where he is. And besides, this way, you and me, we *both* win. I get to be with Elias, and you get to go find the girl you lost. Whoever that necklace belonged to."

When the demon blinks again, a set of black tears trace his white cracked cheeks, and this time, the shock is all mine.

I take care, though, to keep my poker face. Like he said, this is business.

Except we stand this way for a long time. Which, like the tears, makes no real sense to me.

Why isn't he taking the deal?

Why isn't he taking what he *really* wants? The same thing Elias had wanted. The same thing Thea had wanted. And me, too.

"What is hate if not love in hell?"

Elias's words return to me from nowhere. More poignant even than before, since they speak for *all* of us; they echo through the soul the demon has yet to take.

He *should* take it. Would be foolish not to. Unless . . . unless this trade *isn't* what he'd been after. Not really.

"It *wasn*'t worth it," the demon whispers at long last, "was it?"

He's talking about his deal. The one he'd said he'd *needed* to be worth it. The one that had resulted in the death of whoever had killed the first owner of that necklace. The girl he'd loved.

But he wouldn't be asking me this question if he didn't suspect the answer—and hadn't suspected it all along. And something about me, something about Thea—my soul—had answered that for him long before now.

"Maybe not." I shrug. "But at least *I* won't have to ever wonder that. To me . . . that would be the *true* hell."

The demon grits his teeth. He lifts his hand again, claws reclaiming their place beneath my chin.

Our connection is reestablished. He's going to make the exchange.

I know because his eyes once again flicker with humanness—irises transmuting to amber brown, the hue of cherrywood, pupils solidifying into spheres. But the illusion is gone in an instant—as quickly as the change appeared. Or perhaps it's the illusion that transforms them back into twin pits of slit fire.

"It *wasn't* worth it," the demon echoes again, this time more to himself than me. "But perhaps, now that I have what I really wanted, my answer . . . it could be."

He drops his hand, and I'm left standing there before him, my offered soul still, inexplicably, my own.

"I will take no soul tonight," drones the demon, his words aimed at me but meant seemingly for the owners of all the piercing eyes that now crowd in behind him, fuming fury, their gathering whispers like those from a pit of vipers. "Nor ever again."

"Wait," I say, baffled when more white, flaking, and crackled hands emerge from the blackness surrounding him to latch on to *him* now, grabbing him by the arms, the shoulders, his chest, his throat—claws digging in between the fissures that, under the pressure, splinter and widen. "What's happening?"

"Dulcia," whispers the demon, his expression impassive even as the fractures between his skin go dark, spreading blackness instead of light over his frame. "Her name was Dulcia."

With his final utterance of that name I'd accused him of not remembering, his eyes lose their glow, too, snapping off like a lamp does when its plug gets pulled.

Then those countless hands draw him back, rending him as they do. His ruptured form sheds dead ash that swirls after him—into that blackness that evaporates as well.

He and his world—they're gone. Just like that.

Which leaves me gaping into the calm summer night.

Confused, terrified I've *still* somehow lost, I cross the threshold, the shadow of the portico falling over me.

Then I spot him. Elias.

A silhouette, he stands with his back to me, transfixed, it seems, by something in the distance.

"Elias!" I call to him, my heart a sledgehammer against my sternum.

Slowly, he turns to me, the light streaming through the door behind me revealing hair that has gone dark again and eyes that are now *both* that clear storm-gray.

"Jane," he says, the slightest of smiles touching those beautiful lips.

But then his expression darkens, brow pinching.

His knees buckle. I rush to him, arriving just in time to catch him. I can't hope to keep him upright, though, so I guide him to the brick drive, into my lap as he falls.

The light streaming from the manor blots with a new pair of silhouettes. Two that paint Elias once again in shades of darkness. The movements and shapes of these shadows tell me Giovanni and Ingrid have been freed as well, and that they've found me and Elias.

"Jane," Elias says again, blinking slowly, too slowly, as I cradle him against me.

"Elias, I love you," I tell him.

He stills. His eyes find me. His lips move.

He wants to tell me what I already know.

But it's too late.

So, I kiss him. One last time.

To let him know.

I know.

40

They interred Elias in the old Thornfield mausoleum. In the vacant sarcophagus next to Thea's. The spot had remained empty, since Thea's husband was thought to have died abroad during the influenza pandemic.

Elias, sneaky as ever, had the paperwork ready to go. All of it together. Arrangements made.

Mr. Poole had helped him, apparently. Which explained how the housekeeper had known about Elias's impending death, if not how he'd seemed to know everything else as well. More than any of us. Even Elias himself . . .

Standing next to Giovanni, I set a hand on the lid that entombs our friend.

Ingrid sits behind us on the same stone bench Elias and I had occupied together what felt like a lifetime ago.

Per Elias's wishes, there'd been no funeral.

After his death had been attributed to "natural causes"—heart failure—he'd been sealed away.

I lean my head against Giovanni's shoulder. He loops an arm around me.

"Better place, Bird," he manages as he jostles me to him.

Better place.

I hope so.

And Giovanni has to be right. Elias's eyes, they'd returned to their original form. He, his soul, had returned to normal before he'd slipped away. Out of the grasp that, after so long, had only just regained its hold on him.

Which means Bob had simply . . . let him go. Choosing to pay the price of his failure and face that "what else" Giovanni had talked about rather than allowing Elias or me to pay the price of ours.

He'd let us *both* go.

Because he said he'd gotten what he really wanted.

I still wasn't sure exactly what that could have been. Maybe it had something to do with needing to see that love could survive anything.

Even hell.

His refusal to collect on his deal had apparently meant destruction for him. Or maybe, possibly, like Ingrid had said with her cards, he'd just . . . transformed.

Hadn't we all?

"You know, Thornscrub left me the Lamborghini," Giovanni says, his voice inflecting downward.

I can't help it. A laugh bubbles up from the depths of my being, kicking itself out and over the sarcophagus that holds my soul's one true love.

Giovanni has acquired that talent. To make me laugh even in the depths of my sorrow.

Or maybe this time, the joke is truly Elias's.

"Yeah," huffs Giovanni through a watery laugh of his own. "Thing I can't figure out is if he did it because he knew I liked Tilly, or because he found out what I did to her."

"Which one makes you feel better?" I ask.

"Neither," he says. "*Both.*"

I want to laugh again, but I can't. It's like that part of me has to recharge first.

I hadn't thought it ever would after Helen.

"What do we do now?" I ask Giovanni when the quiet swells, and none of us have anything else to say or do. No reason left to remain in this mausoleum except our reluctance to let go.

"We . . ." He trails off.

"We go home, too," says Ingrid as she joins us, her hands lifting to perch next to mine on the cold stone.

Home. I don't have one of those.

Never until Fairfax—which is to be sold. Never until Elias, who had left me behind.

But only because he'd had to. And just for now.

"Home. Where will that be for you, Jane?" asks Giovanni. "I imagine you could take your pick now."

He's trying to brighten the situation, to bring light and a touch of warmth to this dark, cold chamber of somberness and stone.

Elias had left us all money—*way* more than the promised amount. Way more than I even know how to deal with.

In essence? Everything.

That's what those papers Mr. Poole had grabbed off the counter that day had been about. At Elias's request, the housekeeper had helped to arrange for the liquidation of his assets, too, including the cars. All except for the Lamborghini, apparently, which makes me think Elias *must* have found those fries.

Now, at last, I have a possible—a *likely*—answer for what that last-minute "missive" of Elias's must have been about.

Giovanni is probably going to have a rough time selling the car himself after all, unless he decides to import it to the States. Not that it would be drivable there, since the steering wheel would be on the wrong side.

Whatever the case, that particular liquidation is now *his* to deal with. Which *is* pretty hilarious.

The other liquidations? Apparently, they'll lead to still more checks in the mail.

"Cold companions" is all that rings in my head, the words spoken in Mr. Poole's mellow and oddly comforting voice.

As for the housekeeper, none of us have seen him since that last day. The day of Elias's ill-fated birthday party. Which Mr. Poole, along with Elias, must have known *would* be his final.

And the housekeeper, the only one sneakier than Elias himself, had left lawyers in charge, so my guess is that, like Elias, I won't be seeing Mr. Poole again, either.

Our deal. Mine and Poole's. What had it been?

What had *he* been?

The answer to that wants to seem obvious.

Especially since Mr. Poole had said he kept tabs on Elias, that he had "for ages."

At the time, I hadn't realized he might have meant that literally. He'd also claimed it was his "job to care" for Elias. And perhaps it had been—in more ways than one.

So, Thea, after her death, had never stopped trying to get to

Elias. She'd just regrouped. And appealed for backup. Which would explain why Mr. Poole had proposed the idea of hiring psychics. Hiring me. Which had, he'd said, been *my* idea.

Thea's . . .

Another note of irony to this story that, while Elias had made a deal with a demon, Thea would have made one with . . .

I don't know. Not for sure.

And maybe I won't until it comes to be *my* checkout time.

Will I really have to wait that long to find out the truth?

No use in dwelling on it. I'm here, aren't I? My whole life ahead of me. And, like Giovanni had said, I could now take my pick of places to spend that life.

Elias had trapped my heart, but he had also freed my soul. I suppose we'd freed each other's.

Can I leave Elias here in this chamber? Or should I stay close by?

Elias's blanket, his pillow—they're still in their stone nook. And can't I now go find my own Jag to drive anytime I want?

I glance over my shoulder to Thea's sarcophagus. What would she have thought of Elias coming to see her in this mausoleum like he had? What would *I* have told Elias if given the chance?

"Cemeteries are for the dead," I'd have said if our roles had been reversed.

And what would Elias have told *me*? What would he say to me right now if he were here?

I shut my eyes and picture him among our group, and I conjure from the depths of my mind *that* voice.

Let this goodbye stand as the promise of another hello.

Tears burning anew, I open my eyes again.

"I don't know where I'll go," I say, answering Ingrid's question at last. "But . . . I can't stay here."

"Because of the memories," she guesses.

"Because I have a life to live," I whisper. "Elias . . . he's waiting for me. I have to believe that. And, well. I . . . want to have stories to tell him."

Several more beats of silence pass. And then Ingrid steps away from the sarcophagus. She heads out the open and sunwashed doorway, but her fingers pass along my shoulders as she goes.

So, then it's just me and Giovanni.

Because wherever Elias is . . . he's not in this stone box.

No more than Helen is in the ground back in Corydon.

Which means I don't have *any* roots.

The upside to that dilemma is that it grants me wings.

"I'll be outside, Bird," says Giovanni. "Just . . . come when you're ready."

He rubs my back before he departs the chamber, too.

And then it's just me in the mausoleum.

Me and the ghosts of ghosts.

I stay a long time, pressing hands to the lid of Elias's sarcophagus in an echo of that gesture he made when he'd been standing over Thea's. Like *I'm* the one waiting for a heartbeat, a pulse, now.

There's only silence. That and the faraway scents of lilac and honeysuckle, the floral aromas mixing in a way that makes me picture Elias and Helen standing on either side of me.

If they're together, I hope she's cussing his ass out.

I sigh. Because though I want to stay, I *have* to go.

"You put me through hell," I mutter to the marble lid.

And, with that, I push away and stalk toward the door. As I arrive at the threshold, though, I have to glance over my shoulder at him.

"Don't ever fucking do it again," I say, louder this time. So he'll be sure to hear me.

Wherever he is.

And then, without looking back a second time . . . I step into the light.

41

OMG. Finals week is literally killing me. 😵

Send.

I have, like, four exams left and all of them in subjects that stab my brain. 😫

Send.

With pitchforks.

Send.

Too soon?

Send.

Shut up. I know I should be studying.

Send.

It's okay. This coffee shop is open till midnight. Waiting for Giovanni anyway.

Send.

He's supposed to help me with this math crap because I do NOT want to repeat this remedial Algebra bull that's not even earning me any friggin credits. 😑

Send.

Why do I even need math if I'm an art major anyway? WTF.

Send.

Oh, yeah, Giovanni's totally late. Prob cuz he's busy "talking" to his new girlfriend, Lyra.

Send.

They met in the food court first day. Their point of bonding? They both appreciate musical theater. Except Giovanni has never seen a Broadway show in his life and just pretended to know the words to Hamilton to up his chances she'd say yes when he asked her out.

Send.

As if. Girl's got eyes.

Send.

Haven't decided how I feel about her tbh. She's ok. We don't click so well, but she and Giovanni mesh enough. Meaning he's smitten and she's eating up every second of it.

Send.

I'm keeping her on probation even if he isn't.

Send.

Yeah, Baltimore is pretty sweet. Lively. Just like Giovanni said.

Send.

He and I are going to take Ingrid to Little Italy when she comes in for winter break. There's this pastry shop there you would love. And omg, Amici's? Their baked ziti gives me life.

Send.

Giovanni and I have a Zoom chat with Ingrid tomorrow. Which is good. Because I've got questions about her latest Gemini monthly reading posted on her channel yesterday.

Send.

Also, I want to schedule a private reading with her. I think I'm ready. To ask. About him.

Send.

Since he hasn't stopped by at all.

Send.

Probably sitting in on some lectures himself.

Send.

Please say you gave him at least one.

Send.

A text pops up on my phone, diverting my attention from my chat with Helen.

Of course, it's Giovanni telling me he's "almost there."

Which probably means Lyra finally kicked him out of her dorm room so she could get some studying done, too.

Seated in a booth at It's a Grind, the coffeehouse bordering campus, I abandon my phone to the table and sigh down at my open textbook.

The numbers and letters swim on the page, and I have to shut my eyes.

The too-happy classical Christmas music drifting over the sound system should irk the crap out of me, but instead, it entices me to just . . . prolong my break. At least until Giovanni gets here. Because it's not like this alphabet soup of numbers and letters is going to make sense before then anyway.

I grab my pencil and, in the margins, sketch a familiar profile—prominent nose, untamed hair, an eye brimming with secrets. All of which I'm now privy to, if no one else.

Stopping, I force myself to set the pencil down. Because I shouldn't be drawing him.

I shouldn't be drawing him *again*.

But then, there really isn't any hope that I will ever stop.

Especially not when I've been drawing him—*us*—all along anyway.

Shutting my eyes a second time, I lean my head against the winter-cooled glass of the window and just exist for a moment.

Peace settles over me. I tune in to my breathing. And I imagine I'm back at Fairfax. Caught in that gaze of his.

I start, though, sitting up when a ceramic coffee mug shatters.

My attention goes to the counter, behind which bustle a

few baristas. One of them, a man wearing horn-rimmed glasses, busies himself with a broom.

I blink at him several times, waiting for the hallucination to clear. But the man's face never changes. Meaning, it doesn't grow any less familiar no matter how long I stare.

The moment—the vision—stretches on, too. Making it impossible for him to be a mirage brought on by fatigue. Trauma.

"*Mr. Poole?*"

I speak his name under my breath as he returns to the espresso machine, which he putzes with, triggering a burst of steam.

Then, glancing up at me, almost like he heard me, Mr. Poole offers a bright smile—right before refocusing on whatever drink he's crafting. Something frothy for the girl who stands with her back to me, her masses of red curls gilded by the fluorescents.

I'm about to climb out of the booth when someone slides into the seat next to me.

His scent envelops me first: smoke, sandalwood—and that citrus essence I can now, at last, pinpoint as bergamot.

"Do you remember the time," Elias says, looping an arm behind me to rest it along the back of the bench, "when we were in the carriage together? Sitting just as we are now?"

I scowl at him, my mind grasping for grounding.

Elias is here. But just like Mr. Poole, and Helen, he can't be.

Unless this is Mr. Poole doling out hall passes again.

"That ride though the countryside during the heart of midsummer," Elias continues, still hoping to jog my memory, "after you found out the truth. Regarding what I'd done."

I shake my head, fighting the urge to ask him what he's doing here. Where here is.

But then, do I need to know that?

"Carriage?" I echo instead, "do . . . you mean the *Jaguar*?"

He gives me that slight smile, though this time it's colored by a hint of knowing. "It was a bit before that."

I have to touch him. So, I put my hand to his cheek, my movement too similar to his that time I caught up to him in the hall at Fairfax, gazed into that eye streaked with tears for Thea.

For me.

Elias, warm and real, puts his hand over mine.

"You assured me of how love was never a burden," he says, "and always a promise."

"I don't remember," I murmur, shaking my head.

"One day, you will," he says. "Just as surely as you forgot everything, you'll remember what you did . . . to keep your promises. To me. *All* of them."

"Elias, I miss you."

"Mmm, yes," he muses. "Bit of a dumpster fire without me, aren't you?"

I burst out laughing. As I do, the tears that have been waiting to fall spill. Elias laughs, too. Then he releases my hand to tuck my hair behind my ear and trace fingers along my jawline.

"What a love story is ours, Jane," he says, sobering.

"I hate the ending," I whisper, voice pinched with grief.

"You're quite certain it's been written?"

I move in, sliding down the booth the way I'd done in his car that night I kissed him. This time, there's less distance to cover. This time, Elias is ready for me. Head tilting, he leans down, lips closing over mine when we collide.

Our kiss goes on and on and I don't care who is watching. Who sees.

Poole's already witnessed one make-out session, and Helen? She's probably over there with a scorecard.

Me and Elias. We're a ten, but we keep croaking on each other.

Finally, Elias breaks the kiss.

"Next time," he says, "I promise, will be perfect."

"I'd settle for no dumpster fires," I say.

"Write to me?"

I open my mouth to answer. But then someone bumps the table, and I blink, starting awake.

"Word, Bird," Giovanni says as, after dropping his books next to mine and shedding his backpack, he slides into the booth across from me, coffee cup in hand. "Sorry I'm late."

I frown at him, lifting my head from the window to peer to the empty seat next to me. My eyes then fly to the shop counter. A girl from my Drawing, Inquiry, and Expression class occupies the place Mr. Poole had. She offers me a small wave before setting a finished drink on the counter for a guy wearing a beanie.

Numbly, I wave back.

The housekeeper. He's gone. Elias is gone. Helen, too.

I'm back. From the dream. The reality. The heaven world.

"Bird," Giovanni says. "Are you okay? Were you legit asleep? Need another shot of espresso? I just had, like, four. Lookit. I'm already low-key vibrating."

He holds up a hand, which *does* shake.

"No," I tell him. "No, I'm . . . good."

I'm not good. But I also am.

Because now I know for sure. The truth about me. About Helen.

About Elias.

Thea . . .

And, for once in my life, even though I still don't have what I want, even though it will be a lifetime before I ever truly do, I *do* have . . . enough.

Acknowledgments

This book has undergone many transformations since its inception, the story arriving at this incarnation with the help of so many.

I'd like to start by thanking my editor, Dana Leydig, who guided me through each draft and pass, providing invaluable insight and helping me uncover what the story was, and wasn't. Thank you for the phone calls, the many thoughtful notes, and for pushing me to dig deeper with each revision.

Tremendous thanks as well go to everyone at Viking who has worked tirelessly to help me craft the best book possible. I am deeply appreciative of the time, talent, attention, and expertise that my work has received. Thanks as well are owed to Janna Bonikowski for her support and encouragement.

A huge thank-you goes to Jessica Jenkins for her incredible cover design. Thank you as well to the artist, Amanda Larkins. I could not have asked for a more stunning cover.

I count myself among the luckiest of authors to have an amazing critique group. Katie McGarry, Bill Wolfe, Kurt Hampe, Bethany Griffin, and Colette Ballard—what would I do without you? Thank you each for your support and guidance through this novel and all my literary endeavors. Over the years, you've each sharpened my skills and pushed me to become stronger in more areas than just my writing. I look forward to continuing to grow even sharper with the help of your brilliant insight, feedback, and guidance. I am also honored to call you family.

Katie McGarry: I had you on the phone how many times? My favorite instance was when I was walking down the street, talking to you through my wireless headphones, and scaring the neighbors while I ranted to you about "*the demon*!" Thank you as well for helping me find my ending, and for texting me that clip on the Strength card. At every stage, you helped me put *my* cards out of reverse and this story into upright focus.

I am grateful to my friend Bill Wolfe for the many brainstorming sessions. Panera may have gotten tired of us, but I hope they know it was all for the cause! Thanks so much for helping me find the answers I was seeking, for reading and rereading, for offering so many suggestions, for laughing at my in-manuscript jokes, and for groaning over the horrible puns I saved just for you.

Retellings are so fun, but they always come with a unique challenge. As the storyteller, you want to touch on favorite and familiar plot points and honor the source material. At the same time, there's the desire to bring something fresh. Many thanks go to Kurt Hampe for talking me into a "wife in the attic" and helping me to find that wife. Your thoughtful questions led me to unlock that attic door and find out just what dwelled beyond. And that revelation? Game-changing.

Thank you to Jeannine Storm for hashing out plot points with me in Target, T.J. Maxx, HomeGoods, the nail salon, and of course, good ole World of Beer. Thank you for helping me find Jane, and for being my reference regarding elements of her past. Thanks as well for your suggestions regarding the very end. Your idea stuck. More than anything, I want to thank you for being my friend, and for always encouraging me to do the brave thing. Ride or die, Ponie.

To Gina Possanza, who has always championed my writing, you'll never know how deeply I appreciate you. You inspired so much of this story, and I can't thank you enough for being my sounding board at every stage. Your intuition is always spot-on. Thank you as well for being a point of reference regarding Giovanni. Most of all, thanks for being my friend.

An abundance of thanks is owed as well to Nick Passafiume. Thank you for listening and offering suggestions. I'm always amazed when you somehow manage to fix whole issues with one "note."

To April Cannon, thank you for always being there and always reading. Thank you also for cheerleading all my efforts. Thanks go to Tony Cannon, too, for his knowledge about the coolest hot rods and how to fix them.

Much thanks go as well to Anda Thomas, who answered many questions (many times!) about life in the UK. Thanks for fielding my quirky inquiries and for always being up for the next wave.

Chris Reck, you don't know me, but you sure helped a lot! I'm a fan of your YouTube channel, Minnow Pond Tarot, and I gleaned so much insight regarding tarot from your videos and your classes. Somewhat of a sidenote, but your encouragement on the Leo readings has also been appreciated. Thanks for advising us Leos to always "pick the new path." Oh, and because of you, Chris, I choose to be the windshield and not the bug—always.

Thank you to Katie B. I only met you once and very briefly, but that meeting influenced this story. It also influenced my life. I'll never forget what you taught me.

Ethan Creagh, I know I bothered you a ton while I was writing this one, but it's okay because I also made you laugh??? Thanks for offering insight and suggestions on some of my favorite Giovanni one-liners. Thank you as well for schooling me on fancy cars and informing me about serpentines. You're the best, Skillet.

Mom, thanks for watching all those *Jane Eyre* movies with me. I love that you love the source material as much as I do. Thank you also for suggesting the fish sandwich gag, and for always making me laugh. You have encouraged every single creative endeavor, and because of that—because of *you*—I am an artist.

I am grateful to my family, who always offer support and encouragement—particularly my brothers, who inspire me constantly, both with their talent and wit. How'd we Creagh/Miller kids get to be so awesome, anyway?

Thanks are due as well to the incredible Charlotte Brontë, who authored *Jane Eyre*, an enduring classic that I first encountered when I was the same age as Jane. *Jane Eyre* has stuck with me ever since, and it was my honor to revisit this tale of mystery, intrigue, and love.

I also owe a huge debt of gratitude to my readers. Thank you for following me into the dark, for trusting me, and for always asking me what's next. Your support enables me to do the thing I love best, and that is to tell twisty stories of nightmares, monsters, true love, and the kisses that ensue.

Final thanks, as always, go to God. I owe my gifts to Him, and those gifts have brought me here, to the end of this story all about lost souls, lost love, and characters who find more than what they're searching for. I found more than what I was searching for in this book, too. And that, like all my artistic endeavors, brought me closer to You.